Praise for *Checkout 19*

"Singular . . . The prized darkness at the center of the human mind, the place where whatever is really *real* about us resides, is what *Checkout 19* dedicates itself to protecting." —*The New Yorker*

"Wildly imaginative, unabashedly odd, and mordantly funny. . . . This book-full-of-books is a gift and proof of a rare talent. . . . A volume to be consumed whole, on one long, strange trip." —*Los Angeles Times*

"The wonder of childhood reading, the undiluted absorption and imaginative engagement, the capacity to fall madly in love with fictional characters and to fantasize oneself into their worlds—these are the qualities Ms. Bennett wants to celebrate and preserve." —*The Wall Street Journal*

"If you've had your fill of autofiction, thanks—don't lose interest just yet. . . . The life Bennett describes is one blown open by imaginative writing . . . and by the transformative and transportive nature of reading." —*The New York Times*

"Enigmatic and beguiling. Bennett jousts in one sentence and waltzes in the next, her singular style both earthy and soaring."
—Claire Vaye Watkins, author of *Battleborn*
and *I Love You but I've Chosen Darkness*

"Rarely has a book astonished me as much as Claire-Louise Bennett's 2015 debut, *Pond*. . . . So unusual, and so unsettlingly pleasurable, that I thought it would be greedy to hope Bennett's new novel, *Checkout 19*, would be better. Lucky me: it is." —NPR.com

"Sly and strange and deceptively casual. . . . Bennett is trying out a new method of depicting consciousness. . . . She is inviting us to view it from a peculiar new vantage point, somehow both inside and outside at once." —*Harper's Magazine*

"Exhilarating . . . Bennett has an often breathtaking knack for . . . choosing the perfectly uncanny phrase to bring a 'distinct image' into being. . . . [Her] brilliance is that the exchange of pickles and paperbacks between strangers can indeed be made into a story, one that is told twice: first in a sober, straightforward style, and then again in a scrambled, surrealist form."
—*Los Angeles Review of Books*

"Bennett . . . specializes in creating character through details, whether big or small, delightful or dirt-ridden. . . . [Her] humor is often mordant but always on target. . . . *Checkout 19* echoes Virginia Woolf, early Toni Morrison novels, Sheila Heti and Han Kang, and so many others in its insistence on women telling their own stories in their own ways." —*The Boston Globe*

"I fell into *Checkout 19* and didn't want to climb back out. It is wonderful—I'm not sure why, and that makes it all the more wonderful."
—Roddy Doyle, author of *Paddy Clarke Ha Ha Ha*

"The excitement around Bennett's books lies in their willingness to circle back on themselves, lingering in uncertainties and contradictions. . . . Throughout *Checkout 19* stories function as a catalyst not just for thinking but for acting, choices, lived experiences; it feels thrilling to imagine all the books and stories, the reconsidered ways of being, that might come after this."
—*The New Republic*

"A kind of tapestry. . . . Once you allow yourself to get swept along by Bennett's instinctive, synaptic abilities as a storyteller, the vivid textures of her sentences, and her subversive sense of humor, *Checkout 19* is a strange and delicious treat."
—*Vogue*

"Claire-Louise Bennett is a woman writer living in Ireland who writes highly realistic, wildly praised literary fiction. Some of us have developed an incurable condition that dictates we must read every work by every writer who meets this description—please be mindful of this. If that's you, meet Bennett."
—*Glamour*

"I'll remember this book for its disarmingly figurative language and its subtle observational humor . . . [Bennett] traces one person's idiosyncratic, recursive artistic becoming—not just the reading, writing, and cigarette smoking but the relationships and experiences that unlock new ways of seeing." —*Vulture*

"What's amazing for the reader is to see a book so alive, so lively, so aware of what it is made of and yet so itself, so itself really that it eludes review, and ought simply to be read." —*Bookforum*

"[*Checkout 19*] seamlessly moves between literary analysis, fantastical storytelling, and life itself, eventually confronting the realities of sex, violence, and death." —*Los Angeles Review of Books* Radio Hour

"[A] masterpiece . . . [whose] prose is often sumptuously self-aware . . . *Checkout 19* is also a startling meditation on what youth knows and doesn't know."
—*4Columns*

"Bennett has the superb ability to capture the reality of a mind: it is rare to think in fully formed, conclusion-ridden ideas, after all. . . . *Checkout 19* is a fresh take on the coming-of-age novel. . . . Bennett manages to convince the reader that somewhere, her narrator continues to think and ponder and live and wrestle with being in a body, like the rest of us." —*Lit Hub*

CHECKOUT 19

ALSO BY CLAIRE-LOUISE BENNETT

Pond

CHECKOUT 19

Claire-Louise Bennett

RIVERHEAD BOOKS | NEW YORK

RIVERHEAD BOOKS
An imprint of Penguin Random House LLC
penguinrandomhouse.com

First published in hardcover in Great Britain by Jonathan Cape, an imprint of
Vintage, a division of Penguin Random House Ltd., London, in 2021.

First North American edition published by Riverhead, 2022.

The Library of Congress has catalogued the Riverhead hardcover edition as follows:

Names: Bennett, Claire-Louise, author.
Title: Checkout 19 : a novel / Claire-Louise Bennett.
Description: New York : Riverhead Books, 2022.
Identifiers: LCCN 2021022908 (print) | LCCN 2021022909 (ebook) |
ISBN 9780593420492 (hardcover) | ISBN 9780593420515 (ebook)
Classification: LCC PR6102.E562 C54 2022 (print) |
LCC PR6102.E562 (ebook) | DDC 823/.92--dc23
LC record available at https://lccn.loc.gov/2021022908
LC ebook record available at https://lccn.loc.gov/2021022909

First Riverhead hardcover edition: March 2022
First Riverhead trade paperback edition: February 2023
Riverhead trade paperback ISBN: 9780593420508

Printed in the United States of America
1st Printing

BOOK DESIGN BY LUCIA BERNARD

The author wishes to thank the Arts Council of Ireland for their continued support.

Believe me, expression is insanity, it arises out of our insanity. It also has to do with turning pages, with hunting from one page to the other, with flight, with complicity in an absurd, gushing effusion, with a vile overflow of verse, with insuring life in a single sentence, and, in turn, with the sentences seeking insurance in life.

—*Malina*, Ingeborg Bachmann, 1971

There is at times a magic in identity of position; it is one of the things that have suggested to us eternal comradeship. She moved her elbows before saying: "I have behaved ridiculously."

—*A Room with a View*, E. M. Forster, 1908

CHECKOUT 19

I.

A SILLY BUSINESS

One cannot see the future of something learned.

—*A GIRL'S STORY*, ANNIE ERNAUX

Later on we often had a book with us. Later on. When we were a bit bigger at last though still nowhere near as big as the rest of them we brought over books with us. Oh loads of books. And sat with them there in the grass by the tree. Just one book, in fact. Just one, that's right. Lots of books, one at a time. That's it, one at a time. We didn't very much like tons of books did we. No, not really, and neither do we now. We like one book. Yes, we like one book now and we liked one book then. We went to the library for instance and we soon lost the habit didn't we of taking out lots and lots of books. Yes. Yes. Yes we did. First of all of course we took out all the books we possibly could. Which was probably eight books. It's always either six books or eight books or twelve books. Unless it's a special collection of books of course in which case it might only be four. And to begin with we took out as many of them as we could. That's right. We'll take this one and this one and this one, this one, and that one too. And so on. Yes. In a pile up on the high counter for Noddy Head to stamp. And we read not one of them all the way through. It was simply impossible. We couldn't get engrossed. No matter what book we had in our hands we found it simply impossible to refrain from wondering incessantly about what kinds of words exactly were inside the other books. We couldn't help it could we. We just couldn't stop ourself from thinking about the other books and the different kinds of words they each contained and when we picked up one of the other books in order to find out it was just the same. It really was just the same no matter which book we picked up. As long as there were other books we thought about the sorts of words they might contain nonstop and were thus precluded from becoming engrossed with the very book we had in our hands. The very book. A silly business. Yes, it was a silly business. Tossing one book down and picking one book up and tossing that to one side and picking up yet another and so on and getting nowhere. Nowhere at all. Over and over again. And we went on like that for quite some time didn't we until we realised that just because we were allowed to take out six books eight books twelve books four books didn't mean did it that we had to.

No, of course it didn't. So then we took out one book. And of course this aggravated people. Yes. Yes. Yes it did. No end. Is that all you're taking out, they'd exclaim. Go and get some more. Just one—you'll have that finished by tomorrow, they'd say. And we're not coming back again this week. So what. As if the only thing you could do with a book was read it. That's right. We could sit for a long time couldn't we with a book beside us and not even open it. We certainly could. And it was very edifying. It certainly was. It was entirely possible we realised to get a great deal from a book without even opening it. Just having it there beside us for ages was really quite special. It was actually because we could wonder couldn't we about the sorts of words it contained without getting ourself worked up into a ridiculous state. With just one book in the grass beside us we sat there wondering about the sorts of words it contained in a really tranquil and expansive kind of way that in fact enabled distinct images to emerge all of their own accord from who knows where. That was nice. It was actually. The images rarely resembled anything we had seen for ourself directly yet they were not in the least bit vague or far-fetched. Not remotely. From time to time, perhaps to make sure that the images that came about of their own accord didn't deviate too much from the themes and tone and point in time propounded by the text beside us, we'd pick up the book and open it wherever our thumb happened to stop, and we'd read one or two words from whatever line upon the page our eyes happened to coincide with, and those one or two words would be quite enough, wouldn't they, to provoke yet more enthralling images.

When we open a book our eyes nearly always go over to the left page. That's right—the left page, for reasons we have never previously reflected upon, has a much stronger pull on us than the right page. We always look down first of all at the right page. The right page first, that's right. But the words on the right page always seem much too close. Too close to each other and too close to our face. The words on the right page do indeed make us peculiarly aware of our face. Is it our face? Is it? Well? The words on the right seem far too eager, over-bearing, and yes somewhat ingratiating in fact, and very soon our rattled eyes leave the right page in order to seek refuge in the left. We look down at the right page and up at the left page. We do actually. And we nearly always read the left page much more slowly than the right. There seems to be more time on the left page. Yes. Yes. Yes there does. On the left page there is more space it seems, on either side of the words, and above and below every sentence. And the left page nearly always has better words on it it seems. That's right—words like "shone" and "creature" and "champagne" and "ragged" and "clump," for example. Words that really don't require any explanation. Words that happen one by one rather than words that bandy together to try to convince you of something that is not happening. It really can't be the case though can it that these distinct operations that words bring into effect are divvied out between the left and the right pages quite so unerringly. No, probably not. Probably it is more likely that we are much more receptive in fact to whatever we read on the left pages than we are to what we read on the right pages because we look down at the right page and up at the left. We do. We do. Which must mean that the book we are reading does not remain still in our hands. It must mean, yes, that after turning the right page over so that it becomes the left page we shift the book slightly upwards. Upwards, yes.

We have a tendency don't we of reading the last few sentences on the right page hurriedly. We do actually. We enjoy turning the pages of a book and our anticipation of doing so is obviously fairly fervid and undermines our attention to such an extent that we can't help but skim over the last couple of sentences on the right page probably without really taking in a single word. Quite often when we make a start on the left page it doesn't make a great deal of sense to us. No. No. No it doesn't. And it is only then, isn't it, that we realise, somewhat reluctantly, that we didn't read the last few lines of the previous page properly. Quite often, we are so reluctant to acknowledge that this makes any difference, we carry on reading. We carry on that's right even though we can't make head nor tail of what we are reading. We carry on regardless because we are vaguely convinced that, surely, if we keep going, the way these current sentences relate to all the sentences we've already read will, actually, sooner or later, make itself perfectly apparent. We don't get very far. No, we don't. We nearly always flick back. We do. And we are nearly always surprised by how much salient detail was in fact contained in the last few lines on the previous right page and we are surprised even further by a very unreasonable thought that comes to us from who knows where which proposes that the typesetter of the book is really quite irresponsible, that they should allow such important sentences to appear at the very end of the right page. Surely the typesetter must be aware that many people derive a great deal of pleasure from turning pages turning pages and as such cannot be expected to read the last couple of lines on all the right pages with consummate diligence. You would have thought so. Turning the page. Turning the page.

Turning the page and holding the book up a little higher. And the reason we do that, now that we are reflecting on it, is because once we have turned the page we feel inclined to lift our chin and gaze upwards. And the reason we feel like gazing upwards is because we have turned over a new leaf. A new leaf!—that's right. We have turned over a new leaf and as such we feel instantly youthful and supremely open-minded and that is why we quite naturally adopt the uplifted mien of an urbane albeit slightly indulged protégé every time we turn the page. A new leaf. Yes. By the time we get to the bottom of the right page we have aged approximately twenty years. We are no longer holding the book up. No. No. The book has dropped. Our face has dropped. We have jowls. We do. We have a double chin. That's right. We wallow. We wallow. We are wallowing in our chins. We really have aged at least twenty years. It's no wonder then is it that we don't read to the very end of the right page properly. No. No. No wonder at all that we are itching to turn it over. No wonder whatsoever that we anticipate turning the page so very fervidly. As if it were a matter of life or death in fact. Life or death. Life or death. It is a matter of life or death in fact. Yes. Yes. Yes, it is. Turning the pages. Turning the pages. When we turn the page we are born again. Living and dying and living and dying and living and dying. Again, and again. And really that's the way it ought to be. The way that reading ought to be done.

Yes. Yes. Turning the pages. Turning the pages. With one's entire life.

It could be said couldn't it that strictly speaking there are no left pages, just the other sides of right pages. That could very well be said if one is assuming that the book is faceup. Faceup. Yes. Faceup in the grass. Yes. There in the grass a book right beside us. Faceup. Faceup in the field in the grass beside the great big tree. Just one book. Yes. And in fact as far as we were concerned nobody else had this book apart from us. Nobody. Nobody. Not a single soul. No one else had it and furthermore no one else had ever even seen it. It was just ours. Ours entirely. We knew very well of course that that wasn't the case at all, but that's how it felt nonetheless and in fact even now from time to time with certain books the very same feeling returns. It does actually. Erroneous yet compelling. This book is ours and ours alone. Perhaps this atmosphere of exclusivity occurred in the first place because there weren't very many books at home and the few books there were were out of sight inside a corner cabinet in the dining room along with candles and napkin rings and a gravy boat our mother had taken an abrupt and supreme disliking to. Out of sight yet at the same time curiously present. Disturbingly present. Omnipresent in fact. More present yes than rows and rows of books arrayed quite openly on bookshelves one walks past umpteen times a day. And of course "Little Claus and Big Claus" was very present because mother used to follow us up the stairs and into the bathroom reading out the grubby tale of Little Claus and Big Claus's absurd scheming and callous buffoonery. Gee up my horses! Gee up my horses! That's right. Mother loved that. Laughed her head off. She did actually. And even when we were older she came after us up the stairs laughing her head off with "Little Claus and Big Claus" wide open in her hands. Gee up my horses! That was kept upstairs on a shelf with all our other books side by side in the spare room. The playroom. Yes. Whereas mother's books glowered like intricate secrets inside the corner cabinet. That's right. Very occasionally we'd slowly twist the small brass handle to silently release the door of the corner cabinet and we'd peer in at the wakened spines of the books lodged in amongst the candles and the napkin rings and the spurned gravy boat and we could hardly breathe. It made us feel nervous. It did actually. We were looking at things that were no business of ours. Illicit things. Yes. Yes. Illicit things that looked back at us and saw something. That's right, something inside of us that we in fact knew nothing about. The books looked back at us and something inside of us stirred. Yes. One of those books was *Switch Bitch* by Roald Dahl and we had books upstairs by Roald Dahl such as *Danny the Champion of the World* which was our favourite Roald Dahl book and we had read them all hadn't we, but we hadn't read this book. No, we knew nothing about this book. Not a thing. Yet it was quite obvious wasn't it that this book wasn't like any of our books by Roald Dahl on the shelf upstairs and wasn't meant for us. No it wasn't. It was a book meant for adults. That's right. We could see that straightaway. There was a photograph of Roald Dahl inside the jacket cover just like there was a photograph of Roald Dahl inside the jacket cover of each of our books by Roald Dahl. And the photograph was more or less in the exact same place. That's right. But he looked completely different inside the jacket cover of the book our mother kept tucked away in the corner cabinet beside the candles and the napkin rings and the decommissioned gravy boat. He did actually. He wasn't looking at the camera for one thing. No, he wasn't. And he wasn't sitting down either. No, he was standing up. And he was outside. Outside in the wind. In the wind, that's right. It was quite obvious he was standing in the wind because of the way his hair which was thinning lifted away from his head. It occurred to us didn't it that there was probably a small propeller plane nearby. Yes. Yes. And he wasn't looking at the camera. No, he wasn't. And that more than anything made it quite obvious that this book had been written with adults in mind. Adults in mind, that's right. That and the title. The title, of course. *Switch Bitch. Switch Bitch.* Whenever we overheard our mother reading *The BFG* to our younger brother we would see a woman with a black netted veil over her eyes and a small neat nose and large dark red glossy lips mouthing the word "bitch" back at her slightly out-of-focus reflection which was tremendously exciting though we didn't fully understand why it was and in fact the excitement this image brought on soon troubled us because it was of an unprecedented nature and all too quickly made us feel guilty and alone and afraid of who knows what. We didn't know. No, we didn't. But were afraid nonetheless.

A Start in Life was in there too. *A Start in Life*, that's right, by Alan Sillitoe and not Anita Brookner. We read that in no time one summer in the back garden. There were two sun loungers on the patio in the back garden and one summer when we ought to have been reading books from the reading list we laid down upon one of the sun loungers in a halter-neck black bikini with a packet of Dunhill cigarettes and read *A Start in Life* by Alan Sillitoe instead. Later on in the afternoon when she got back from her ten till two in the department store our mother would come out onto the patio with sun cream and lie down on the sun lounger beside us in her fluorescent yellow strapless bikini and we'd read bits out to her that we'd already read and reckoned to be highly amusing. She liked that. She did like that she'd laugh. She'd laugh in nearly all the same places where we'd laughed earlier on. It was a very entertaining book. She would lie there smoking Benson & Hedges cigarettes on the sun lounger beside us. Laughing. Laughing and flicking ash down onto the patio. It was a long time ago. It was actually. It was one of the last summers. We can't remember what *A Start in Life* was about. We haven't a clue. Though we can recollect the gist of the bit that amused us. Yes, the bit we found amusing and so did mother was when the narrator suggests that not everyone is cut out for loafing around day in day out and that really instead of regarding people who do diddly-squat all day with irritation and disdain they ought to be thought of in the highest of terms because actually doing nothing at all day in day out is not nearly so easy as it looks.

There's a fine art to being idle in fact. That's right, there is an art to it, and very few people are naturally in possession of the gumption and fortitude necessary to pull it off. Reading outside on a summer's afternoon. When there have been weeks and weeks of hot sunny days one after the next. There really is nothing else quite like it. We liked nothing better. A tiny dotted beetle might hoist itself up onto the cover of the book faceup beside us. The book that had never before been handled or seen by anyone else. Out of the dishevelled grass, up onto the venerable tableau that was the cover of what— Plato's *Phaedrus*, for example. The columns the platters the pewter the vine leaves the drinking vessels the swarthy shins the lemony lemons the chiaroscuro. We could easily have squished it with our thumb gently applied if we were so inclined. Yes. Yes. Yes, we could. There it was. Little dotted beetle. Stopping and starting. This way and that. Around and around the venerable tableau dottily for ages. Around and around. Quite unable to find a way to properly immerse itself in the moody scene's alluring sagacious gloom. We weren't inclined to flatten beetles dotted or otherwise were we. No, generally not. Or ants. No. Nor spiders even. Vessels. Vessels. And in a way we couldn't tell could we whether the little beetle was from now or from then. No, not really. Not even when it tipped off the cover and beetled back into the grass.

II.

BRIGHT SPARK

One day we'll domesticate him into a human,
and then we can sketch him. Since that's what
we did with ourselves and with God.

—"BOY IN PEN AND INK," CLARICE LISPECTOR

At the end of term the English department sought to recoup all the books that had been gamely issued to each pupil at the start of term. Books hardly any of the pupils had bothered to look at in the meantime, yet now, at the end of term, they felt no compulsion whatsoever to bring them back. This must have been infuriating for the department. The pupils simply had no interest. Not in reading books, nor returning them. Their principal interest, right up until the very last bell, was to disrupt the flow of information and ideas, which the teachers attempted each lesson to set in motion, with all kinds of never-ending pranks. Though, actually, their repertoire, despite being perseverant, was not especially varied. Every term in fact the pupils became fixated on a particular stunt and took great delight in pulling it off in just the same way day after day for most of the term's duration. It was quite perverse. Like performers in the avant-garde tradition they were alert to the ways sustained repetition produces subtle and absurd variations that are as transfixing as they are subversive. Such recursive hijinks were most often deployed in the science labs, where the pupils' incendiary hands might easily alight upon and combine a spectrum of appliances and substances that could be counted on to interact with each other in a palpable and fairly predictable fashion—though the exact scale of the ensuing reaction could not be quite so reliably gauged. The combination of knowing what would happen without knowing to what degree seemed to excite them very much, and there was no such thing as a disappointing outcome—if anything the pupils derived greater satisfaction when an operation fell flat. There was something about an anticlimax that really seemed to tickle them. Lemon Head, the chemistry teacher, found this recurrent animate response vexingly ludicrous and not a little unsettling. It was idiotic, and, worse than that, it was inscrutable. Why was it indeed that the brief whooping that went up all too quickly following a beautiful bright explosion sounded dutiful and hollow, yet a damp squib elicited a cacophony of cheers and plaudits that were genuinely gleeful and ever so slightly ominous? There certainly was an element of darkness to it. Could it be that the pupils knew very well that they wouldn't ever amount to anything much themselves? Knew that the system was rigged against them, could feel it in their waxing bones— their bones which were also their mother's and father's bones, and their mother's mother's and father's bones, and their father's mother's and father's bones, and so on and so on, a long line on all sides of rankled, rigged against, and put-upon bones. And as such the present fresh-faced custodians of these burgeoning yet bridled bones concocted a controlled scenario that occasionally culminated in a flashy climatic blast but more often than not only fizzled pathetically, leached and dripped and abated. Failure after all was inevitable wasn't it, so why not make a neat little routine out of it and laugh again and again in its dour face with mirthful derision, as hard and as often as they could. Their future was mapped out for them on the smallest scrap of paper. Just as it had been for their parents and their parents' parents and their parents' parents' parents and so on and so on and why would it change now? How well they did or did not do at school wouldn't make a blind bit of difference. All of this sitting up at a desk in this or that classroom day in day out, taking in every word and committing it all to memory, what a complete waste of time, it was an absolute farce, and they didn't have to go along with it did they, they didn't have to be obedient and diligent and tight-lipped like their parents and their parents' parents and their parents' parents' parents had been, the teachers had no powers whatsoever anymore—throwing a board rubber across the room so it smacked you hard on the head, striking you ten times upon the backside with a cane, or twenty times across the palm of your bold raised paw with a ruler—the willy-nilly meting out of heavy-handed punishments such as these had been outlawed years ago—the only way, now, that continuous rectitude could be achieved was if the pupils could be induced to self-govern and made it their business to sit still and pay attention, and they would only do that wouldn't they if they thought it would get them somewhere, and so, to this end, weren't they told, time and time again, that the sky was the limit, that they could achieve anything at all, if only they put their minds to it, and wasn't it reiterated over and over that the very town they lived in was in fact the fastest-growing town in all of Europe, all of Europe, the opportunities available to them therefore were real and endless, aim high and aim higher again, and there were one or two of course who happily fell for all that soft-soaping claptrap, who were only too pleased to cultivate fanciful notions and far-fetched goals and thus gladly toed the line, the little egg-heads, and didn't those one or two live in detached houses in tendrilous cul-de-sacs off in the suburbs already in any case. The majority did not and did not fall for it, and so most lessons were more or less catastrophic from start to finish. Each teacher therefore had no option but to develop some method or other to use in the classroom at times when it all went to pieces so as to arrest the pupils' willful dereliction and inculcate a little order, however short-lived that invariably turned out to be. This mostly involved shouting which was often accompanied by slamming. The teacher, at the end of his or her tether, would get to their feet of course in order to shout. And while they shouted their hands rifled atavistically across the desk for something to throw. But they were no longer permitted to throw board rubbers or anything else at the pupils, so whatever item they'd got hold of had to be slammed only, again and again against the desk, again and again, and that in itself could in fact be fairly purgative and quite often brought into effect a subdued slightly embarrassed hush that heralded a brief spell of heaven-sent respite. There was one teacher who didn't like to shout, perhaps he couldn't, not everyone can. He was tall, with a soft beard and blue wholesome eyes, and often wore tweeds. He looked Swiss, or Victorian. That's to say he looked like he ought to be outside, leading a keen and harmonious expedition through some lovely mountain range in May, stopping now and then to make a note of this or that flower and butterfly and bit of lichen. That's where he ought to have been. Up there amongst the nascent edelweiss, not down here in a classroom rife with goons running about with Sellotape around their heads and their thumbs on fire. His name was Aitken and his disciplinary method involved holding up his hand, nothing more. He didn't say anything, he didn't even get up out of his chair. He stayed where he was with his arms on the desk and simply raised his hand, usually the left one, so that his big benign palm faced the class. His fingers were closed together. He had long shapely fingers. Tapered fingers. Nimble fingers. Fingers made for unhooking briars and finding things in the grass. The pupils immediately fell about the place laughing at this entirely incongruous signal. They'd scramble back to their desks, straddle their stools, and up their hands would go—"How!" they would say. "How!" Over and over in deep solemn voices and then the war whooping would start up, their hands now flying on and off their upturned mouths as they yowled and hooted. And still Aitken didn't say anything. He went on sitting there in his mellow tweeds with his peace-seeking palm facing out and his polymathic eyes twinkling with sublime forbearance. Sometimes it looked as if the shenanigans amused him. Did he feel a part of it? It was his distinctly slender yet enduring gesture after all that they were all having a great time riffing on. Mimicry can be unkind, but at least it acknowledges that you're there. The comic dimension of the pupils' self-generated antics on the other hand was often so cryptic as to be incogitable, and their escalating laughter perplexing and downright unnerving—at least this way the teacher was in on the joke. Indeed, sometimes it looked as if he were smiling through his soft beard. Or was he grimacing in fact, putting on a brave face? Was he in fact going round the bend? The very same bend Frau Floyd went round. Frau Floyd. Where exactly did she end up? One day she was there, as she'd been there every day for years and years with her emphatic der, die, and das, and then she was gone. Never seen again. Frau Floyd. Stringent and humourless, with a bombshell bust—and German, yes. The pupils had a field day. Little shits. Little buggers. Give the bloody books back! But the pupils would not give the books back of their own accord. Their unheeding palms had to be greased in some way. And so it was that at the end of term the department sought to recoup all the books that had been gamely issued to each pupil at the start of term by offering a bar of pretty decent chocolate for every book returned. It took a little time for this tactic to gain traction—pupils were initially suspicious, presumed there must be some sort of catch. Their reservations were soon dispelled however by the sight of a few unfazed sorts casually brandishing Twixes against the wall at break time. Then, of course, the little fuckers couldn't get their books in quick enough.

One lunchtime, on a Wednesday let's say, five or six girls met up in a classroom on the ground floor of the English block to start work on a presentation they were to give in front of the class the following week. They pushed together two desks and sat around them and one of the girls was me. And what exactly do I know about her, this girl at the table who would be me? I know she would have much preferred to come up with a presentation all by herself. She might have even asked the teacher if she could work on her own. Sometimes Mr. Burton would let her do that, work all on her own, but he couldn't permit it every time, no matter how much she squirmed, no matter that she knew he knew she'd come up with something memorable all on her own, no matter that he knew she knew that, what could he do—I have to be able to report, he said, that you are able to work well with other people. But I could not work well with other people. Working well with other people meant keeping my mouth shut unless I had something entirely extraneous to say. If I dared to make a useful suggestion it would be automatically resisted by the group because in fact I wasn't half as smart as I thought I was and the group was always very keen on letting me know that. It was strange to sit in the classroom without the rest of the class there. Without Mr. Burton. We were lost at sea. The room was just a lot of cold furniture and stagnant reflections, it was difficult to imagine anything. I didn't feel like staying long. Nothing was coming together in any case. Nobody seemed willing to say very much. The contributions were sketchy and disparate, the discussion gathered no momentum, and so there was nothing at all to hold our attention.

Within a short time we all became agitated, and actually it seemed as if it might turn a bit unpleasant. I could feel two or three pairs of eyes appealing to me to say something and even though I had plenty of ideas I kept hold of my tongue, it just wasn't worth the hassle to do otherwise. Probably I had just one idea in fact, a kind of blithe vision of how the presentation should unfold—the atmosphere, the tone, the denouement, and so on. There had been occasions when I'd tried to convey what I'd identified to be the mechanics of my various visions, the brass tacks as it were, but they seemed not to make a great deal of sense when said out loud and I remember a particular girl looking at me with hatred while I attempted to put into words what was going on inside my head, an attitude which didn't aid my efforts at all. I sometimes wonder if my inclination for abstruse ideas wasn't in fact a form of passive-aggression. There was a large window along one side of the room that went from floor to ceiling so you could see across a large tarmac square to another building that contained changing rooms, the main hall, and the canteen. There were a few thin trees near the window, on the left. Whenever I think of them they have no leaves. I often felt shivery at school. Once my period leaked onto the stool during a science lesson while the teacher was demonstrating a Van de Graaff generator. There was a so-called hand hole in the middle of the stool's varnished wooden seat and the blood spread across the varnish with alarming rapidity and dripped through it straight down onto the floor. It was one of my first periods and I'd just started to use tampons and evidently had left this tampon in much too long. I very quietly told the girl beside me I'd leaked and without taking her eyes off the generator's hair-raising dome she gave me something out of her bag which I immediately scrunched up and stuffed into my cardigan sleeve. Then I put up my hand, the hand that had nothing up its sleeve, and asked the teacher for permission to go to the toilet. He looked at me over the top of his glasses and nodded with the same surliness with which he always nodded his almighty yet somehow squeezable-looking head. It was a relief to see him nodding in his usual surly way because that surely meant everything was still going on just as normal. That apart from the girl beside me, not one person in the room knew or suspected there was a small pool of blood on the classroom floor, warm and human, directly beneath my wooden stool.

I stood at one of the spotless white sinks and held my skirt under the cold tap and watched as the blood came streaming out of the pleats and swung around the silver plughole in beautiful unfurling plumes. I always liked being in the girls' toilets during lesson time. It was nice to be on my own and to see my face there in the mirror with nothing but clean white tiles all around me. There are lavatories everywhere and there have been for centuries so it didn't feel like I was at school or even English. I felt safe and far away, and as such I was tempted to sing. I was curious to know what my voice really sounded like. Who knows what would come out of my mouth as I stood out of time. Perhaps I am a nun in the north of Italy rinsing out skeins and skeins of bandages and outside in the woods tired filthy men are advancing and shooting at one another from behind dripping trees and they shall all be halted in their deplorable tracks the moment they hear me sing. You learn early on that you use cold water to get blood out of fabric. It's very effective if you do it straightaway while the blood is still wet and red and not yet a stubborn brownish stain. I don't know how many times I've had to wash blood out of knickers, jeans, the backs of dresses, dressing gowns, sheets, cushions, car seats. At least on one occasion every month twelve months a year for twenty-seven years, and I suppose if I were any good at maths I could work out just how many times that amounts to. On it goes. Only two weeks ago I had to take my culottes off and rinse them through at the kitchen sink. Afterwards I shook them out and examined them, front and back since I wasn't sure which was which, then draped them over the balcony railing. Not a trace! Plus it was a sunny afternoon so they were dry in no time. Still I was annoyed with myself. How many years have you been having periods, and still you manage to get blood everywhere? You should know by now exactly how this goes. There was a time in my twenties when I derived voluptuous satisfaction from going around dripping blood everywhere. I am a bleeding bloody creature, see how I bleed and bleed, look at all the blood crinkle-oozing out of me, onto my ankles, onto the ground, onto the street, onto your smart shoes. Bright as a ruby, dark as a garnet. She'd given me a pair of her knickers. They were wrapped very neatly around the sanitary towel I'd knowingly stuffed up my sleeve. I hadn't known anything about the knickers however and was amazed to be standing there holding them. I looked at the label to see what size they were and where they'd come from. She was one size bigger than me. They were nice, white I expect, with small flowers or balloons or sausage dogs on them, and very clean. They didn't have any bits like pencil shavings sticking to them so she must have kept them separate, tucked into a special little emergency pocket with a popper fastener I should think, just inside her rucksack. It was exciting, standing in the girls' toilets during lesson time all on my own surrounded by small shining white tiles with blood drying on the insides of my thighs and another girl's clean pair of knickers in my hands. It made me think of the First World War, though many things then made me think of the First World War. Freewheeling on my bike in the summertime, past all the hedgerows and that brown farmhouse with the tall chimney stacks near Purton—that almost always made me think of the First World War. And crows in the hard empty fields on Sundays in November—I couldn't help but think of the First World War then, but in a different way, because I would stand still for a while with my hands in my pockets looking at the crows drift back and forth over the tilled fields, and the thoughts you have about the First World War while standing still like that in the freezing cold are obviously of a very different nature from the kinds of ideas about the same subject that go on in your head when you're hurtling in the sunshine down narrow empty country lanes on a bicycle in July. Doing toast on the fire in winter and glancing out the corner of my eye at my mother reading a book and smoking a cigarette on the green-gold sofa in the evening. Getting up for school when it was still dark. The sound of hot water in the pipes when it was still dark and the mirror in the bathroom in the dark and the bathroom cabinet opening and closing with a nice neat click, all of that always made me think of the First World War. And the empty milk bottles in my mother's mother's kitchen, though never the ones in ours, probably because ours were so very very clean, practically sparkling, whereas the ones in my grandmother's kitchen looked like they contained fog. The whole lot of us running cross-country in the winter. Running through all that rain and mud on Thursday afternoons week after week right up until Christmas. All that mud and rain splashing up our bare legs, and all of our trainers, pairs and pairs of them, slung off and muddled up against the changing room wall, all caked in mud. All absolutely caked in mud. And mud of course would always make me think of the First World War. There was a lot of clay in the ground near where we lived. It was grey and smelt clean and was lovely to dig down and press into. Clay is completely different to mud and didn't ever make me think of the First World War. On the contrary. It made me think of half-baked pots and potteries and skittish spiders in the corners of flaking windowsills and narrow overgrown garden paths besieged by enormous crisscrossing moths and cardies on the backs of chairs and jam jars brimming with warm rainwater, and those are things I've always associated with the interwar years. Jumbled-up footwear of any sort piled high all the laces trailing and the rumpled tongues spilling makes me think of the Second World War and when I say that what I really mean is the death camps. Heaps of clothes and personal belongings, especially watches and umbrellas and shoes, always made me think of the death camps and the first time I went with my grandmother to a jumble sale in the community centre the sight of all those thin cardigans and nylon scarfs and gaping shoes heaped up on trestle tables end to end the length and breadth of the hall made me short of breath with thoughts of all the hundreds of thousands of women and men and their children who were dispatched in those wretched cramped cattle cars from all across Europe week after week straight into the barbaric ineludible core of the death camps. The best thing to do immediately upon entering a jumble sale, I quickly discovered, was to go over and stand around for a little while near where the two ladies in blue and pink turtlenecks were selling apple turnovers and butterfly cakes. And then, after listening in to them discussing Weight Watchers and rheumatism and rhododendrons and so on, I'd shoot off all of a sudden and join my grandmother at one of the tables and zealously root through the piles and piles of cast-offs alongside her. Looking for something with snazzy buttons on it I expect. (Just like a good little eagle-eyed Kanada Kommando.)

I used tampons almost as soon as my periods began because for one thing my periods began long after everyone else had got theirs so there wasn't time to be fannying around with towels. Sanitary towels weren't cool at all by the time I began my period, tampons were the thing because they let you carry on as normal since all you had in your knickers was a little white string, which would hardly get in the way of all the activities the adverts showed menstruating girls doing, such as swirling around on roller skates, leaping into the air to catch fluorescent-pink Frisbees, riding white horses across tremendous golden beaches, and so on. A lot of propaganda that was. In reality of course what carrying on as normal actually meant was, don't even think about skipping PE or sloping off early—don't lie down in a mute ball in the middle of the day—don't bellyache and groan at any hour of the day—don't expect to be excused from the table or let off from drying up—show up, join in, be productive—don't let the side down, never miss a day. By contrast, it was generally agreed that wearing a sanitary towel got in the way of everything. It was like having a sheep between your legs, everyone said. Only abnormal girls who had no friends in the first place and nothing to do besides didn't mind going around with a big smelly sheep wedged between their thighs all day long. Then, after years and years of wearing different sized tampons each month, and still never getting it quite right, I found myself orientating towards towels instead. It was dawning on me that I won't go on having periods forever—at some point they will splurge, then weaken, become erratic, and then they will stop altogether. I should make the most of them while they are still regular and strong, and not block them up. Blood should flow, it's not a wound after all, it doesn't need to be staunched. It's peculiar, how you can do something a certain way automatically for years and years, then, when you stop and begin to do it another way, you look back on the way you did it for so long and you can't quite believe it—how you just went along with a trite and manipulative depiction of something that's in fact such an integral part of your intimate reality. Swoosh. Leap. Twirl. Shameful inculcatory nonsense. Never miss a day! I didn't even stop to consider it really, I just went along with it, hardly gave it a second thought. Until one afternoon, when I stood in the bathroom and looked at my blood and womb lining, there on a tissue, and I thought, I'll miss this when it's gone, and I realised I didn't want it congealing invisibly inside of me anymore. Towels aren't entirely plain sailing though either. I never seem to get it in quite the right place—I still manage, almost every time, to stick the bloody thing too far back along the gusset.

On the first day the colour is very pretty—it's a shade of red I've been looking for in a lipstick since forever. Neither too dark, nor too bright. Not too pink not too brown not too orange. More than once I've imagined taking the blood-stained tissue into a department store, up to the Chanel counter, the Dior counter, the Lancôme counter, and saying "Look, this is the red, this is it, this is the most perfect red in the world. Let me see a lipstick at long last in this most perfect shade of red." Needless to say I've never done it. Month after month I ruefully drop the most perfect shade of red down the toilet and flush it away. Quel dommage. I have this idea that Marilyn Monroe stayed in bed when she got her period and bled all over the sheets, and I'm not sure where I derived it from. It's been in my head since I was approximately ten years old. My grandmother adored old Hollywood stars and had a particular penchant for Vivien Leigh and Marilyn Monroe, so it might have been from her I got it. But I can't imagine my grandmother telling me a thing like that. Perhaps she said it to my aunt and I overheard—I wasn't a snoop, but I did have sharp ears. My family relished exchanging grisly tales, though usually I'd only ever catch a snippet—which, severed from the full body of the story, became disturbingly visceral and took on a lasting and malignant life all of its own. I shall never forget the heinous image that assaulted my imagination when I overheard, for example, my other grandmother saying to her son, my father, "and she'd bitten all the skin off her fingers. Imagine that, eating your own hands." Stupidly I repeated those words to myself verbatim, many times over. My tendency to take every word I heard absolutely literally paradoxically meant I very often got the wrong end of the stick about quite a lot of things on a daily basis—and surely I had got the wrong end of the stick about this conversation—surely the girl, whoever she was, hadn't really eaten her own hands? It occurred to me that I probably hadn't understood what my grandmother had said correctly, that her words meant something else, something entirely innocuous—however, instead of just brushing them off it came to me that perhaps if I only repeated the awful phrase enough, the real, innocuous meaning that it obviously contained would eventually surface in all of its forgettable ordinariness, and the gory apparition of the girl greedily gobbling up her own hands, and all the blood crawling down her arms and dripping thickly from her elbows, would go away at once. That's not what happened. On the contrary, a new terror was released upon me—ironically by the most humdrum word out of them all. After many repetitions the word "and" lodged in my throat, expanded barbarously—I practically choked on it: *and*?! And she'd bitten all the skin off her fingers?? So in fact there was another thing she did, before chewing off her hands, possibly something much worse. Would my grandmother say the worst thing first? Probably she would. (My father's mother was dramatic and liked to make maximum impact when she told you a story whereas my mother's mother recounted scandalous news in a roundabout sort of way, pulled back and forth, again and again, by uncertainty and a preoccupation with peripheral details. Apparent shortcomings—oh come on, spit it out—which often nonetheless conspired to plant a strange and robust seed.) What exactly had the girl done before she chewed off the skin on her fingers? On this occasion my imagination was uncommonly considerate of my fainthearted disposition so that instead of conjuring up the absolute worst it very quickly installed a relatively tame image of the girl tearing out her blond and lank hair, thus preventing anything truly horrific from emerging that would scare the living daylights out of me. Tearing out her hair seemed to make sense anyway: "She'd torn out her hair in great big clumps, and she'd bitten all the skin off her fingers. Imagine that, eating your own hands." Yes, that made sense. Clearly it was the eating of the hands that my grandmother wanted to leave my father with, so, in all likelihood, the prior diabolical action very probably wasn't anything worse than that. And in fact, now that the hand-eating was prefixed by another grim act of self-mutilation, it wasn't nearly as frightening anymore. In fact it made me laugh.

I don't know whether Marilyn Monroe did stay in bed and bleed all over the sheets, but if she did I wouldn't blame her. Especially since she had endometriosis which meant during her period she suffered from intense pelvic pain and excruciatingly severe cramps. Sexual intercourse with male lovers would have been really uncomfortable for her a lot of the time too. My grandmother certainly wouldn't have mentioned any of that to me. She did tell me that Marilyn Monroe liked to read. "You wouldn't think so to look at her, but she always had her head in a book. Like the way you are." My grandmother often said "You wouldn't think so to look at her" about some woman or another. It seemed to me that it gave her enormous pleasure, to think about women doing things and behaving in ways that were entirely at odds with what they looked like. She rarely, if ever, said such a thing about a man. She didn't talk about men very much. I got the impression she was of the opinion that, as far as men were concerned, you could tell exactly what they got up to just by looking at them. And of course you could tell what they got up to just by looking at them since they went around getting up to whatever they pleased with no compunction whatsoever—women, on the other hand, were secretive and hid things and though it may have looked like they were doing one thing they were in fact quite often doing something else entirely. By the time I was born my grandmother had already been divorced many years and would soon be living alone again since by the end of my first year in the world the younger man she'd found some overdue happiness with died of leukaemia just after Christmas. She carried on living alone until she died approximately forty years later at which point I hope that her dream of being reunited with this man she'd never stopped missing came true. It was unusual for a woman of her generation to live alone like that, for all those years, though it never seemed particularly peculiar to me growing up. We saw her often since she lived close by, and I liked going off to see her on my own, she baked fruitcake, for one thing, that tasted of marmalade and cigarettes. It was there, already cut into big squares, inside the red and cream container on the right when you went into the kitchen—or else it wasn't because she hadn't made any and that was disappointing, even if she did have something else for you. Whatever it was wouldn't taste of smoke and oranges. While I sat there eating cake, or else corned beef and beetroot with a hard-boiled egg, she'd empty her coat pockets onto the kitchen table. She was always picking things up off the street. And if you saw her in the street she'd say, "I think I dropped something under that bench, have a look for Nanny will you." She hadn't dropped anything of course—I was more agile than she was and could bring my eyes into places that hers couldn't investigate. "Have a good look," she'd say as I scrappled around beneath the bench, without ever saying what it was exactly I should be looking for. Leave no stone unturned. No. No. When I was older I worked weekends on a checkout in the local supermarket and she would often come in and watch me with abstracted admiration as I scanned frozen vegetables and tinned food. "You look ever so smart in that uniform," she'd say to me. Several years later I moved to another country and so I didn't see my grandmother so often anymore. We wrote to each other now and then. In her letters she nearly always mentioned that the lady in the cigarette kiosk had asked after me. Whenever I returned and visited her we'd always have tea and fruitcake, and smoke whatever brand of menthol cigarettes she happened to prefer at the time, and then, when it was time for me to make tracks, as we always said, she'd dally up and down the hallway, offering me an assortment of things which she'd dust off with a corner of her cardigan before showing me—telephones, tea towels, slippers, irons, iced buns, umbrellas, candlesticks, air fresheners, photograph albums, gloves, fifteen-denier tan tights, knitting needles, manicure sets—and each time I'd explain to her regretfully that I was flying back and couldn't bring much with me. "You're a free spirit," she'd say. "I don't blame you, my dear. You're better off." Her flat was a trove of disparate objects, some mysterious, some commonplace, some utterly defunct— most of the grown-ups in my family, I noticed, seemed to think she ought to have "a good clear-out." Yet I suspect that le Comte de Lautréamont, macabre poet and darling of the surrealists, wouldn't have endorsed their breezy incitements to declutter at all, would in fact have felt right at home in my grandmother's flat exactly as it was, since, as far as he was concerned, a sewing machine and an umbrella upon an operating table was a chance encounter of some considerable beauty. No doubt he would have found her book collection a source of considerable inspiration too. In addition to mawkish biographies of Hollywood legends my grandmother possessed an impressive range of sensational hardbacks containing photographic accounts of the vilest Victorian murders. Which is just the sort of singularity that gives an otherwise run-of-the-mill room an exciting air when you're a child. Sitting in proximity of those slashed and mangled corpses rendered in delicate monochrome made my heart thump its way into my throat in the manner of a maimed troll heaving its smeared bulk up a wishless well by the mulish efforts of its one remaining weevil-ravaged fist. I swallowed hard, again and again, until my ears thrummed, in a bid to get my heart down to where it ought to be.

I'm not long for this world.

I'm not long for this world.

That's something I grew accustomed to hearing my grandmother avow while waiting for instance for the kettle to boil. The dull infinite rumbling sound of water shuddering to vapour heaven knows can all of a sudden bring on such celestial yearnings. Or perhaps after, seated. While she stirred sugar into her tea and I herded cake crumbs about the tea plate on my knee with the small engrossed pad of my middle finger. She said it one day while we were both sat waiting for pudding in the living room of my aunt's house near the brook and my aunt came flying in from the kitchen holding up a large steaming spoon and said very crossly, "Mum! Don't say things like that in front of her." But I didn't mind, I didn't mind one bit. In fact I rather liked it when she said that and said it myself later on when I got home and was sitting on the edge of my bed. I am not long for this world. I am not long for this world. I was already experiencing the sensation by this time that I was outside of the world, looking in, and the feelings that sense mostly gave rise to were ones of forlornness and anguish. Sat on the edge of my rosebud-patterned bed, repeating my grandmother's mantra, however, I felt noble, mysterious, and independent. As if I were only visiting this world in any case and had somewhere a million times better to return to. I am not long for this world. I am not long for this world.

On top of one of the cupboards pushed back against the wall in the classroom that uninspiring Wednesday lunchtime was a box and inside the box were a lot of copies of the same book. The very book that the department had lately been extracting from the pupils by dint of the unfailing pull of handsome bars of chocolate. My eyes, always searching, and especially then since my mind's eye had clouded right over, landed upon the box and couldn't help but be pricked by its significance. My mouth opened and my finger pointed. Yes, it was my mouth. Yes indeed it was my finger. In the blink of an eye the girl who was so adept at finding one reason or another to look at me hatefully was up on the table beside the cupboard, hauling the books hand over fist out of the box to the other girls who were right on her heels, their flexing hands fanning the air as they each reached up to grab one. I stood up where I was and saw it all. The girl jumped down and the table wobbled. I saw her skirt flare out and the table wobble, and while I was coping with this sudden disturbance of the box and the table and the air around both, a book was rammed directly into my chest with such force it knocked my own small portion of air right out of me, and there, suddenly, was a pair of dark contemptuous eyes, exactly opposite my own. I looked into one and saw there around the iris something more unsettling than hatred even, something like an ouroboros covered in a glittering chain of small obsidian mirrors. Something in my own right eye twitched, violently. Whatever it was clearly did not have its tail in its mouth. Its riled unswallowed tip twitched again and my eyelid came right down over it and stayed down. "It was your idea," she said, pushing the cellophane-wrapped hardback into my barely-there chest. I had a lot of ideas and most of them stayed where they were and nothing gave me greater pleasure than to sit in the grass and go over them again and again. Turning them this way and that, buffing them with the fringed edge of my entangled imagination. I would never dream of taking them out—how did this one get out? It was not down deep enough. The only parts of me that had been involved in this were my eyes first of all and my mouth and then my finger. Extremities! Or was it my finger and then my mouth? Yes, of course it was my finger and then my mouth—I would hardly have said "Look" before pointing my finger. "Look," I said, my mouth catching up with my finger that was pointing up towards the box the eyes had seen on top of the cupboard against the wall. The eyes, the finger, and the mouth, yes, and its utterance, last of all. Look. And that's all I said, not a word more. Yet if that doesn't quite constitute an idea I surely would have known very well where such demonstrations lead—no child says "Look" without meaning for something to happen. A child's eyes are instinctively and never-endingly searching for some little thing amongst it all that just like that upends the whole lot. I carried on looking at her with just one wide-open eye. It amazed me how easy it was to do that on and on while keeping my right eyelid firmly closed and heroically smooth. I felt mythical and unassailable—on the edge of something.

Clearly I wasn't winking at her—it wasn't remotely like a wink. She knew that. She knew there was something I wasn't letting her see. Whatever creature I had, coiled up and hankering inside of my right eye, was none of her business.

All thoughts pertaining to the nonexistent presentation have gone out the window and are mingling dolefully with the scant swaying branches of the trees, there to the left of the empty tarmac square.

The others all race on down the corridor to the department office and the one now in charge knocks on the door, impatiently, insistently, expectantly, many times. It's quite shocking how commanding her knock is.

The door opens, nothing is said.

The books are proffered, someone short fires out the bars of chocolate without question or thanks, and they're off again. Just like that.

Charging back up the corridor towards the bright grey sunlight.

Where am I? I have hardly moved at all. I stood halfway outside the classroom watching the backs of them as they ran off, each clutching a book, down the corridor towards the door of the office. Am I holding a book? Probably not. I don't know what I did with it. I did not get up on the table and drop it back into the box. That really would have been ridiculous. Impossible. There was no going back. What could be

done with it? Perhaps I left it on the table. Yes, of course. Yes.
I left it on the table. That's right. Exactly in the spot where I
sit every lesson. Then I stood, empty-handed, one foot in the
corridor, the other still in the classroom, and watched them
running down towards the door. I saw the door open. I saw
the brightness of the room behind. Whoever had opened the
door was just a silhouette, a short squat silhouette. I heard
nothing, nothing was said. The door closed and the light
went. In no time at all the corridor was cool and dark once
more and the girls came bobbing back up, their hands now
gripped around gratis bars of chocolate and not books they
had zero interest in. Just like that. By then I was extrinsic,
invisible. One foot in one foot out. They passed me by. Only
the ouroboros flashed briefly in my direction. Up ahead the
grey light outside shone with a strange grainy brilliance that
turned them all into black gelatinous blobs—inkblots or
tadpoles—and then absorbed them completely. Looking neither left nor right I shifted across the corridor and disappeared into the toilets. I looked into the mirror straightaway
and saw there the only girl in the whole wide world. Such an
apprehensive-looking thing! My hands gripped tightly on either side of the ice-cold sink and that was something I had
never done before. Yet it felt as if I had been gripping the sink
tightly like that since forever, and would go on gripping it just
as tightly until at least the end of my life. My mouth tasted of
cucumber and elastic bands. I had no urge to sing.

They all adored Mr Burton, he was their favourite, by miles. He wasn't like other teachers at all and his lessons weren't like other lessons, he was lively and his classes were lively and exciting and fun. He was very funny. The boys loved that, they lapped it up. The boys liked to think they were funny and some of them were funny, but he, generally, was much funnier without really having to even try. It seemed so effortless when he was funny and of course he was always a few steps ahead of them, and they knew that of course, they could feel it, that's what made it so exciting. It was a kind of sport in a way, this sparring that went on, with him always a few steps ahead, except for the occasions when one or another of them misjudged where they stood and went too far. It was a thin line and they'd overshot it. They'd realise too late that they'd gone too far, too far in the wrong direction perhaps, was there a direction, was any of this leading somewhere, who knows, well now it had been brought to a standstill and the lesson resumed, which was just as well. Sometimes it seemed to take up an awful lot of time, all this sparring, a few steps forward, a few steps back, and to begin with, yes, it was quite exciting, for the first couple of months like everyone else she'd found it all tremendous fun, it made such a change after all, all this levity—you'd hardly ever feel chilly in that classroom, on the contrary—and then it wasn't a change anymore.

She became irritated. She wondered actually if he wasn't becoming a caricature of himself. She could feel just like everyone could feel that he was a few steps ahead always, but that didn't stop her from feeling that he was stooping to their level. A few steps ahead, yes, but ahead on the very same level as them, when really he should have been on another level altogether, shouldn't he? She couldn't help but feel he was kowtowing to them and that made him seem a fool and that vexed her, that really put her out, she didn't like to think of him as a fool so she resolved not to go along with it anymore. She stopped laughing with the rest of them because really it wasn't that funny in any case, over and over again, what was so funny, on and on, she was tired of it, she was tired of his popularity, she was disdainful of popularity in fact, of being the one that everyone liked, she couldn't see what the attraction was. When people liked you they had a habit of hanging around you and quite often they'd be scoffing something overwhelmingly vinegary, and as often as not there would be someone else with them, someone else they liked, though not as much as they liked you, and predictably whoever that was wouldn't like you very much, because of the way their friend liked you the most, and you liked neither of them particularly. But there they both were, all the same, one of them loudly munching space-invader-shaped crisps and probably offering the bag to you and the other one—probably to you first since you were their favourite, and you wouldn't dream of putting your hand into that revolting bag, lined, you knew, with horrible greasy crumbs—and you could tell, even though you'd looked away, that the other one couldn't wait to get her hand in there, and then her hand was in there, right the way in, rummaging about the disgusting bag, noisily and greedily, the back of it getting covered all over with those horrid bright orange crumbs, and then it was the two of them standing there, crunching obnoxiously on this odorous crispy snack, and there you were, somehow caught between both, even though you hadn't said a single word to either of them. That's just the kind of uncomfortable scenario you'd find yourself in if you were popular, she knew that very well—she knew that popularity meant being trapped at every turn— no, it held no attraction at all and she was fed up of seeing how his popularity meant that they expected him to be fun every single time. What if he didn't feel like it? Was he afraid of letting them down? The boys thought they were ace, they really did, it was quite astonishing. They never tired of the sound of their own voices, not for one minute, and the sound of some of their voices had changed—their voices had broken, apparently. Whenever she heard that peculiar phrase she imagined something down in their throats tearing, a thin pink membrane, not unlike the hymen perhaps. She knew about that, about how that got broken, everyone knew about that, but she didn't know what caused a boy's voice to break. Perhaps talking all the time was what did it and that's why they wouldn't shut up for even five minutes. But Woody hardly ever said a word and when he did it was obvious he had the deepest voice of them all so who knows what makes that thin pink hymen in a boy's throat give way so that their voice issues from a deeper chamber and resonates with an apparently more serious timbre. The male's voice breaks, the female's hymen breaks, and then what? The boys with the broken voices, she noticed, wouldn't mess around so much anymore, they were too mature now for that kind of thing. That's right, they were grown up now and wanted everybody to know about it, including him. They especially wanted him to know it. They still liked the sound of their own voice, she noticed, if anything they liked it even more now, because it was deeper and obviously a deeper voice sounded stronger and much more manly, which meant, she noticed, that those boys fancied themselves to be men, and occasionally he would, she noticed, talk to them slightly differently. He'd make asides to them from time to time, and they'd laugh, together they'd laugh, knowingly, and that really disgusted her—that sort of phoney male comradeship really got her back up. How easy it was for them to be taken seriously, to be let in on something—a female teacher would turn on her in a flash if she tried on any of that. Female teachers didn't want you getting too close, they blew hot and cold in fact—mostly cold then all of a sudden out of the blue, hot, hot, utterly dazzling, perfumed, then away again, the cold shoulder. The big freeze.

As if she'd tricked them into dropping their guard. It was quite startling. Everyone knew that one of them had a scar like a feather across her throat which she nearly always covered over with a scarf and one day she did not. One day she stood at the front of the classroom without a scarf around her neck and they could all see the scar across her throat, just like a feather, but it was her eyes really that were unforgettable. Her eyes were pale green. She was probably no age at all. She wore boots and long skirts and long scarfs nearly always. And then, after calling her Mrs Hurly for two years, her name changed. That's right, they were to call her Miss Selby from now on, which was much nicer and suited her better. That's her maiden name, someone said. Her maiden name. So it was no wonder really was it that it sounded all satiny and sibilant and suited her so well. His name would never change would it, his name had always been that, Burton, always Burton, since he was a boy, and it would be the same for them wouldn't it, their names wouldn't ever change. The boys would always be called what they were called now, Robert Ellis, and Liam Sykes, and Paul Carter, and Mark Kuklinski, and so on. She really was fed up with every single one of them, and was intensely put out by the way that more and more of them could insinuate themselves with him simply on account of their voices being suddenly deeper, as if that was something they'd managed to bring about themselves according to their own wits and erudition. It cut her to the quick. Was he really that much of a fool that he supposed that that alone made them men who knew what they were talking about because from where she was sitting they didn't look or sound remotely like men who knew anything at all. No, he wasn't a fool, of course not. He was very sharp in fact and she heard him snap at them occasionally, that's right, they'd gone too far, so in fact there were limits, there were still limits, and they didn't know where these limits were of course, they hadn't a clue when they'd got above their station. He knew. He knew! He was the one in control, and occasionally he'd snap and they'd know about it then, and that pleased her. It pleased her when he put them back in their place. He could be very cutting actually, and that really gave her a great deal of satisfaction. They'd sit there feeling very silly then, she could feel it, how silly they were feeling, how wounded. She wouldn't dare look. If you looked at them when they were humiliated they'd absolutely despise you for it and later on after school they'd do or say something on the way home to humiliate you in a way that you'd never live down. She knew that, she knew that very well, so even though it was immensely tempting to look them straight in their stupid wounded faces she refrained from even glancing over when one or another of them had been put back in his place.

Gloating would be less of a temptation perhaps if there were something out of the window she could look at that would help distract her from all this. But beyond those scrappy destitute branches on the left there wasn't anything at all diverting to look at out of that enormous wide window. Her exercise book was open on the table all the while of course. Yes, there it was, waiting for some mark or other to be made upon it. Unbearable really—for god's sake get on with it. It's not surprising in the least that she often took up her pen and began doodling on a page somewhere towards the back. That's what she wanted to be doing really, committing something or other to the page. It was always a relief to doodle in the back of her exercise book—just small intricate doodles while all the nonsense was still going on. If she had been able to draw she might have sketched some actual things, she might have sat there in fact and sketched the things around her, pencil cases, people's faces, but she was hopeless at drawing anything in front of her. She occasionally wondered if her lack of interest in the things around her wasn't in some way due to her inability to accurately depict them, or perhaps it was the other way around—her inability to accurately depict the things around her was due to her lack of interest in them. But she was interested in them, she was extremely interested in nearly everything, just not so much with how they appeared. She was distrustful of appearances, which was hardly surprising since her mother's mother seemed to think that almost everyone was a wolf in sheep's clothing, a point of view made doubly woolly by her father's mother's perennial observation that so-and-so was in fact mutton dressed as lamb, and wasn't her own mother forever opining that there was more to this or that than meets the eye, and indeed time and time again many things that looked perfectly decent turned out to be rotten to the core, so it was hardly surprising was it that she wanted to get beneath the surface of things, find out what they were really like, and it was that desire perhaps, to know what something was really made of, that interfered with and hampered the pencil. The resulting depiction would bear hardly any kind of resemblance to its subject, achieving a credible likeness just about eluded her, and she resented having to try and try again. What exactly was the point of reproducing an illusion? For a little while she tried to draw birds from memory. The beak would come easily enough and a beady eye, then a careful flick over there for a tail and flecks for feet somewhere beneath. But she could never join up these various stations, it seemed intrusive to try. She made shapes, she made symbols, she made patterns. Patterns and doodles intruded on nothing she could see—they gave shape to something she sensed was there but couldn't see. Then, one afternoon, out of the blue, there came a few words, just a few words at the tail end of a face. A face, yes—his face in fact, though he was nowhere to be seen. No, he wasn't there that day, a replacement teacher was there, and what a waste of time that was, since he was irreplaceable. Everyone including the replacement teacher was in a very bad mood, it was a shambles, where on earth was he, it was a shambles. They hadn't been told why he wasn't there, it wasn't any of their business they were told, he would be back next week, that was all they needed to know—they didn't like that, they didn't like that one bit. They all sat there with folded arms in intractable silence, as if they'd been wronged. As if he had no business at all being anywhere else but right here. She quickly discovered she liked him not being here because it meant she could think about him and about where he might be and what he might be like there. She thought it served them right that he wasn't here and she was pleased with him for being somewhere else. She imagined him putting his jacket on, a jacket she'd never seen. She imagined him driving a blue car with sunlight moving across the windscreen, she imagined him crossing a street quickly, she imagined him going up the clean grey steps of a municipal building, she imagined him passing by other people, she imagined keys in his trouser pocket, she imagined other people out in the world noticing him. Women—she imagined women noticing him. It was exciting to think of him that way, to imagine him out in the world. What kinds of thoughts, she wondered, would he have out there, as he buttoned up his jacket and crossed streets and waited at traffic lights. She imagined she was with him, in the car, on the pavement, crossing the street—maybe they'd take a train to the next town, or perhaps they'd drive in his blue car past trees and hedgerows out to one or other of those charming villages beyond the suburbs—perhaps they'd be carrying boxes or a trunk—perhaps she'd be wearing a hat—perhaps they'd stand on a small old bridge and look down into a river and perhaps she'd drop something down into the river like a reed or a catkin and then what—they'd run to the other side no doubt—perhaps they'd take off their shoes and she'd see his feet and his ankles—imagine that—his bare feet and naked ankles. She found she could imagine him very well when he wasn't here and she didn't want to stop. His face was in her mind and she could see by his face that the thoughts going on in his mind when he wasn't here had nothing at all to do with boys or school or books or with anything particularly funny even. Out there in the world he had a life of his own. She could see him, she could really see him, now that he wasn't here, and very slowly she began to draw his face on the page in front of her so that his face stayed right where it was, in the very centre of her mind. Drawing him kept him steady in the centre of her mind and brought him in closer, even closer, blotting everything else out. He wasn't absent—she wasn't remembering him—he was here—he was right here, moving through her mind, making it warm and luxuriant, and he could see of course all the many things she kept stored away in it, though only from an oblique angle—he couldn't see all the way into those things in her mind which were all around him, not yet. Then it all started to go wrong of course because she really was hopeless at drawing, added to which the biro was all wrong, all wrong—the feeling from it was all wrong.

A biro is a cumbersome perfunctory instrument that gives no pleasure to the one who wields it and in her inept hand it soon made her shortcomings in the illustrative mode brutally apparent. One eye was much bigger than the other, would have looked at home on an entirely different creature, and the hair, his beautiful wavy hair, was all over the place, this way and that, the mess of it made her hot with shame. It was shameful—it had to be obliterated—no discernible trace of it should remain. She scrawled all over it, around and around went the pen, forging tight little obliterating spirals, over and over. Strange really, winding up her fist like that—it would not let go. It remained there on the page and the wound-up fist sent the nib across the paper in a wavy line that flew up into exuberant loops, throwing off the tightness of the tight spirals that were a kind of steel wool obliterating the face that was so disgracefully wrong beneath, and then the loops sank down, calmer now, yes, calm now it seemed, a line again, a smooth line relaxing across the page and the line broke off into words, just a few words, then a few words more, and the words set out a story, as if it had been there all along. Within a matter of moments, there it was, a story—small and complete and indestructible. She closed the book, turned it the right side up, put her expended pen down on top of it. She felt insanely hot. No one would know just by looking at her exercise book what was inside, it looked very ordinary yet she knew sat there looking down at it that it contained something more, something that didn't need to be there at all, something voluntary, out of the blue, something secret, something small that had nonetheless disclosed the entrance-way to an alluring and unmapped realm. Come this way, come this way, don't look back. She didn't want chocolate, that's not what she wanted, she'd buy some herself if that's what she wanted, she did a paper round, two in fact, one during the week and another on Sundays, she could buy her own chocolate, if that's what she wanted, but that wasn't it, that's not what she did it for, that wasn't the idea, that wasn't what she wanted at all. She'd got glimpses of him, seen something now and then beneath his skin, amidst his eyes, searching and unsettled, adrift. He wasn't done, far from it. She was tired of being fobbed off, she was restless, hungry—something had to happen, away from this desk, outside of this classroom. It was alright for them, laughing their heads off on and on, they all went off elated and thoroughly pleased with themselves. Something had to break through. She wanted to unmask him, and so she betrayed him.

"Look," I said.
The eyes, the finger, and the mouth,
yes,
and its utterance,
last of all.

Wearing another girl's knickers wasn't something you just got on with. It sort of took over, like keeping a secret, and changed the texture of the day entirely. It was difficult to know what to do with them once you got home and could sprint upstairs to your bedroom immediately and open a drawer full of knickers and put on a spotless pair of your own. Some girls didn't want them back after and other girls thought that if you didn't give them back it was because you wanted to keep them and if you wanted to hang on to a pair of another girl's knickers that meant you were scavvy or peculiar. It was quite a complicated business. Added to which, I never really liked my mother knowing I'd worn another girl's knickers and if I put them in the laundry basket she'd notice them right away and want to know where they'd come from. My mother was very particular about where things came from and didn't like it very much if something or other just turned up out of nowhere. "Where on earth have these come from??" she'd exclaim, holding up a pair of Garfield-patterned pants for example, eye level and at arm's length between the tips of her fingers. My mother didn't like other people's things getting in with our things and I thought there must be a good reason why she didn't so I became very conscious of our things and of other people's things and I was constantly amazed at the way other people didn't seem to be conscious of their things at all—they were very slapdash with their things I couldn't help but notice whereas it had been instilled in me to be very careful with mine. This disparity between how things were treated did mean that other people's things, which were frequently chucked about any old how, had a completely different aura from those things that belonged to me. Their things seemed cheaper, more disposable, and my things seemed rarer and much more valuable, practically irreplaceable, and I was distractingly terrified of losing or ruining them. Having said that, I had a terrible habit of "dapping things down." Of taking things off and leaving them behind in the grass for example. Easy come, easy go, as they say. As my father often said in the hallway as I went on up the stairs, with that soupçon of chipper sarcasm that typically permeates the many pithy observations of the proletariat. Easy come, easy go, eh? My alleged couldn't-care-less attitude made this self-starting man turgid with disapprobation, while his native substance lit up and rejoiced at how little importance I placed upon having this, that, or the other. A conflict simmered on and on in my father—on the one hand he was rightly proud of the progress he'd made in his chosen trade and of the top-drawer material comforts he was able to consistently provide his family with because of it, yet on the other hand he also felt like a bit of a mug for going along with it all—working and buying and working and buying—working harder and buying better—it was all a big game after all, wasn't it, he could see that, and it wasn't a game he was destined to come out on top of, he knew that, he knew that and the conflict roiled away in him, on and on. It sometimes happened of course that somebody might have something even nicer than something of mine, but I seldom experienced any jealousy about it because in a matter of weeks whatever it was they had would seem perfectly average, whereas where my things were concerned the more time that passed the more precious they became. My mother I began to realise did in fact have an eye for the finer things in life and made it her business to choose exceptionally nice things for us all. I wouldn't say she was at all materialistic or avaricious, yet having nice things was important to her. Possibly because when my parents got married and I was born—the two events happening in quick succession—they didn't have any things. Nothing at all and as far as I know nobody gave them anything. Nothing they wanted in any case. They started absolutely from scratch. And so naturally it became important to have things. It helps make unexpected circumstances seem planned and even desirable. Things hold life in place. Like pebbles on a blanket at the beach they stop it from drifting away or flying up in your face. Having nice things makes you feel like you're doing a good job and shuts everybody else up. There's nothing anybody can say to you so long as you have nice things all around you. They can't touch you. And as time went on there were more and more nice things, lovely things.

A white cotton jacket with striped lapels and big square pockets and come September a smart navy coat with two rows of small buttons and a rounded velvet collar. Party dresses with smooth sashes. And oxblood loafers and argyle socks and a rosebud pitcher and bowl and croissants on Sundays and banana shampoo and maidenhair ferns and holidays in the Canary Islands and gold-plated bathroom taps and pavlova and 501s and Flower Fairies and Wayfarers and Feast ice creams and Slazenger tennis rackets and made-to-measure Roman blinds and Betty Boop sweatshirts and Barbour jackets and Pineapple leggings and Wedgwood china and Stag mahogany and Laura Ashley wallpaper and Raleigh racers and ballet shoes and Clinique and Volvo and Thorntons Easter eggs and Chez Fred fish and chips. I had the same bedcover as Helena Bonham Carter. I couldn't believe my eyes when I saw the photograph in the *Sunday Times* magazine. She was sat on her bed with her immense hair all loose and the rosebud cover on her duvet was exactly the same as the rosebud cover on the duvet that I was at that very moment sitting on myself. I would have liked to have torn the page out and slipped it into my rosebud pillowcase that was exactly the same as her rosebud pillowcase. It was intoxicating to look at a photograph of Helena Bonham Carter sitting on a bed that looked just like mine. It encouraged me to feel there wasn't a great deal of difference between us—as I gazed at her romantic mass of twinkling curls I could feel my own sullen slew of rats' tails augmenting magnificently. Next to my bedroom was the bathroom and one day not long before I left home to go to university in London a duck appeared on the bathroom wall just above the toilet cistern. I couldn't believe my eyes—where had it come from? My mother had painted it. "What do you think?" she said. "Does it look daft?" It came all of a sudden, all at once, and brought with it a terrible wind. Soon after it arrived all the nice things my parents had worked so hard to gather and had arranged so beautifully were blown right off the life they'd held so firmly in place, were wrapped up in newspaper and put into separate boxes, and some of those boxes went who knows where and some of them ended up in my father's mother's loft, and nobody can remember what's inside any of them. All this time later I find myself holding on to certain things I don't even like that much, for no other reason than that I have had them for so long. A somewhat tautological reason. On it goes.

Mr Burton was very angry. The books were all numbered of course and the returned ones ticked off as they came in and put away into boxes. When he entered the classroom the door swung open violently and hit off the wall behind it. He walked directly to his desk fast and with his head down. I felt sick. I throbbed all over. All over. It was very exciting. I don't remember what he said. He didn't look up when he said it. He was looking down at his desk and he was moving some paper around and what he said only made sense to our table and the other girls couldn't care less and barely took any notice. Hateful eyes had clocked it all of course. She smiled at me with utmost insincerity and mouthed the words "well done." I couldn't take my eyes off him. His face. How the skin rippled, twitched, with agitation. I felt tremendously bad. And then I felt bad, just bad. What had I done? He wouldn't look me in the eye. For the whole lesson he didn't look at me once. Perhaps he would never look at me again. If there had been somewhere to sob I would have gone there at once and sobbed my heart out and never left but there wasn't anywhere so I could not sob I could only go around and around for the rest of the day feeling bilious with all the tears pent up inside of me. Perhaps I would be drowned by them. Perhaps it would serve me right. Perhaps it would be for the best—what if he never looks at me again? I couldn't bear it so the only thing to do was to go and see him and hadn't I known all along from the moment I pointed my finger that I was setting in motion a situation where the only thing to do in the end would be to go and see him? It was a Friday. Fridays always felt different anyway. Friday afternoons especially. Everyone felt it, pupils and teachers alike. You could get away with more on a Friday afternoon because no one was entirely there anyway. Everyone was on a sort of threshold and often did and said anomalous things with the tacit understanding that in the cold light of Monday morning whatever had been said and done last thing on a Friday belonged to a completely different world and ought not to be acknowledged or referred to in any way, now that we were all so firmly installed back in this very familiar and boring one. The staff room was on the ground floor of the English block at the end of the corridor. I say corridor as if it were a narrow passage—it wasn't, it was wide. I don't remember there being any narrow passageways in any of the buildings except where the offices were of course and you'd never walk down that corridor even though it connected the language block with the main hall—the only reason you'd ever be in that corridor was in order to wait, either for the nurse or for the headmaster. I don't know what the flooring in the English block was made of but whenever I think of it it is always dark and resinous, and always has light moving across it, and reflections, shadows, all at the same time. It is more present than the doors, there on all sides, to the classrooms, to the staff room. I knocked on the door to the staff room and the door opened right away and so yes I really had knocked on the door. He was inside the staff room and I was standing outside of it looking at him and then behind him. It was quiet. Nobody else was in there. I could see to the end of the room and I could see there was a window that went from floor to ceiling, just like in the classroom. It faced out onto some shrubs that were tall and bushy and had thick leaves all over them making an area that was inaccessible, private. When the teachers were in here they didn't want to see us and that was understandable. It was strange to see them outside of a lesson anyway, awkward really—yet I had longed to see him somewhere else, my idea of him could not be contained by the classroom any longer, it had outgrown it, outgrown it. I stepped into the staff room and he closed the door behind me and now I was in a room with him, just him and no one else. It was quite a small room. Everything seemed so very still and watchful. There were bookshelves all around and chairs pushed up against them and the chairs had foam cushions and pale wooden arms. Some of the chairs were light blue and some were pale peach. I see my jacket on one of the chairs. Sometimes I see a green jacket and sometimes I see a purple one. I can remember both of those jackets, they each had shoulder pads and fabric-covered buttons. One of them had belonged to my mother, the other one I'd bought in a sale from McIlroy's. It was far too big for me. Whichever one it was I must have been carrying it if it ended up on a chair, I certainly wouldn't have taken it off. Why didn't I go on holding it, it wasn't heavy or encumbering. He must have invited me to put it down. Maybe he took it from my hands and put it down himself. And why would he do that? Because I was crying, sobbing my heart out at last, and perhaps holding on to this grown-up jacket while I sobbed my heart out was just too pitiful a sight. Perhaps even though it was not heavy or encumbering it was in the way. Something, yes, was lifted, removed, put to one side, when it was taken and laid down upon a chair. A green or purple jacket on a peach or a greyish chair. I don't really remember a single word of what I said. I remember his head was bowed because he was quite tall and I was very short and he was looking down at me and we'd never stood as close to one another as this. His eyebrows were raised incredulously and I think he said something about so many tears coming out of such a small girl and probably that made me cry even more because it was such a tender and funny thing to say and I would have been so relieved to hear him talk to me that way because when he didn't look at me at all the world seemed completely bland and indifferent and interminable and I felt so very odious. Probably I told him I was sorry and he probably said he knew it hadn't been my idea and I no doubt became indignant then and told him it had been my idea, all my idea, and I don't know why I needed to make that so very clear. To dispel any ideas he had of me as being good through and through very probably. To show him there was a lot more to me despite how small I might appear. That I was studious and diligent, yes, but that didn't prevent me from having wild and boundless thoughts. And then he played it down I expect, said something like it wasn't the worst thing in the world, that we all do things we're not proud of from time to time, it's only human—he had an admission of his own to make in fact. He'd looked in the back of my exercise book he said. Yes, I remember that. Of course I remember that, it shocked me.

What on earth! Teachers never went looking in the back of your exercise book, goodness knows what he was doing there, in the back of my exercise book. Strange to think. But really it wasn't his confession that struck me, it was the sound of his voice while he made it. So soft, vulnerable, almost imploring—unbearably endearing. Nobody had spoken to me with a voice like that before. I wanted to reach up and take his face into my hands. He'd gone somewhere he shouldn't have gone, and had found something curious there. A curious little story, he said, and he asked me if I'd made it up myself and I said yes I had and he asked me if I had any more stories and I said yes I did even though I didn't and what did he say then? "Can I read them?" "Would you like me to read them?" I don't know exactly how he put it. It was a very beautiful moment. It was beautiful at the time and now looking back it is perhaps even more so. It is precious. A precious moment. He'd been somewhere he ought not to have been, and he wanted to go there again—that's how it seemed to me. OK, I said, I'll bring some in for you to look at, and that's what I did. I wrote stories and brought them in for him, every Friday.

I experience, every few years, an urge to recall this moment and the events that preceded it. Not only to recall it, but to write it down, again. Again. Write down again how he had discovered something secret in the back pages of my exercise book and asked me if there was more. He wanted more of something that I created, that I had, that I was—I couldn't tell these things apart—it is the attention of a desired man or woman that will blur the lines that distinguish them. Again and again I recall how I wrote stories on loose unlined sheets of A4 paper my father brought home from work. My hand-writing was joined up, just like it is now, but much neater I should think. I would staple the pages together and that wouldn't always work out the first time—I've never been very adept with staplers, or photocopiers. And then I'd hand my new story to him on a Friday. What were the stories I wrote? Little things. Something about a bus shelter being like a living gallery because of all the things written and drawn all on top of each other across its walls. Something about a boy with AIDS sitting in the library looking out of the window cut off from the playground seeing all the open mouths roaring roaring and not being able to hear a thing. A hated cat disturbing the peace and intensity of a summer afternoon reading in the back garden. The pensive girl in a white vest hears the slamming of brakes and a yowl and believes the cat has been killed and so shimmies smugly, down into the sun lounger, deeper into her book. Why so much hatred for the cat? The cat reappears, steps into its saucer of milk and tiptoes off indoors, tail in the air, leaving white paw prints all over the place, as if to say, I am here, I am here, I am here and here, I'm not going anywhere. I gave him the stories on a Friday so they were in his home for three nights and two days. Lying there somewhere in his house. Absorbing this environment that I could never go to. His Saturdays. His Sundays. Who was he on those days? What clothes did he wear? Where did he sit? Where did he read my stories? Near a long window, on his own, of course. In an armchair but not a big one, not a soft squidgy one, something quite elegant and angled towards the window that might be a door and the garden beyond really was like a jungle, full of vines and brambles, rosehips and elderberries, little birds, apples, pears, old trees and startling ferns. I was with him. I'd done it, I'd crossed over a boundary. I was somewhere I shouldn't be. I was with him—and he was with me. All weekend I felt him with me, wherever I went, all day and at night. He was with me very strongly when I lay in the dark, it was almost as if I was made of him. Writing could do that. Here was a way of reaching someone, of being with them, when you were not and never could be. Here was where we met. Here was where the distinction between us blurred. When he returned my story to me the following Tuesday the paper was covered with him—touching it was like touching his skin. My fingertips slowly spread out and up the pages. Here and there in pencil he had written comments, brief and encouraging. They meant nothing to me, but I liked to see his handwriting beside mine, sometimes overlapping mine. It was unlined paper. I wrote with a fountain pen. I still do.

III.

WON'T YOU BRING IN
THE BIRDS?

For books are not absolutely dead things, but do
contain a potency of life in them to be as active as
that soul was whose progeny they are; nay, they
do preserve as in a vial the purest efficacy and
extraction of that living intellect that bred them.

—*AREOPAGITICA*, JOHN MILTON

When I was in my early twenties I began to write a story about
a man named Tarquin Superbus. Tarquin Superbus was a very
elegant sort of man who lived in a very elegant European city
sometime in a previous century. I didn't mention in the story
which century the unfolding events described took place in, I
simply wrote "long ago" at the beginning of the tale and left it
at that because I wasn't really sure myself when exactly or
where exactly the story happened. In fact my sense of when

and where swung back and forth, from one century to another, from one European country to the next. Sometimes as I wrote it seemed to me that my portrayal of this character Tarquin Superbus and the apartment and the city where he lived were very much in tune with the 1800s. At other times it seemed to me that the vibe of what I was writing exemplified the mores of a much earlier time, somewhere around the beginning of the long Renaissance. Setting this particular story around the time when Europe was on the cusp of modernity made sense thematically, but whenever Tarquin Superbus opened his mouth and had conversations with the Doctor for example neither of them spoke in the manner of that era—their way of speaking was much more in line with the way I imagined gentlemen in the mid-1800s to speak—byzantine, comical, and portending. In addition to speech there was also the matter of Tarquin Superbus's attire and apartment to consider. The image I had of him fluctuated. Sometimes he appeared to me as a trumped-up figure from commedia dell'arte, the next minute he is looking spry in a perky tricorne, other times he is cossetted by an elaborate puffy ruff, sometimes he sported pearly white hose—lo and behold here he comes, light on his feet, in outlandish cross-gartered stockings à la Malvolio. He often wielded a swinging cane with a silver top and sometimes that silver top was in the shape of a Goyaesque owlet with hungry outstretched wings and other times it was the dour tapered mask of Il Dottore, and other times still a plucky vole. Yet regardless of which sartorial flourish bedecked his attire, Superbus was nearly always swathed in a cape or a cloak. Mostly a cloak that swelled and swung behind him as he strode past dim lanterns one after the next down this or that dark passageway. Sometimes it seemed there might well be a dagger or some such dastardly device tucked deep within its dark folds. Various accessories occurred to me on and on, popping up one after the next, as if from out a magician's hat, and it vexed me that the marvellous mishmash of glad rags and clandestine accoutrements that came to mind whenever I thought about Tarquin Superbus would ultimately undermine the credibility of my story if I set them all down, but set them down I did, all the same, anachronism upon anachronism, because it was immensely enjoyable for one thing and—historical incongruence notwithstanding—it seemed to me that such details lent the tale so much atmosphere and intrigue. Long ago, long long ago. Indeed, isn't that when all fairy tales occur—long ago, no one knows quite when? As far as his apartment was concerned, the image that most came to mind was that of an aubergine.

I've always been very taken with aubergines, with the way they are so tightly sheathed in a shining bulletproof darkness. When I was a dismayed student in London I often fantasised about hanging a great many aubergines from the square ceiling of my sketchy boudoir. Imagine lying there beneath such a pendulous chandelier of lambent gloom—imagine

the transporting reflections slipping across their sleek herme-
tic skins, the assuaging shadows they'd cast as degradation
tipped them into slow stately revolutions, the whisperings,
the whisperings, the sighs, the melancholy glow. I lay there
and imagined it often but couldn't realise my dream of course,
aubergines were expensive and I would have needed at least
ninety of them. I'd had some rather fanciful ideas about what
studying literature at university would entail. The sorts of
mellow rooms I'd pass through, the views I'd come upon, the
crepuscular light, the animated hush, the slinking patina and
recurring fleur-de-lis, the bicycles and small bridges, everything on the turn, and, most of all, the sharp and charming
people I'd meet. In fact as it turned out a great many of them
liked nothing better than to sit in the middle of their beds in
the middle of the day, watching Australian soaps cross-legged
with the door wide open. "Do you want a cup of tea?" they
would sometimes ask when occasionally I leant up against
the door frame and scowled within. "No," I would invariably
reply, and thereupon carry on down the corridor with the in-
tention of having a very long hot bath once I got to the end of
it. The communal bathroom in halls was basic, austere, and
cold. The mirrors were frameless and thin, the tiles white and
the grouting between them black and crumbling like bone-
yard soil, and the stark taps obdurate and shrill. The water
that twisted out of them however was clear and soundless as
fresh-blown glass. There were showers of course but I almost

never used them because communal showers almost always reminded me of the death camps so I preferred to take a bath and there were two baths I think, though there may have been only one. Certainly there was one. In a small room with a sloping ceiling. That's right. And an off-kilter wooden chair beside it. It was a very deep enamel bath, somewhat discoloured, and the water that billowed from the hot tap was scalding. The bathtub was where I felt private and absolutely away from everyone and everything and perhaps I pretended some things while I was in it. Perhaps I pretended I was in an asylum at last, with nothing much to do and no expectations upon me. Or perhaps I imagined I was a maid in a big house doing her ablutions on a dismal Sunday evening before a rapid and somewhat violent assignation with sir halfway up the furthermost stairwell. In my own quarters I quite often threw furniture and smashed things. Someone I've known since then maintains time and again that I once flicked a chest of drawers across the room with just two fingers. "Don't exaggerate," I always say. "Two," he always says back, holding two fingers up in the air meaningfully—is he swearing the truth or showing me what two fingers look like? I drank a lot of lapsang souchong then and would leave unfinished mugs of it here and there, which meant that when a piece of furniture plunged vertical several mugs went right along with it, flinging these perfectly round velvety tapestries of mould up ahead. Until they flapped and landed, like creepy little doilies, all along the scruffy bookcase. And I drew on the walls, nothing sinister, waves mostly, with a nub of blue cue chalk I'd slipped off the pool table into my pocket at the King's Head one evening. The walls of Tarquin Superbus's apartment were without a doubt the colour of aubergines, and so were the long heavy drapes, and so too was the wooden floor. There were white things here and there and those white things seemed to float, gloves becoming doves becoming skulls, suspended as they were in this shining sealed darkness.

And where exactly was this apartment? Stockholm, Malmö, Basel, Stuttgart, Lyon, Madrid, Turin, Trieste. Never in England. Never ever in England. Mostly either in Vienna or Venice in fact. Whenever Tarquin Superbus was triumphant about something, pleased as punch with a new filigreed trinket, or undulant with amorous joy over an erotic bauble perhaps, he was most certainly in Vienna. It is also in Vienna when Tarquin Superbus is shovelling into his quail eggs and caviar with a nifty little silver spoon while sitting at a small round table which has upon it the whitest cloth right there beside an open shutter through which he can easily see devil's ivy and star jasmine growing around and around the wrought-iron scrolls and laurel leaves and quinces that decorate the very elegant balcony railings. It is also Vienna when Tarquin Superbus tucks into cake. Small, infused, and intensely fragrant cake from the East that sticks to his thumb and finger. If Tarquin Superbus is licking his fingers and thumbs chances are he is in Vienna. It is also Vienna when Tarquin and the Doctor are sat in a relaxed sort of way, amiably discussing perhaps a light piece of conservatoire news. If there is a bevy of hen's eggs squelching away in a pan of oil on a small squat stove on the other hand then Tarquin Superbus most certainly is in Venice. Fried eggs are a long-standing source of comfort to Tarquin and if Tarquin Superbus needs comforting he is undoubtedly in Venice. If Tarquin Superbus is in foul humour he is in Venice. If he is sulking and feeling hard done by, he is in Venice. If it is night and all night through he cannot sleep, he is in Venice. If there is a waning fire lolling and catching sporadically in the hearth. If he fills his wineglass again and again to the brim. If he is especially feverish. If he is irate with paranoia. If he can't remember where he left his slippers. If the conversations with the Doctor are erratic and cabalistic and cunning. If his grasp on reality is a little shaky to say the least, Tarquin Superbus is in Venice, because, after all, what reality is there to be found in Venice? It is a place that is constantly playing tricks on you. You retrace your steps, you swear you came this way, you recognise that clock face, that one-legged beggar, that balustrade, that sign—look, isn't that where you had your coffee only an hour or two ago? You hurry, you hurry, you hurry back to your lodgings, yet with each glancing footfall you are in fact moving very efficiently further and further away from where you came. The fact of the matter is, Tarquin Superbus is frequently made a fool of. It's easily done and sends him into such a resplendent rage—it's exceedingly entertaining— he's fallen for it, all over again! Tarquin Superbus is a spoilt nitwit who fritters away the immense family fortune on esoteric fads and gastronomic mainstays and naturally he is perennially defrauded by this or that enterprising impostor, of which, of course, there are multitudes.

His only ally is the Doctor, who has probably known Tarquin Superbus since the day he was born and probably the Doctor made some sort of pledge to Tarquin's diaphanous mother just before she expired—a sudden tragic demise that occurred of course when Tarquin Superbus was still only a small boy, and oh what a darling little pursed-lipped amoretto he was. In the story I wrote many years ago I gave the Doctor a name, I suspect it might have been a German name. I remember there was something slightly off about the Doctor and although I can't pinpoint what exactly the nature of that anomaly was, dwelling on it now brings a feeling of uneasiness strumming about my ribs. I don't think he was unpleasant. Perhaps he was three hundred years old. He was certainly extremely pale, his long fingers were practically white, and his visage was so white it shone. Perhaps that was the strange thing—he was a doctor that looked like Death. There was nothing inside of him, he was vaporous, empty as a hologram, he achieved movement not via the mechanism of his body but by the fact that he consisted of a substance lighter than air—Death. He floated, he hovered, he arabesqued, he seeped, he vanished. Was he a ghost then? No, I don't think he was a ghost, nor a vampire either. Though perhaps he was. Perhaps he was after all and I didn't know it. Didn't realise, not until now, looking back. Ghostly. Hovering. I can hear him saying, "I'm not in any hurry—on the contrary, I've all the time in the world." And how many times in a day would he say that? And just how many days had he been saying it for? Superbus had acquired a library—that was the story's chief event. He was desperate, always, to be taken seriously, and everyone knows if you have a lot of fine books about the place people are likely to automatically infer that you're a serious sort of person who thinks things through thoroughly and deems deepening their knowledge of all that went on in the world and continues to go on throughout its fractious territories a valuable way to spend their time. Tarquin wanted people to have those sorts of thoughts about him so he went about procuring an entire library of books and these books arrived in wooden crates and from where they came exactly was something of a mystery. I can see those wooden crates very well. I can also see the long metal implement used to prise open the crates' wide slats, though strange to say I cannot see the person levering it. The wheels of a wagon are also very distinct. I see the whole wagon but it is the wheels that are clearest to me, the spokes of the wheels particularly. They are cream and unfeasibly clean. I can also see a thin whip flashing like the tongue of a viper through the air—but again, I cannot really see the zealous bedlamite cracking it. Only the peak of his unctuous hood. The wagon is going crazily fast, the enormous wheels are spinning up a lot of dust, the road is winding, the road winds like a river, like a drawing of a river. Nothing else has been drawn—no tufts of long grass here and there, no craggy milestone, no half-timbered inn, no little rocks, no cumulus clouds, nothing beyond. I imagine there were many many carriages transporting Tarquin Superbus's books, there must have been, yet I see only one upon this sinuous bare-bones road. It seems to me these headlong crates also spent time bobbing in the hull of a boat throughout the night. I can see them being hauled up out of the boat just before daybreak and I can see the water contained in the dock—dark and shining and restless. There is the bottom half of a man's legs, he is standing with his feet wide apart. I can see his hands, there on either side of a crate, yet I cannot see his face. I can't see his face but all the same I know his hair is dark brown and often falls into his eyes though right now it is sticking to his forehead and I know that there is engine oil all along the creases around his eyes.

Boxes and boxes and boxes. It was quite a big deal. Everyone was clutching their handkerchiefs with both hands and looking around corners qualmishly when they arrived and were unloaded one after the other outside the magnificent residence of Tarquin Superbus. Birds scooted along to the ends of their preferred branches to see it all better. Tarquin was very excited and hopped about like a puffed-up bird himself. Not really having anything to do he knocked his silver-topped cane on the side of a crate proprietorially and was delighted to discover that such a gesture immediately made him feel sagacious and discerning, so he kept it up, leaping about this way and that, knocking his silver-topped cane off the side of all the crates. Naturally he'd rounded up a few local ne'er-do-wells and set them to work unloading the boxes and installing the thousands of great tomes upon the shelves of his bespoke ebony athenaeum. Yes, that's right, lustrous black shelves from floor to ceiling. Inlaid with opals, Tahitian pearls, and ivory. Copper and gold. Burmese rubies and lapis lazuli. A windowless hexagonal chamber glimmering darkly right in the centre of his roost that Superbus occasionally popped into thereafter in order to pitter-patter his pudgy fingers along the soft leather spines of his prestigious collection. And then, hardly a fortnight later, the rumours began to circulate, and the attitude of deference that had emanated from the townspeople with such gratifying and smooth palpability following Tarquin Superbus's noble acquisition began to bristle, the atmosphere turned positively scabrous, as if rubbed up the wrong way, and Tarquin, who for many splendid days now had enjoyed parading up and over the canals—for this is all surely going on in Venice—shaking hands here and there, tipping his tricorne and tapping his cane, generally basking in the new and clement climate of belated admiration, began to experience a sudden numbing chill all the way up his backbone whenever he went out and made his way round and about, from one campo to the next, because, all of a sudden, no sooner had he passed a group of washerwomen, or ragazze, or altar boys, or stone carvers from Cannaregio, a silvery tittering would break out and follow in his wake, swooping and darting all about his ankles, his elbows, his earlobes, like a small excited flock of inseparable swallows. What the devil were they laughing at? Superbus was furious, and confounded—a terrible combination that sent him careening blindly through his apartment, flinging open doors, kicking cats into leaf-strewn corners, toppling collectibles willy-nilly with his dependable cane. I see things, vague things, crashing and falling all around him, dry crinkled papers go fluttering up into the air, pale grey birds with silent fantails—probably doves—fly directly into the windows. Grapes, apricots, and walnuts from Grenoble roll like tumbleweed across the credenza. A lamp shatters, tongs clatter, tassels whip the air. Carvings worth their weight in gold tremble volcanically upon their marble plinths, portraits seesaw on the walls, keys of all sizes drop out of aghast locks, escutcheons cloud over. Dead leverets bicker side by side in the pantry, chandeliers splash bright sulphurous tears, shutters bang, and the aromatic vines around the balcony writhe and retract. Tarquin collapses of course into his favourite chair. His chin drops, his swollen hands resemble a pair of cuttlefish upturned in his flaccid lap, his stomach distends fully, he breathes through his mouth begrudgingly, and these attributes taken together indicate that Tarquin is well and truly ensconced in the plush familiar hub of a gigantic sulk. The Doctor is summoned. He hasn't seen the Doctor for some time, not since he's acquired all these magnificent books in fact. Where has the Doctor been? Bologna very probably, at the university. Yes, the Doctor has been giving lectures on mesmerism of course at the university in Bologna. But now he is back and he must come at once! Tarquin will be able to show him his incredible library—the Doctor will be amazed! Tarquin cheers up considerably at the thought of the Doctor visiting—everything will quickly be fine, he thinks. The Doctor will come and together we will stand in the library and we'll raise a toast to knowledge and everything will be just fine. And so, moments later, the Doctor appears.

The Doctor appears and Tarquin leads the way, down an infernally dark passage. He holds a candle and the candle is white and its flame ducks down again and again as if to avoid something or many things flying about them fast and low up and down the passageway and then the Doctor is in the library, down a very narrow aisle of the library with a book in his hand, and it's just as if he was already there in fact, as if he's been there all along. I can see his profile, concentrated and relaxed, quite at home, his long slender nose, in its element, pointing down towards the pages of the book that lies open in his left hand while his right hand turns the pages, turns the pages. The Doctor is turning the pages, slowly at first, slowly and with extra care. The Doctor is turning the pages of the book slowly and carefully, and then more hurriedly, and much more hurriedly again. Tarquin is burbling on by the fire. At intervals, and for madcap reasons of his own devising, he swings his brimming glass up towards this or that painting, there above the mantelpiece, most of which are of small fleets of capsizing ships upon a raging sea. How he loves to swing—a glass, a cane, a mouse, a cape, a cloak— indeed, when he was a small child Tarquin Superbus loved nothing more than to be swung up into the air himself. Lightness, lightness, air. Following his mother's death, the romantic chintzes, the pastoral toiles, the delicate panels of lace which made such delightful shadows upon the pale blue walls and across the blonde oak floors were darkened bedimmed extinguished, by heavy drapes and the colours of nightfall. Tarquin's father no longer wanted to see where his wife wasn't and would never be. In the meantime, since his father's death, Tarquin has reversed not one funereal detail, he just can't bring himself, and anyway there is always the kitchen and the kitchen is and always has been Tarquin's favourite place. The kitchen is and always has been a lovely bright and warm room with its walls as white as sieved flour and its white lappato tiles above the smart cast-iron stove and its smooth rounded shelves the struts of which blend into the wall quite harmoniously and there upon them are all the little bottles and jars and ramekins turned this way and that each holding its own delectable though not always readily detectable specimen, capers, for example, capers, cornichons, cockles, truffles, tamarind, nutmeg, goose fat, juniper berries, olives, oregano, lavender, tapenade, sloes, apricot jam, onion chutney, preserved lemons, sauerkraut, vinegar, mincemeat, vanilla pods, squid ink, saffron, candied angelica, piccalilli, porcini, cherries, cloves, and beneath the shelf the shining pots and valiant colanders and glinting utensils. The whisk is Tarquin's most favourite kitchen utensil of course. How he loves to lean on the counter dabbing sugar and sucking on cold strawberries, watching the sweet-cheeked cook beat so much air into a large blue bowl of immaculate cream. Lightness, lightness, air. Yes, Tarquin loves the whisk! He loves meringue and soufflé, and spoondrift and froth and lather and spume—bubbles, yes, and baubles—baubles, bubbles, balloons, and ballerinas—ballerinas!—my god they spend every hour of the day training every joint and muscle in their body to lift them high into the air, to catapult them skyward, away from this earth, right up into the heavens. They stretch and leap and spin, leap and spin and stretch, moving very quickly across the world on the very tips of their toes, oh they have about as much contact as a pair of compasses with terra firma, it makes Tarquin's heart swell like a sail to see them take off—up they go, up, up, up, and down they come, and sometimes they stay down and remain very still and that makes Tarquin's innards churn and clench right the way through, to see the little ballerina standing there as if her shoes were suddenly fastened to the floor. Look how her wings have dropped and her hands are turned in towards each other so sorrowfully. The dear fingertips of both hands are almost touching almost touching and her little head is dropped and she gazes so sadly down at the small heartbreaking gap between one hand and the other—what does she see there, is she falling, falling, is she a child again, was she always only a child, whose voice does she hear, her eyes are so sad, so enormous, she is a crestfallen abandoned soul, indeed seeing her this way causes Tarquin a great deal of anguish, my god he feels the weight of the world upon his heart and cannot breathe, he can't take another breath until she takes to the air again, all is stagnant, stale, historical, until she is once more mixing with the air, bringing it all to life again, and the elation then, as her beautiful slender arms lift and yes all at once the weight of the world swings away from him, my god his spirits are thrown high, high, higher, and they too mingle, up there in the prolonged present—no past, no future, only the exuberant now and always. Tarquin rejoices, he is saved, in the same way he is saved by the soprano at the opera when her voice soars, reaches the very top notes, how light Tarquin is then, lightness, lightness, air, but again and again he is brought down to earth nonstop by long-faced reminders that these are dark times, very dark times indeed Tarquin, over and over, the words descending on him like brushes, like awful brushes upon his head, getting him to be still, still in front of the mirror, the child Tarquin stands rigid in front of the mirror and sees his stiff collar and straight socks and the neat little garters holding them up, they are green, and the brush—keep still—coming down, again and again, this side, the other side, this side, the other side, again and again, brutally scuffing his ear, and who is holding the brush and dragging it like that—keep still I say—so close to his scalp through his soft hair scuffing his small ears again and again, who is it that stands behind him, morning after morning, not smelling pleasant at all, who, he doesn't want to stand there a moment longer, he doesn't want to keep still, he wants to run, out of his room, down the corridor, down to the kitchen, where he can kneel upon a stool and look down at a pan full of eggs frying just for him and feel behind him the breeze coming in through the window, behind him, ruffling his hair, Tarquin can feel it, ruffling the hair on the back of his head so very gently, but Tarquin the world is a very serious sort of place. Yes, yes, he has heard it so many times. Like the bristles of a damned brush hard against his skull. And so here he is, isn't he? In his important library, with its black glittering shelves stacked with weighty tomes that go way back, way back. Rows upon rows of sacred teachings about how the world was made, and the significance of all the things upon it—lizards, birds, streams, wheat, sheep, clouds, gold, fire, apples, human beings, oxen, and all the great seas, and all the great planets and stars that circle about it. Here he is and there is the Doctor—there is the Doctor at last, thank god! Cupping a book with his left hand and turning the pages with his right.

Turning them in rather a hurry Tarquin can't help but notice—perhaps he is looking for something in particular. Yes, of course. Despite being a man of his time and having, accordingly, cultivated a great variety of interests, the Doctor doesn't deal in theories or generalities—an anecdote or a case, a conceit or an anomaly, those are the specific elements that the Doctor's mind takes to. Something exceptional, something unsettled, something with life force. No doubt about it he is on the hunt, turning the pages, turning the pages, not for affirmation of this or that point of view but for some enigma he came across many years ago, an episode or a turn of phrase which brought on an enduring golden-pink aura within a certain recess of his mind, all that time ago, yet the precise details of which always evaporate the very instant his memory reaches out to grasp them. Is there any greater pleasure than being reunited with details such as these? Don't the years simply fall away? Sure enough the Doctor returns the book to the shelf and immediately slides out the one beside it with a great deal of urgency, looking for something, yes, abeyant treasure—the bedrock of himself in other words. He opens the next book, cups it in his left hand, and once more the Doctor turns the pages with his right, turning the pages, turning the pages, what is he looking for, what on earth is he looking for? He is turning the pages so quickly that surely it's impossible for him to register a single word on any one of them. Superbus has quietened down, settled his glass upon the mantelpiece, something is horribly wrong, the atmosphere is stomach-turning all of a sudden. He draws in closer to the Doctor and he sees the Doctor's hands are shaking—it's no use of course to say the Doctor has gone very pale, that establishes nothing since the extreme paleness of the Doctor's face has already been attested to, perhaps then it has gone green. The Doctor's face is quite green and glistens obliquely like jade, his hands shake as if inside of them there crouches a pair of opposing primeval life-forms on the brink of busting out and having at each other after multiple years of seething dormancy. Biding their time, biding their time. He returns the book and takes out another, and another, and another, holds each one unsteadily in the left hand, bats the pages erratically with his right, turning the pages, turning the pages—"Tarquin," he says, suddenly, looking up, his face— his face!—green and marbled and all a blur—"there isn't a single word on any one of these pages!" Yes, that's exactly what the Doctor says—I remember it very well: "Tarquin, there isn't a single word on any one of these pages." Tarquin, by this time, is equal parts inebriated and hungover and doesn't have the vim to blow a fuse. Helpless and leaden, he allows the Doctor to turn him around and shuffle him back towards the fireplace and the tempestuous canvases, in front of which there are two leather chairs and a chess table. They sit down and Tarquin immediately starts up prodding the bronze studs around the end of the chair's warmest arm. The studs are practically red-hot. Tarquin prods and presses one after the other nonetheless as if determined to ascertain which is the very hottest. The Doctor has sat in one chair and watched Tarquin prod peevishly at the calescent studs on the warmest arm of another for many years and witnessing him doing so now is oddly reassuring, even though the Doctor knows it is a categorical sign that Tarquin is shaken to the bone and a gesture of much bigger and more calamitous proportions therefore is inevitably in the offing. I'll deal with that when it comes to it, he thinks, not for the first time, and makes the most of this period of calm, even if it does presage a storm, to gently impress upon Tarquin Superbus some singular though entirely unsubstantiated facts pertaining to his library that he apparently has not been furnished with.

It is quite clear that Tarquin had not opened even one of those thousands of books himself since they came into his care—the Doctor however makes no mention of that. There are more important things to be addressed for one thing, and, for another, the Doctor is one of those rare human beings who derives no satisfaction whatsoever from making another person feel silly or remiss or just plain bad. It very quickly dawned on Tarquin of course that the cretinous sneaks who helped to unload and install the books must have had a good grope through three or four of them and thereby ascertained swiftly enough that there was damn all written in those books nor all the rest. And there amidst the hubbub was I, Tarquin Superbus—"si signore," "no signore"—prancing this way and that, tap tap tapping this crate and that shelf with my trusty silver-topped cane—ha! What a colossal chump! Off they'd skedaddled, shifty bunch of hyenas, down to whatever filthy bàcari they hang about in, and mouthed off to the other slack-jawed ingrates. Bet they couldn't wait. Couldn't wait! The smeared speckled mirrors, the flaking golden letters, the bitter smoke, the small scratched glasses of firewater, the scarred hands and sallow pitted foreheads, and the laughter, the laughter, hacking its way up through tar and bile, before ricocheting out of their jabbering muzzles. Well, that explains it—that certainly explains all the nudging and tittering that has spread throughout the sestieri and dogged Tarquin Superbus like a foul common cold these past few weeks. Superbus is relieved to have finally uncovered the source of this most recent and virulent bout of mockery, no one likes to be left in the dark, yet now he has the cause itself to confront and he hasn't encountered anything like it before, not even close, he is terrified—his relief is short-lived—he'd much rather feel perplexedly vexed than panic-stricken. He wants to get as far away from those disgusting books as possible. What are they? What kind of sickness are they?! Tarquin presses the pad of a finger against the hottest bronze stud, is soothed by the clarity of the localised scalding pain and murmurs, madre, wake me from this nightmare. Does he hear what the Doctor imparts? Bits and pieces. He hears the Doctor's voice, and that is enough. The Doctor's voice, it has hardly altered at all in all these years—always so even and unhurried, and unattached—as if there were something speaking through him in fact. Tarquin hears him mention the Medicis, the Borgias, the Gonzagas, and something about the Inquisition—there is always something or other about the Inquisition—and it is such a salve to hear these familiar venerable words, they chime upon the air like spheres, each one entire and unsnagged. Tarquin dares to close his eyes. The Medicis, the Borgias, the Gonzagas, the Inquisition, yes, yes, all is as it was and as it should be. And then come strange words, stranger and stranger, words Tarquin can be sure he has never heard before, words like Popol Vuh, Amduat, Apaurusheya. Make them stop—make them stop at once! He can't open his eyes, he can't open his mouth, his tongue is thick and a thousand colours, his skull feels absolutely enormous, his entire head is an enormous luminous dome, there is nothing outside of it. In the whole world there is only this huge white dome with its little ledges and stray crumpled vines and faded frescoes and dust motes and pale grey doves—the pale grey doves soar and swoop, vanish and reappear, in and out of conspiring columns of light, and these doves are the Doctor's voice: "No one knows where this collection of books originated from," and then, nothing—all is quiet, vast—dust motes, little ledges—a dead leaf scratches against ancient lime plaster. And then: "It is said to have circulated throughout the world for many many hundreds of years, thousands of years." Dust motes, light, little ledges, faint scratching. "Strictly speaking, one does not acquire the library—it comes to you." Faint scratching, faint scratching, vast, vast. "And when you have learnt from it, it moves on." Learnt from it! Learnt from it! Tarquin snorts derisively at this, and feels all the better for it. The Doctor, realising that Tarquin has in fact been taking in what he is saying, looks at Tarquin and addresses him directly—his words take on a more purposeful tone, no, they are no longer lucent doves and Tarquin's head is no longer a huge white dome—it feels like a lone mushroom or a whacked catfish—the underside of his chin feels preposterously vulnerable, but at least now he is able to move his tongue about and open his eyes, indeed both appendages glide slickly and instinctively in the direction of the mantelpiece, to where

Tarquin put down his glass of Barolo what seems like a lifetime ago. The Doctor gets up and retrieves the libation, he wants Tarquin to be as comfortable as possible. He takes a sip from it himself before relinquishing the glass, settles himself back into his chair—the Doctor isn't inclined to puff out his chest and hold forth from the mantelpiece—and continues. "The pages are all blank, it's true, Tarquin, it's absolutely true. Thousands of books, and thousands upon thousands of blank pages within them—of course I can see why you would be alarmed, consternated, disquieted—provoked—by this. It is a provocative state of affairs indeed. And there is more. The pages, Tarquin, are all blank, except for one page. Within the collection there is one page that is not blank—at least not entirely. It has upon it one sentence; that's all, that's it—one sentence. And this one sentence contains everything. Everything. Whoever comes upon it undergoes an immediate and total awakening. Even an illiterate child would experience this revelation, and that is because this sentence, this one sentence that is everything, is not read—it is seen. It cannot be comprehended through the intellect—it is not understood because what it contains is beyond our intellectual powers of understanding, and so it completely bypasses the mind, it has no interest at all with the mind. The words, how can I put it, are alive and distinct, they are like organisms, yes, exactly like organisms—and they are supremely potent. When at last they come into contact with a pair of eyes they vibrate immediately and imperceptibly, they come to life and emit intensely powerful and advanced waves which the eyes accept, and in this way, through the eyes, these extraordinary vibrations stimulate and ease open pathways deep in the consciousness of the perceiver. There are no more blockages, no more demarcations, no defences, nothing in the way—he or she, the perceiver, is released completely, and immediately transcends all definition. He or she is free then to participate at once in the greater imagination, what some go so far as to call the world soul. Importantly, the sentence cannot be shown to anyone else—it is an impossibility. It connects with and emancipates only the person who discovers it. Once connection has occurred, and the awakened state has been achieved, the sentence disappears from the page. It vanishes completely, Tarquin, in an instant, and materialises somewhere else, on another page, another page god knows where inside these thousands of books. So, you understand, it is quite impossible to show the sentence to anyone else. Which of course rules out the possibility of enlisting the assistance of hundreds of page turners in order to track the formulation down. It is a solitary task, Tarquin, that must be carried out only by the one who attracted it in the first place—a daunting, arduous search if ever there was, naturally some of those who have been chosen by the library have been driven right around the twist by the endeavour. Who knows why it finds its way to one household and not another. Possibly it goes to where it is needed most. Is it a gift, or is it a curse? That all depends. That all depends. It is a weight, Tarquin, no doubt about that, a formidable and unquantifiable weight. And so what you have upon all these shelves that surround us my good and dear friend is the ultimate paradox, because some-where, somewhere within this terrific burden, is a key: a key to complete and infinite lightness."

The Doctor provided no explanation of this sort in the story I wrote all those years ago. The pages of Superbus's library were blank, and that was all there was to it. It seems in the retelling I have got carried away. But then I have read so much and written so much since then it is hardly to be wondered at that in the meantime some ideas pertaining to the potency of the written word, based upon direct and seismic experiences, have been developing inside of me and should find their way out—albeit somewhat hackneyed, with something vaguely remembered from Hermann Hesse hovering close by—through the Doctor's mouth, now that I have opened it once again, some twenty or so years later, in order to impart to Tarquin that his whole library is filled with blank pages, but for one sentence. But for one sentence! No, I could not leave it there. Strange to think but when I first wrote the tale I hadn't yet read a single word by Italo Calvino, Jean Rhys, Borges, or Thomas Bernhard, nor Clarice Lispector. I had read *Of Mice and Men*, and *Lolita*, and "Kubla Khan," and *The Diary of a Young Girl*. I had not yet read *The Go-Between* or *Wuthering Heights* or "A Season in Hell" or *Orlando*. I had read *Jacob's Room* and *Nausea* and *The Fall* and *Tess of the D'Urbervilles* and "The Hollow Men" and many Imagist poems, one of which had snow in it and a white leopard I think, or, more accurately, it was a leopard that had no outline— maybe it was penned by Ezra Pound, I don't remember. I hadn't yet read *A Sport and a Pastime* or *Wittgenstein's Mistress* or *Moon Tiger* or "The Pedersen Kid" or "A Girl of the Zeitgeist" or "The Letter of Lord Chandos" or "The Trouble with Following the Rules." I had read *Oranges Are Not the Only Fruit* and *Confessions of an English Opium-Eater* and *A Sentimental Journey* and *One Hundred Years of Solitude* and *The Silence of the Lambs* and *The Sea, the Sea*, which I bought from a stall at Glastonbury festival and read lying down in the top field with a paper cup of chai tea and a packet of Jaffa Cakes. It's a very long book and I did not read it all at the festival since of course there were other things to do there—I finished it in the back garden at home, during what remained of the summer holidays. I recall that the main character of the book, who I'm almost entirely certain was a man, made coffee with the same water he'd boiled eggs in, and that struck me because it might have been something I'd do if I drank coffee, which at the time I didn't. Though I did wee in the bath from time to time, which seemed to me on a par with drinking coffee made from the same water that eggs had been boiled in. I had not yet read *Cassandra at the Wedding* or *The Calmative* or *Unfinished Ode to Mud* or *Birds of America* or *The Grass Is Singing* or *The Notebooks of Malte Laurids Brigge* or *The Man of Feeling*: "Manur lowers his glasses though he does not take them off, and peering over the top of them with eyes accustomed to being flattered by the things of this world, he does not reply immediately" is a line I've copied out of Marías's novella with a trembling hand into more than one notebook. I had read Plato's *Republic* and Aristotle's *Nicomachean Ethics*, and *The German Ideology*, by Marx and Engels, which we all referred to as "The GI," and *On Liberty* by John Stuart Mill, and a book on ethics and animals by Peter Singer, and a badly printed book by Edmund Burke— the letters were so thick and small and all cramped together, and *Thus Spoke Zarathustra*. I had not read *Das Kapital* nor anything by John Rawls and I still haven't, and I certainly hadn't read anything at that time by Vivian Gornick or Natalia Ginzburg or Lynne Tillman or Joan Didion or Renata Adler or Janet Malcolm or Marina Warner or bell hooks or Anne Garréta. When I was doing my A-levels in Philosophy, English Literature, and Psychology, I worked in a supermarket, mostly on the weekends, though occasionally weeknights too, and there was a large Russian man with long white hair who used to come in and he'd always have a basket, which he'd hold quite a way out in front of him, and he used to walk at such a terrific speed—it was just as if it was the basket in fact that was leading him up and down the aisles because actually he did always seem bewildered—as if he'd landed there in the supermarket quite by chance—and he'd be going up and down the aisles for a long time and the basket out in front of him would be empty and I never saw him stop anywhere and take anything from off a shelf, but somehow very quickly a few things would find their way into his basket and that was quite sufficient, he could leave now, but not before going to the checkout of course, and he'd always come to my checkout, even if the queue for the checkout in front or behind my checkout was shorter, he'd always come to mine, and I knew very well as he stood there waiting he was looking at me through his thin round glasses, and he'd look at me when I scanned his few things, tinned fish and pickles and so on, and he'd look at me when I took his money, and he'd look at me when I gave him his change, and I'd look just over his shoulder always and he didn't ever say anything and it wasn't at all as if we were in a supermarket, and one day I was not at a checkout, I was walking down an aisle towards the checkouts about to begin a nine-hour shift on checkout 19 wearing a horrible skirt that managed to swivel around and around my waist even as I sat still in it all day long, and his basket was very close to me, then he caught up with it and there he was and he really was very large and he said "Here, it's all yours" and he thrust a book towards me. I was already holding a biro and then I was holding a book in one hand and a biro in the other since it seemed I should keep them apart and I continued making my way to the checkouts and when I got to checkout 19 I put the book on a shelf beneath the printer that printed out receipts all day long and the book was written by Friedrich Nietzsche and it was called *Beyond Good and Evil* and on the cover was a painting of a woman with large naked breasts and her hands are resting down, her hands are resting down because she is a sphinx, a sphinx as depicted by Franz von Stuck in 1895, and it was funny, the way her hands rested down like that, exactly like the way my hands rested down on top of the dark brown lid of the till when there was no one there and nothing for me to do, so even though my small breasts did not resemble her large dusky-looking ones at all, my hands were like hers, exactly like hers, and I couldn't help but believe that the Russian man must have thought so too.

I had not yet read but have done since the diaries of Witold Gombrowicz and though I had read many novels by Milan Kundera I had not yet read his gallant essays in *Testaments Betrayed* which I read with a great deal of pleasure some years later and which might have put me on to Gombrowicz, as well as Calvino perhaps, and definitely Fernando Pessoa. I had not yet read any Hofmannsthal or Handke, or Goethe, or Robert Walser. I had read *Death in Venice*. One of the first serious works I ever read was *The Tin Drum* by Günter Grass and I got that from the library and it was a very big book and

I read it during that week or so when my bedroom was being painted and I slept in the spare room on a sofa bed. I really liked sleeping on the sofa bed even though I found it more difficult to get up in the morning when I slept in it, probably because of it being so low down, and I preferred that room to my own room, even though it was much smaller. I've always preferred to go to sleep in a small room. They have more atmosphere and it's easier to imagine things far away in a small room—in a large room it's impossible to imagine anything— you're in a large room and that's all there is to it. It won't go away and neither will it take you anywhere. If you've bagged the bigger room you'll realise all too soon and much too late that you're trapped in it. Thinking about *The Tin Drum* now I recall a scene where the boy tries to get on a bus but he can't because he's much too tiny. I can see him, standing on the kerb, looking up into the bus. He is holding something in the crook of his left arm, a tin drum probably, though in my mind the thing wedged into the crook of his arm looks more like a medicine ball. The bus driver who has a hairy face and damp curly hair is shaking his head. And that's it, that's all I am able to recall from that book, which is kind of astonishing considering it's a very long book, and even then I might be mixing up that scant scene of a boy trying to get on a bus and not being able to for one reason or another with another book I read around the same time—*A Prayer for Owen Meany*. I'd read plenty of Sidney Sheldon, one or two of Jeffrey Archer, heaps of Danielle Steel, a couple of Jackie Collins, and some James Herbert. The names of these authors were always printed in large embossed letters on the book covers, in gold or silver of course, because they were bestsellers. There was a book of James Herbert's about an infestation of rats in a beautiful old house in the country that a newly wedded couple had just bought and moved into. I think the woman was pregnant—women in horror stories often are pregnant. I hadn't at the time read any Marguerite Duras or Colette or Madeleine Bourdouxhe or Annie Ernaux. I had read a few books by Françoise Sagan, including *Bonjour Tristesse*, which I discovered she'd written when she was just eighteen, and that threw me into a tizz for a little while because I would have been that exact same age when I read *Bonjour Tristesse*, but the things I was writing at that time when I was that age had none of the clarity and assuredness of Sagan's work, they were autotelic and inscrutable and quite often when I read back over them I didn't understand them at all, they perplexed and disturbed me, they didn't tell a story, they expressed confusion and despair and desire and anger, irrepressible forces which issued out of the dissonance that existed between my interior life and the world around me, and nobody would want to read that, and I didn't want anyone looking at any of it anyway, apart from my friend Natasha. Natasha said my writing reminded her of Anne Sexton's poems, had I read Anne Sexton, and I told her I hadn't, that

I didn't want to get into all of that. Natasha shrugged. She was an Erasmus student from Nuremberg and lived a few doors down from me. Most of the books she had in her room were by Horkheimer and Adorno and Habermas and they were in German of course and had very austere covers. I liked flicking through them, seeing all the long serried German words, they evoked the forest, as if each unit of a word was a tall coniferous tree, all packed in close together exhaling cold air and vibrating with animals on the hunt, like in the Black Forest, the Bavarian Forest, where I once went, and I recognised some of the words or perhaps just a part of them, because I had studied German at school and had done very well in it, knew without fail more or less when to use der, die, or das, and Natasha gave me a new word, a word that I have retained while all the others, the hundreds and hundreds of others I recited and copied out over and over, have fallen away: hirngespinst. She also had a lot of books in English, one of which was *The Female Malady: Women, Madness, and English Culture, 1830–1980*. It had a dreadful cover that featured the artwork *Pinel Freeing the Insane from Their Chains*, which was painted by Tony Robert-Fleury in 1876. One woman at the very edge of the picture is on her knees, gratefully kissing the plump ringed fingers of Pinel, her saviour. Pinel stands with his cane held gallantly to his chest, looking at the pretty young woman at the centre of the tableau who is being released from her shackles. Her hair is loose and tousled, and her dress is falling off her shoulders. Meanwhile on the ground behind her a woman is depicted in a hysterical arc-de-cercle posture, gasping, and pulling at her clothes, gratuitously revealing a pert breast. It is a very lurid kind of scene—the way these distressed and vulnerable women are sexualised made my skin crawl. However, since Natasha said I could borrow it I felt obliged to take it back to my house a few doors down, up to my bedroom—which was the same room in my house as Natasha's bedroom was in hers—and make notes from it in bed during the afternoons while wrenching open pistachios one after the other and drinking Ribena through a tiny purple straw. I collected tokens from the Ribena cartons which was fairly organised of me and eventually received a free Dino bubble watch for my efforts. I was very pleased with it, until somehow, inexplicably, Dino turned over. His underside was flat and pale blue like Blu-Tack and entirely featureless, it looked just like Blu-Tack, and despite patiently flipping that watch over and over, ankles crossed and a cigarette sloped in my free hand, in a kind of relaxed yet dogged trance, Dino never came back round and was eventually buried beneath the bedside heap of sliding pistachio shale. The things I read in that book by Elaine Showalter were absolutely harrowing and upset me a great deal. It described in painful detail various so-called therapeutic practices that have been used on women in order to bring them back to their senses—and back into line. These depictions were vivid and sickening and they shot right in beneath my skin, into that place between the nerves that is not me or even mine, that unseperate place where my mother's mother and my mother's mother's mother are softly present, like supple shadows overlapping in a sacred alcove. I had known from a young age that my mother's mother and my mother's mother's mother had both spent time in psychiatric units and I knew my grandmother had had electroconvulsive therapy, maybe she was still having it then, when I was grown up in London, reading Showalter's book upstairs in bed, I don't know. Showalter's study argues that cultural notions about how women ought to conduct themselves have made women mad—a point of view I shared, though in a more nascent unspecified form. It was just a feeling really. As I read on this feeling soon began to deepen and darken emphatically and as it did so another feeling surged upwards with such force it winded me and that feeling was very distinct, it was outrage, it was outrage because it was obvious wasn't it, so absolutely obvious, that if a person has no autonomy, no income, has so many restrictions imposed upon the course of their life and their daily round, is belittled, undermined, ignored, is misinterpreted on and on, is in the dark sexually, goes up to bed without knowing when or if their husband will come home, spends hours and hours and hours alone or with three children all under the age of six, of course they are going to go out of their mind. What are they supposed to do? Carry on cooking and cleaning day in day out and open their legs with a smile whenever it's required, just as normal? Surely only an incapacitated sort of person with barely any of their faculties intact would be capable of putting up with conditions such as these. And there you have it. I didn't finish reading *The Female Malady*. It was unbearable. It roused in me an inherent anger that was ancient and bloodthirsty. After having several extremely violent nightmares I returned it to Natasha and admitted I couldn't finish it and she confessed to me that it had overwhelmed her also and she hadn't been able to finish it either. We were sitting in her kitchen probably, which was much nicer than the kitchen in my house even though they were more or less exactly the same, and I expect we were drinking Earl Grey with Baileys in it which was her invention and one we often enjoyed together in the afternoons once the days started to get chillier and shorter, and very likely the book was on the small Formica table between us and if it was I would certainly have turned it facedown so as not to see any longer that ludicrous piece of so-called visual documentation that testified to Pinel's great service to insane women by Tony Robert-Fleury. Many years later I will come across a phrase in a slim book with a black and white cover which I will take to my heart at once: "the glow of grime." The glow of grime. Just a few words yet how they soothed me. On and on I experienced gaping periods of time when I was flattened by a sense of doom. Quashed completely by deep despair and anxiety which was relieved now and then by anguished though relatively merciful bouts of sobbing. I had no small children, no errant husband—I had plenty of friends, was getting educated—the world, I was told again and again, was my oyster—I could go anywhere, be anything. Yet in my heart I was bereft, grieving—homesick for a place I had never seen. For a place that doesn't exist, yet I belonged there nonetheless. Ridiculous really. Ridiculous, yet so acute and abiding. At such times I could see no way ahead. "I suppose I shall sound terribly defensive if I say that Westerners attempt to expose every speck of grime and eradicate it," wrote Junichiro Tanizaki, the author of *In Praise of Shadows*, "while we Orientals carefully preserve and even idealise it. Yet for better or for worse we do love things that bear the marks of grime, soot, and weather, and we love the colours and the sheen that call to mind the past that made them." A place that values worn and sullied objects. That favours darkness, patina, and fragility. Indeed, compared to the West's obsession with light-filled rooms, sparkling appliances, spotless surfaces, and having the latest thing, such a place sounded like paradise to me. Tanizaki suggests that these esthetic differences are indicative of attitudes to light and dark on a deeper level. He surmises that in the West we are fearful of shadows and seek to banish them, while the Japanese are more inclined to "guide shadows towards beauty's end," and in doing so are able to live cheek by jowl with phantoms, mysteries, the ancient, and the chimerical. I don't believe for one moment that cultural ideas about how women should live and behave have ever been any better in Japan, not at all, but that doesn't detract from the virtue of Tanizaki's notion of "visible darkness"—a perhaps inadvertent inversion of Milton's "darkness visible" which indeed flips the hellish connotations of that chilling oxymoron by inferring that the blackness within you is stilled, is transfixed perhaps, when it has in its gaze the blackness without. That preternatural and particulate place, "where always something seemed to be flickering and shimmering [. . .] This was the darkness in which ghosts and monsters were active, and indeed was not the woman who lived in it, behind thick curtains, behind layer after layer of screens and doors—was she not of a kind with them?" According to Tanizaki's evocative descriptions, the home is not so much a boundaried static place, sealed off and impervious to external and previous influence—Japanese interiors are permeable and transmogrifying, infinitely capable of "luring one into a state of reverie." Yes, that sounds like the kind of place where I might feel at home. Modern homes, now frequently referred to as bases and living spaces, are becoming lighter and brighter, homogeneous in their increasing need to be increasingly operational. And who, exactly, is doing most of the work required day in day out to ensure that all these homes are unfailingly lighter and brighter and operational? Convenience replaces ritual, devices replace daydreaming, spotlights replace shade, and the discord between one's inner world and their immediate surroundings goes through the roof. Fastened, by so many cables and leads to its functions, possessions, and gadgets, switch by switch some cosmic link is short-circuited, and the house is no longer a doorway to other worlds. And whoever lives inside there is bewildered to her wit's end that she experiences such a penetrating and abiding—almost accusatory—sense of estrangement in a place where she is surely supposed to feel inspired and at ease. When everything is illuminated and the shadows have been sanitised, where goes the creature inside and what happens to her need for reverie? Perhaps she takes to her bed, perhaps she throws furniture, perhaps she draws on the walls, perhaps there is suddenly a duck, perhaps one day she simply leaves it all behind her. Communing with the dark, in all its primordial and transformative potency, is somewhat unsettling, certainly. But who on earth wants to keep their feet on the ground on and on? It seems to me entirely indefensible that anyone ever thought it necessary and correct to send an electric current blazing through the furrows of anyone else's mind in order to dazzle the intimate blackness at its core into rapid extinction.

I'd read and loved poems by William Wordsworth, and shall always remember the one about Goody Blake and Harry

Gill. She is so poor she can't afford wood for her fire, and the winter is so bitterly cold. After a great wind she goes down the lane, picking up twigs that have snapped off of Harry Gill's trees, and she gathers them up into her apron. Harry Gill comes out of his house, comes mincing down the garden path, all red-faced and arms waving, and he shouts at Goody Blake, tells her she has no business taking those twigs, probably calls her a wicked thief. Goody Blake is mortified of course and very apologetic and off she scuttles, all the scrappy twigs tumbling from her thin apron. Harry Gill has an enormous fire day and night of course and many luxurious blankets—it's very easy for him to get snug as a bug on a cold winter's eve. Except on this night, the night after he'd reprimanded Goody Blake for gathering up a few twigs broken off by the wind, on this night Harry Gill can't seem to get warm at all. He piles more and more logs onto the fire so the fire roars brightly and throws out a tremendous heat, and he piles more and more blankets and maybe even some sheepskins onto himself, but it makes not a bit of difference—he is frozen to the marrow. His teeth chatter and his fingers and toes go numb and the insides of his miserable old thighs clatter against each other like long cold swords and there is nothing he can do to thaw himself out and feel warmth coursing through his veins once more. He never ever feels warm again, always cold, always freezing cold. That made a deep impression on me because at the time it seemed to me one of the very worst things that could befall a person was to be cold in bed and find it impossible to get warm, and yet of course it served Harry Gill right. It was the perfect punishment for being such a mean and nasty man, and making Goody Blake feel so bad and wretched for doing nothing wrong at all. There was another one, "We Are Seven," and that was very sad—no, the child says, after one of her siblings has died, we are seven, we are seven. And Andrew Marvell, reading his poems brought about beautiful crepuscular images in my mind, glowworms and paper lanterns and dens twisted up out of long bluish grass and those winking white flowers in the shape of a star that become more and more luminous when night starts to fall. And I'd read Blake of course, Blake, and Byron, and Keats, and Thomas de Quincey and William Godwin. And I'd read Mary Wollstonecraft's *A Vindication of the Rights of Women*, though I confess not all the way through, and I'd read Turgenev's play *A Month in the Country*, two or three times, though not yet J. L. Carr's beautiful novella of the same name. I hadn't yet read any Saul Bellow. A boyfriend read out bits from *Herzog* while we were having a picnic up the Town Gardens one afternoon and that annoyed me because he had a very insistent way of reading and really I just wanted to lie there quietly with my eyes closed and listen to the little birds twittering until it finally occurred to him to snog my face off.

Years later another boyfriend recommended *Seize the Day*,

and I read that and enjoyed it a lot because of where and when it was set. I could easily imagine the young man in the smart restaurant with the older man who was perhaps his uncle. Whoever this older man was, I think the young man was asking him for some advice about business, or perhaps even for a favour that would help get him started in an area of business the older gentlemen had a lot of connections in going way back, or perhaps it was about a woman, or perhaps the young man simply needed some money. I know that when the waiter came over to serve them drinks he was wearing a dark red waistcoat and had to go up a few marble steps that had big plants in big glazed pots on either side of them and the glasses were on a silver salver and contained a top-notch kind of brandy, and owing to those kinds of details and the way these two men conversed I recommended it to a boyfriend I had a few years after the one who had recommended it to me and he didn't like it at all. He didn't enjoy any of the books I recommended to him, he only liked biographies of very eminent men such as Napoleon and Beethoven and George Bernard Shaw. I once gave him a book of stories by Maeve Brennan when he had a cold and he hated that and went on and on for ages saying he couldn't understand what on earth I saw in a book like that—he wanted me to explain it to him, what it was exactly about this particular book that appealed to me so much, because he thought it was very dull and couldn't see anything interesting in it at all, and I wouldn't say anything in response to that because I was very put out by his attitude and considerably embarrassed, though if it was for him that I felt embarrassed or for myself I couldn't quite distinguish, and I vowed not to give or lend him any more books after that and whenever he asked me what I was reading subsequently I would answer most mellifluously, "Something that you'd find very dull but that I happen to like a great deal." And we'd both laugh at that, which was better than the air turning sour, and then he'd tell me all about the life of the great man he was currently reading up on and it seemed to me that the biographies he read were always very flattering, I was surprised he was taken in by them—that he read biography "in a state of bovine equanimity" as Janet Malcolm memorably puts it in her gripping investigation of the subject, and then I realised he really did want to believe in greatness and had no interest in reading a more critical or evenhanded assessment of this or that man's life, and I realised too that he wanted very much to impress upon me this idea of greatness which was so fundamental to his outlook, so sometimes I suspected that he wasn't telling me the full story, that he was glossing over the parts of this or that man's life—including his own— that were not so great at all, as such I invariably found what he told me lacking in nuance and credibility and so boring therefore and he probably sensed that, which again made things a bit strained between us, but of course it would never occur to him to say "something that you'd find very dull but that I happen to like a great deal" whenever I asked him what he was reading. I hadn't read any Georges Perec or Robert Musil or Hermann Hesse or Stefan Zweig or Paul Bowles. The boyfriend who recommended *Seize the Day* gave me *The Sheltering Sky*, I still have it, he wrote inside it. I was amazed by that book, totally seduced by it, and then, when I was in Tangier, six or seven years after we broke up and he got married, there was a bookshop on the main street that had a small selection of English-language books and of course they stocked many titles by Paul Bowles since he'd lived in Tangier for almost fifty years, which is something I knew at the time. I also knew he'd grown up in New York, but it was a while later that I found out he'd spent some time studying music composition with Aaron Copland and it was with Aaron Copland that he first visited Tangier and it was later again that I discovered that Gertrude Stein had been the one to recommend they go there. On leaving New York, he once said to an interviewer for the *Paris Review*, "I had a fairly good idea of what life would be like for me in the States, and I didn't want it." "What would it have been like?" asked the interviewer. "Boring," said Paul Bowles.

I've never forgotten reading that, how could I?—what kind of person, who had the kinds of connections and opportunities that Paul Bowles must certainly have had, feels that life in New York would be boring nevertheless? One day my friend and I were walking through the Petit Socco when we bumped into an American folksinger and her husband. We'd met them and some other people up in a club, not too far from where our apartment was, a few days previously. We'd been in Tangier for about three weeks by then and were planning to go down to the desert soon, via Fez. We told the singer and her husband, who was a musician, about our plan and she said they were playing a concert in Fez soon. She told us the date of the concert because we asked her when it was, and it was a good week or so after we planned to be in Fez— my friend and I looked at each other and said: "We'll be in the desert by then." I'll always regret that we didn't see the concert in Fez because once I got back to Ireland I looked her up and found plenty of her songs online and she has the most extraordinary voice. While we were all talking in the Petit Socco, me not knowing at all what this woman's voice sounded like when she sang, I noticed a young woman standing on her own, looking at me, then I soon realised she wasn't looking at me—she was looking at the books I was holding. I smiled at her and said hello and she came a little closer. "Do you like to read?" I said, and she nodded and said she did, and she told me she was learning English. "It's hard to get books," she said. She had a very clear face, and eyes, and her voice too was very clear. I told her I had some books that I'd finished with and would she like them, and she said yes she would. I looked over at Café Tingis then turned back to her and said, "If I leave them in there for you, can you go there and collect them?"

She said yes, that would be fine, so I told her I'd leave them in there for her around lunchtime on Friday. She told me her name, I can't remember it now though I recall at the time thinking that it didn't quite suit her, and Friday morning I collected up the books I'd already read, two volumes of the *Neapolitan Quartet*, and *Practicalities* by Marguerite Duras, and I tied them with string I found in a drawer in the kitchen of the Spanish Colonial apartment my friend and I were staying in. I wrote a note and tucked it into the book on top of the pile, it said I would leave some more books for her at the same time the following Friday. The day after that me and my friend would be heading down to the desert, via Fez. I didn't have any more books to give her but it occurred to me that I could go to the bookshop, the one on the main street, the same bookshop where Jean Genet used to go to collect his royalties sent over from Gallimard, though I didn't know that then, and buy some for her, so that's what I did. I don't remember which books I chose. There weren't so many to choose from. Maybe there was something by Hemingway, I don't know. When I went in with them on the following Friday the same man was standing behind the counter in Café Tingis so I asked him if the books I'd left the previous week had been collected. "Oh yes," he said, "she came in right after you left." I don't know what she made of those books. I don't know where she read them. I wondered if she read them secretly. The picture that came to mind was always of her sat with them alone at night in a room with a very high ceiling and pink plaster walls and cushions piled together in the middle of the floor. She sits cross-legged on a big round cushion, sometimes it's a ruched cerise one, sometimes the softest leather stitched with white and gold diamond shapes. Thin apricot-coloured cloth with golden thread running through it flutters gently either side of the long open windows. There is a low square table with candles and a lamp and a pot of tea. Not the sugary mint tea everyone drinks there, something else, English tea perhaps. She was learning English, but English isn't just a language is it? I'm glad some of the books I gave her were by female writers from Italy and France. I wonder what they awakened and stirred up inside of her. What did they make her yearn for and set out to meet? I wonder, especially, what impact Lenù and Lila had on her heart and on her ideas for the future. What seed did they plant? Where did she go? And when she got there, was it how she had imagined it to be? I no longer have my copy of *Let It Come Down*. It wasn't one of the books I left for the young woman in Tangier though—I'd wanted to keep it, I'd underlined sentences in it with violet ink.

It came back with me to Ireland and was put in a stack along with the other Penguin Modern Classics piled up against the blue wall in my apartment and then one day I was coming home from the market and was almost at my apartment building when I saw up ahead of me a bunch of wildflowers fall off the back of a bike that I realised was being pedalled by someone I know. The flowers fell into the middle of the street and a car went over them immediately. They were completely flattened. The guy who I know and whose lovely flowers had just been pulverised by the stinking hot tyres of a car carried on cycling until someone called out his name. They had picked up the flowers and were holding them out to him. The flowers were very droopy. They looked like weeds. He looked at them sadly and flopped them across the back of his bike, which he parked up outside the bar, and then he went inside the bar looking defeated. He hadn't seen me. I went upstairs to my flat and searched for *Let It Come Down*. I'd told him about it just a week or so ago when I was last in the bar and he said he'd like to read it sometime. So after finding it quickly enough and freshening up I went down with it, to the bar, thinking giving it to him now might cheer him up. I perched up at the end of the counter and right away he began to tell me what had happened to his flowers on the way back from the market. "I saw," I said. "You saw?" he said. "Yes," I said, "I was coming home from the market too, and I saw them fall off the back of your bike into the road." "Did you see the car going over them?" he said. "Yes," I said, "I did. Sorry about that." I'm not sure if I was saying sorry about the flowers getting squashed or for having seen the flowers getting squashed, because actually he did seem a bit put out by the fact that I had witnessed the whole episode for the reason that, since I'd seen it, I'd deprived him of the opportunity to tell me all about it, and I could tell he was itching to tell somebody about his flowers being run over. I gave him the book and told him he could keep hold of it for a while, but I'd like it back somewhen because I'd underlined sentences in it. "Plus I bought it in Tangier," I said, "and I have some cool memories attached to it." He said of course and thanked me, but I can't say he received it with much enthusiasm. He was still sulking about his wildflowers being run over and every time a new person came into the bar he told them all about it in the exact same way with the exact same degree of umbrage each time. In fact, if anything, he was getting more and more worked up about the incident as the evening went on. With repeated telling, I noticed, it had accrued metaphorical significance—wasn't the incident a perfect expression after all of how the small man's attempts to introduce a little natural beauty into his daily life are ruthlessly steamrolled again and again by the big man's obnoxious SUV? Maybe, but I didn't feel sorry for him anymore, I felt sorry for my book. It was just sat there on the bar, redundant—he hadn't so much as leafed through it. It may as well not have been there. I saw that, I saw that whenever I looked at it—it may as well not have been there. Indeed, my book had not changed a single thing, all that had happened was that for the time being it was separated from me and as the evening went on that made me feel more and more morose and separated from everything else. I was tempted to reach across and slide it back towards me when he was looking the other way, all caught up in telling someone else about his innocent flowers and the heinous motorist. I went off him a bit after that. And he hasn't given me the book back and I know he never will, and I know he hasn't read it, and probably never will. It bugs me that my underlined sentences are somewhere in his house up the road, bright violet inside a book that he ignores. Sometimes I think of asking for it back. But I can't bring myself: "Can I have my book back please?" No, I am just quite unable to say that. I can buy it again of course, and one day that's what I'll do I expect. And as I go along reading it again I'll underline sentences here and there once more, but they won't be the same sentences—it's very likely that the sentences I'll underline in future will be different from the sentences I underlined in the past, when I was in Tangier—you don't ever step into the same book twice after all.

I read Henry Miller for the first time in France, one evening while my friend was out with her boyfriend, and I hated it, I found its bombastically vulgar language unbearable, which made me feel disappointed in myself and I wondered if perhaps I'd happened upon one of his duds and if I tried another I would very likely enjoy it much more and understand right away why people considered him to be such a brilliant writer.

I still haven't tried another so as far as I'm concerned Anaïs Nin is a much better writer than he is, not that they need to be compared of course, it just gets on my nerves that for expressing a comparable eschewal of sexual and artistic convention she is thought so little of and he so much. When she died in 1977 the *New York Times* obituary said she was survived by her husband, Hugh Guiler. The *Los Angeles Times*, meanwhile, reported that she was survived by her husband, Rupert Pole. Both accounts are correct—Nin was a bigamist, but big deal, really. People just didn't like her did they. I picked up several of her books, four novels and *Under a Glass Bell*—a collection of short stories—in a Paris bookshop during springtime a few years ago because somewhere or other around that time I'd come across a quote of hers that had really made me feel better: "We do not grow absolutely, chronologically. We grow sometimes in one dimension, and not in another; unevenly. We grow partially. We are relative. We are mature in one realm, childish in another. The past, present, and future mingle and pull us backward, forward, or fix us in the present. We are made up of layers, cells, constellations." I began to read the first story of the collection while standing in a narrow aisle of the Paris bookshop and the story takes place on a houseboat docked in the Seine. The king of England is about to visit Paris so of course the authorities want to clear the riffraff from off the quays, consequently the people in the houseboats all receive notices telling them they have to sling their hook, tout de suite. The bookshop I stood in while reading the story was itself on one of the quays beside the Seine and after I paid for the books and put them in my bag I took a walk along the great river, thinking about how strange and wonderful it must have been to have had a houseboat on the Seine in the middle of Paris in the 1930s. Nin describes the people who lived and congregated around the quays with candour and sensitivity, with affection I suppose is what I'm saying—the way she writes of the tramps dipping their combs into the river is to my mind particularly tender, and naturally there is throughout the tale that element of fantasy and sensuousness for which she is known, as for example when she describes her body being like "a silk scarf resting outside the blue rim of the nerves." The blue rim of nerves. Later that same year I went to New York and various people at a party asked me what had I been reading lately and when I said Anaïs Nin many of them were noticeably thrown off guard—Nin was not à la mode and hadn't been for aeons—they had nothing up their sleeve at all to say in response and replied, in a dismissive yet wistful sort of way, that they'd read her years ago, when they were at college—as if that was the only time in life that Anaïs Nin should be read. I said it really was worth reading her again. I said that I'd been particularly struck by the way she writes about sexual relations as a way of uprooting herself, of remaining unfixed, of transgressing the familiar lines of her personality. In fact, if anything—though I did not say this—

Nin should be read later on in life, when one has solidified and feels so very sure of themselves and would perhaps benefit from coming undone, from perhaps going out of their minds. Nin did not shy away from the phantoms and fantasies that haunt and goad us—on the contrary, she cajoled and probed them. Sex, as far as she was concerned, was as much an existential adventure as it was an erotic one. Something that took me by surprise when I read *Henry and June* was discovering that Nin had been to Innsbruck—"I have Austrian money in my bag and a ticket for Innsbruck." I just couldn't imagine her in Innsbruck at all. I also know—and knew then, when I read that—that Clarice Lispector spent some time in Innsbruck, but that is understandable since Lispector's husband was a diplomat which meant they spent time in all sorts of places together. Not that she enjoyed moving about particularly, in fact she said travelling in an official capacity was awful—"it's serving out sentences in different places," she wrote in a letter to Portuguese poet Natércia Freire in 1945. "The impressions you have after a year in a place end up killing your first impressions. At the end of it all you end up 'educated.' But that's not my style. I never minded being 'ignorant.'" It's not really so much that Lispector liked to remain ignorant—it's very likely that she was averse to the way people in diplomatic society took it upon themselves to condescendingly hold forth on another country's "situation." She was certainly alienated by their snobbish chitter-chatter and exhausted by the merry-go-round of judgements and opinions that they continually rolled out—"I've never heard so much serious and irremediable nonsense as over the month of this trip," she wrote while staying at the Brazilian legation in Algiers in 1944. And in a letter written in 1947 she wrote, "I was truly fatigued in Paris by all those intelligent people. You can't go to a theatre without having to *say* whether you liked it or not, and why you liked it and why you didn't [...] I end up really not wanting to think, besides just not wanting to say what I think." I don't know what she made of Innsbruck, probably not much. "I see very little," she said in one of the many letters she wrote to her sisters, adding that all the places she passed through looked "pretty much alike." Lispector was homesick when she was away from Brazil. Despite her glamorous worldly looks a life spent going from one country to another didn't suit her at all. The most important thing in the world, as far as she was concerned, was being close to the people she loved. When Nin was in Innsbruck she stayed in Hotel Achenseehof. When I visited Innsbruck I stayed in an apartment that belonged to a translator who was in Porto for three weeks and needed somebody to take care of her plants. I had planned to do a lot of walking in the Alps but as it turned out I couldn't walk up in the mountains as often as I had dreamily anticipated because of a heatwave that just got more and more stifling—what I needed to do was to find some water to cool off in. So one day I took the train, and then a bus, to Lake Achensee, which is in fact right beside where Hotel Achenseehof once was. I remember that I didn't get into the water straightaway once I eventually got to the lake even though I was absolutely dying to, for the reason that no one else was bathing—perhaps it wasn't allowed? I stood smothered in sweat at the edge of the beautiful blue water and experienced that oppressive and immobilising confusion which often sets in on me when I am in a different country and makes me lose all common sense and behave in a freakishly stupid manner. Then I watched as two men went in and I got my answer—they roared and gasped and jumped up and down—evidently the water was very cold. That was no deterrent to me, however. I live beside the Atlantic and am used to swimming in frigid temperatures—these two men were probably used to only ever swimming in the Adriatic Sea. I walked into the lake as the men were walking out, having gone in to only halfway up their thighs, and the water was fresh but not especially cold—I plunged down into the lake so elated to feel cool and fresh at last, and when I popped back up I saw that the two men were stood with their hands on their hips and the water around their calves, looking at me, and looking as if they had half a mind to go back in, but they didn't, they returned to their towels and glanced at me a bit sheepishly when, a while later, I came out of the water and walked reborn and dripping wet back up to mine. I got the last bus from Achensee, which would bring me, or so I blithely imagined, to the train station, and from there it was a short ride back to Innsbruck. As it turned out the bus terminated in a small village several stops before the station, which sent me into a panic that didn't go unnoticed by the bus driver. He told me he lived in Jenbach, which is where the train station was, and he'd drive me there once he'd taken the bus back to the depot. So I stayed on the bus, what choice did I have, and we drove around a field of long grass and he stopped the bus beside a wire fence and took out the cash box and walked with it towards a small breeze-block building. "I won't be long and then we'll get going," he said over his shoulder. I went and sat in the field and tried to read but I couldn't concentrate because naturally I was wondering about how trustworthy this bus driver was. I don't know what book it was, it could have been anything. One belonging to the translator perhaps, she had many books, including something by Elias Canetti, which I read in the Domplatz several days later, safely back in Innsbruck. "I have one hour remaining," I wrote in my notebook while I sat in the Domplatz with Elias Canetti and a coffee, "before I head back to the apartment, put away the washing up, fold up the laundry, take a last look around and depart for the Hauptbahnhof to take the bus to Munich, a journey which takes 2 and a half hours. I am very unhappy about leaving, mostly because of the weather which continues to be beautiful. So I am in the Domplatz again, about to copy out some sentences I underlined in *The*

Conscience of Words by Elias Canetti. I don't know if I'll have time to transcribe all the sections I underlined and perhaps, as I read them again, I won't want to." I did in fact manage to write down several citations from Canetti's book before returning to the translator's apartment and taking a last reluctant look around after checking for the umpteenth time that I'd locked the windows and turned off the hob. One such passage reads: "The other speaker is grasped not so much in the way he thinks and speaks. Broch is far more interested in finding out in what specific ways the man makes the air shake." Below that I have written "Dialogue with the Creul Partner" (I nearly always misspell the word "cruel"), and beneath that, "you will need to have this," possibly referring to Canetti's book—possibly to Broch's—who knows—something, anyhow, that I didn't need right then, but "will," in some unspecified but certain time to come. Before I left the translator's apartment I wrote her a note, and in it, amongst other things, I apologised for burning a cork tablemat and for underlining sentences in her Canetti book (with a pencil)— "I quite forgot it wasn't mine," I wrote—which was an out-and-out lie. Apparently, Jane Baltzell Kopp borrowed five of Sylvia Plath's books while they were both at Cambridge and she made pencil marks in all of them, which made Plath apoplectic—"Jane, how could you?" she said, and then in a letter to her mother she wrote of the incident: "I was furious, feeling my children had been raped, or beaten, by an

123

alien." Perhaps making marks in five books is rather taking liberties. Then again perhaps Kopp's pencilling wasn't as completely brazen as it seems—it was seeing Plath's underlinings, she said, that "emboldened" her to make a few of her own.

I'd read plays by Euripides, Racine, and Molière, Chekhov, Pirandello, Ibsen, Strindberg, and Shakespeare—of course. At college we'd studied *The Tempest* and *King Lear*, which I found quite distressing, and we also read *Racing Demon* by David Hare. I never really got over the title. Racing demon, racing demon, and all men of course. All men with feeble hands is all that comes to mind now, superfluous hands and static hair—and argyle cardigans: green, navy, maroon, grey. That's how I imagined them at the time I suppose—argyle cardigans are in fact very much of that time. I don't think I was grown up enough to read it properly, to take the intended meaning from it. Instead I got caught up in peculiar masculine details and likely missed all the pertinent themes that the exam papers would undoubtedly ask me to identify and wax eloquent about later on in the year. You come across all sorts of men in literature, it's very interesting—especially at that age, when you're probably coming into contact with only one or two sorts of men on a regular basis in your own life, sorts that of course you're already bored to death with. I don't believe we ever went to a staged production of *Racing Demon*, and we used to go to the theatre—we used to go to the theatre in Bristol fairly often, it cost five pound. The landlord from the pub behind the college used to come too. I don't know how he managed that since he was neither a student nor a teacher. Possibly the proximity of the pub to the college and its popularity with both students and teachers encouraged everyone to feel, including himself most certainly, that it was part of the college, which made him a part of the college too. He had a lot to say for himself and would shout things out, on the bus there and back, and in the theatre during. People thought he was "a real character" and seemed to get quite excited whenever he was about. I thought he was a pisshead with a big gob who had read a few recondite verses and I didn't like him one bit and was glad when at last he buggered off to a bona fide college bar in Oxford for good. They'll make mincemeat out of you there, I thought. After that, *Equus*, which bothered me greatly. We took turns reading out parts. Wilcox said, "You read that exceptionally well," which made me livid. What are you getting at? I thought. Whenever anyone like that said anything at all to me I nearly always felt sure there was a connotation there somewhere that I was failing to grasp, an insinuation I couldn't fully decipher. The dreadful low-lying sense that there is something I'm just not getting has never fully abated. When I was a student in London, just a few years after *Equus*, a man in a baseball cap and Red Wing boots told me my response to questions, even routine ones that no one really cared about the answers to, was far too defensive. "It makes you seem juvenile," he said. "No one is attacking you, you mustn't take everything so seriously." Well naturally I was very put out by this, mortified and humiliated—my nose felt horribly swollen and I remember my cheeks were prickling with embarrassment, and probably indignation too. I was just about to open my mouth to reply "That's easy for you to say" when I realised of course I couldn't do that. There was nothing for it but to hold my tongue and accept every slighting word. He was right really. I was, overall, far too reactive. Just like a child. After that I did manage to be less touchy, mostly, but then it returned, this unsophisticated tendency of mine. It came right back many years later, making a little fool out of me. The shame and confusion I'd feel after flaring up again towards the end of dinner, and again I was advised to turn the other cheek, this time by the man who liked to read fawning biographies and hadn't the heart to be moved by the bittersweet observations of a smart Irish woman assuredly adrift in Manhattan—or no, not that, the other one—to "let it go over my head." To let whatever had got to me go right over my head in future. And what then, I thought, but didn't say, cowed as I was once more into holding my tongue. Later, I said it, when it came about another evening. "What then?" I said. "Then I'm only paying you half my mind. Is that really what you'd like? For me to stop taking you seriously? What then?" He was forever saying I was so serious. I wasn't really. I was often uncertain about who he was and what he'd got up to in the decades before we met, and that uncertainty from time to time did indeed make me pensive and cagey. Exactly how much does one need to know, I wonder, or how little do you need to care, in order to lift up your skirt and feel truly lighthearted? One day he asked me why I hadn't married someone well-off when I was younger; "I think it's very strange," he said. "It's not that strange," I said. "Things have changed a lot since you were young, women make their own money now." "You don't make any money," he said. He had a point there. I must admit sometimes I have kicked myself that when I was younger and had the chance I didn't get in with a man who had a lot of money but whenever I met one I quite often didn't enjoy the way he spoke to me. "I suppose you didn't move in those kinds of circles," he said. "What do you mean?" I said, "I met lots of men with money for your information and they got on my nerves." "Are you referring to when you were a waitress in the Royal Enclosure?" he said. "Possibly," I said. "Amongst other things. I don't know why you keep on asking me questions that you already have a fair idea of the answer to." "Now, now," he said. And I laughed, I always laughed when he said that. Now, now. Looking at me over the top of his glasses. "It's nice to see you laughing, love. I'm just saying you're very independent, that's all." (He was rarely vexed or put off by any outcome, no matter how much it contrasted with his purpose, it didn't or what you said, it didn't matter a damn did it, try as you might it was impossible to surprise or defy him, everything carried on in just the same way. You felt like you were going out of your mind. It didn't help did it that you couldn't describe any of this, not to anyone, not to any of your friends, you couldn't tell a single one of them who he was or what he was like, you couldn't tell yourself, you never could find the words, sometimes, rarely, you did succeed but your triumph was short-lived, very quickly those words seemed uncouth and unkind, they made you feel so naïve and ashamed that you ran to him, caught his hand and let it loose beneath your dress. Occasionally you came across him eloquently depicted in someone else's words, a man's words usually. There he was again one day, on page thirty-eight, in a short book by Alfred Hayes this time, his name this time is Howard. Howard: it is New York City after all, around 1950, and there he is, the president of a big company, textiles or chemicals, something like that. Howard, in Café Paris, of course. Of course that's where he is, chomping steadily into a premium cut of beef, and what happens when you come across him in someone else's words, what do you do, you write the fluent sentences down gratefully of course, you write them down in the notebook you bring with you wherever you go, with so much relief and gratitude your hand trembles: "he isn't the kind of man who behaves as though there's such a thing as winning or losing, what he thinks is that the world and everybody in it are a certain way, a way he says they are . . ." and after you have written it down you sit back in the chair don't you and you take a deep breath and you read out loud, he isn't the kind of man who behaves as though there's such a thing as winning or losing, what he thinks is that the world and everybody in it are a certain way, a way he says they are, and it's exactly as if you are at last speaking your own mind—now, finally, you are saying something you have for so long struggled to say, so naturally your voice disintegrates, of course you are crying, you are so relieved, where are you this time, you're in Innsbruck, in the translator's apartment, and you're crying with both of your elbows on the translator's round table near the bookcase poor thing and your heart is full and warm as a baby again because you know, perfectly well, that when Howard orders his steak, he says "fill-ay" too.)

I'd read *Frankenstein*, and *Anna Karenina*, and *Madame Bovary*, and *The Wife of Bath*, and *The Woman in White*, and *Sons and Lovers*, and Bram Stoker's *Dracula*—for years I read it at the beginning of every winter—and I'd read *A Room with a View*, by E. M. Forster, and after I read it for the second time I got it into my head to go on a trip to Italy, on a wild-goose chase in search of Love. I went to the travel agents beside Devon Savouries and after looking through some brochures in the BHS cafe opposite with a couple of girlfriends I booked a package deal for the three of us and paid off my share in instalments with the money I earnt at the supermarket. We were seventeen, which was the same age Lucy Honeychurch was when she set off for Italy with her aunt, Charlotte Bartlett. We travelled by coach, all the way, it took a day and a half and we went through Luxembourg and late at night we skimmed around Lake Como. I could see little lights up in the hills through the coach window. I've always loved to see little lights up in the hills through a car or a bus window, especially when there is water below. It all looks so magical—a world unto itself. How nice it must be to have a house up there in the hills with all those trees full of russet animals and speckled birds and knowing lights twinkling around you and the deep still water below. My two friends had not read *A Room with a View*, they were studying other subjects, and knew nothing about the Italy that it depicted and that I was fully expecting to discover. Very early one morning at my behest the three of us set out on a day trip to Florence and when we arrived we ran away from the coach and all of its English passengers smartish and once we were satisfied we'd given them the slip we stood about in a square deciding what to do next and a man who was obviously not Italian almost immediately came lumbering over to talk to us. It was very annoying—he was from Wootton Bassett, it quickly transpired, which was a village just a few miles outside of the town where we all lived and went to college. He bragged about how he was playing two market traders off of one another—soon he'd have himself a shit-hot leather jacket for practically peanuts he said—indeed he was very pleased with himself and obviously thought we'd find his acumen impressive too. I did not, I was really annoyed and wanted to get away from him at once. I couldn't understand why my two friends went on talking to him, he was really uninteresting and his antics quite inane, furthermore he came from a village just a few miles from where we all lived—I wanted to be neither reminded of where I came from nor of the monkey business that people from that same place typically got up to, wherever they happened to be, while I was on this trip. His presence in Florence was ruining everything. I stared across towards Santa Croce and fixed my gaze and spirit on a statue there in an effort to blot him out and augment my connection with the Beauty and Love and Courage that E. M. Forster's novel had prepared me for. I wanted to stand as she had stood, with my elbows upon the parapet. I wanted to walk where she had walked, amongst the churches, the Basilica, the statues. To see those things and be overcome. I did not count on seeing a murder by the fountain as she had done. I did not count on seeing blood, real blood. I would see Christ, yes; Christ wounded and suffering and bleeding on the cross, and my own blood would be shaken from my heart, like Dante's blood was once shaken from his, and I would swoon as Lucy Honeychurch had swooned. Except I wouldn't faint exactly. I had more space in me than she did. Quite literally. She wore a corset after all. It's probably very easy to be overcome and pass out if one is trussed up in a corset. After swooning, sans corset, in Santa Croce, I'll make my own unsteady way to the River Arno and there I'll put my elbows down upon the parapet and stare intently at last into the green tumbling water. And what then? What then? Will I throw postcards into the River Arno? That seemed to be the point—that seemed to be what it was all driving towards—at least that's how it seemed to me when I recollected it some years ago and wrote about it, for the umpteenth time. Wrote about how early one morning we went off to Florence for the day so I could visit Santa Croce and see the churches, the Basilica, the statues, the fountain, the fountain where Lucy Honeychurch had witnessed a man being knifed, stabbed, fatally wounded, had seen with her own eyes the man stagger with arms flung wide, his dark eyes rolling heavenwards, and blood as red as carmine spouting from his mouth. I wanted to see Jesus's blood in Santa Croce and to be overcome, I wanted to flicker through the clandestine arcade onwards to the Arno, to stand above the cool wide river, with my hands, yes, trembling and white over the parapet and to throw something, yes, postcards, yes, just like she had done, and to watch them flutter, wildly, yes, before landing upon and being carried off, away, yes, by the River Arno. That's how I always remembered it, for years and years. That was the image I had for years and years—me, somehow fused with her, and she was Helena Bonham Carter of course, dressed in white, eyes dark and possessed, hair writhing closely beneath a ruffled hat, tossing postcards with arcane conviction, as if it were a rite of passage, into the Arno. George Emerson is beside her of course, this is his opportunity. Death as they say is a great leveller, and surely this sudden melodramatic Latin laceration has cut through the suffocating façade of Lucy's Edwardian middle-class life. What are they? What are they really? They are a young woman and a young man in Italy for goodness' sake, and doesn't death make that gloriously apparent? Emerson talks on in an excited sort of way because he senses that Lucy's petulant surface does not correspond one bit to what she is truly made of. Lucy Honeychurch has promise—that's been clearly intimated several times along the way. Mr Beebe, in the chapter just prior in fact (of course) to the Arno chapter, recalls an occasion in Tunbridge Wells when, performing on the piano for the women and men of the parish, Lucy selected to play "Opus 111" by Beethoven, a perverse choice, according to one guest, to which Mr Beebe counters; "If Miss Honeychurch ever takes to live as she plays, it will be very exciting—both for us and for her"—yes indeed, Lucy Honeychurch has promise. Well we all have promise, don't we? We all feel it thumping in us, especially around that age, seventeen, and it's irksome. What are you going to do? Everyone wants to know all the time what you are going to do and nothing makes them quite so cross as when you don't want to do anything at all. Do something! Do something! At that particular instant Lucy doesn't do anything—how can she?—none of this relates to anything she has been prepared for. At the same time however it is all completely momentous for George, it's precisely what he's been waiting for, so it's awful for them both—his spirit soars, yet he can't inspire her, nor can he leave her, he can't do anything—they are in a kind of impasse, a classic impasse that is customarily seen off with a passionate kiss, instigated by the man of course. But it is too soon for that, it is much too soon for him to make any kind of move, it's up to her to do something, what does she do, she throws what's in her hands into the river of course, and let that be an end to it. Let that be an end to it—for now. Down into the River Arno in Santa Croce in Florence, Italy, at the beginning of the twentieth century. Less than one hundred years later I'll go there myself, to the River Arno, because I want to stand as she had done, yes. At that time it seemed to me that the River Arno in Santa Croce was the only place in the world where I might stand and allow my promise to thump away inside of me, madly, madly, without feeling irked by or terrified of it.

This image endured for many years, seemed almost to have a life of its own—so autonomous was it, I never doubted its accuracy. It was the beginning. Something in me began or was perhaps realised when Lucy Honeychurch threw her postcards into the River Arno, and twenty or so years after reading *A Room with a View* for the first time I went back to it, because I had a need, as anyone does when they feel they've lost their way, to get right back to the beginning of myself. The story unfolded much more rapidly than I remembered— and there was a lot more straight-talking than I recalled. One thing directly after another—and all very external, brusque even—and it was very funny. It just wasn't a book you could get lost in, and yet at one time I had got completely lost in it—and what a very beautiful unsurpassable sort of raptness that had been. As I read on I understood that my memory had isolated and preserved several images in such a way that they were deprived of any interwoven meaning they might possess—which of course they possessed—much to Forster's displeasure *A Room with a View* is a very well-made thing— too well made, in his view—as such, these images I'd circum-scribed did in fact strategically foreshadow subsequent scenes, and yet, in my mind they stood alone and exerted a more abstract and expansive significance. As I got closer to the mo-ment with the postcards at the Arno I noticed I was begin-ning to feel anxious because events leading up to it were depicted and dealt with very differently from my memory of them, as such doubts started to creep in, and so I read on slowly, in order to delay discovering something completely at odds with my cherished memory—my bedrock—and then I read very quickly, turning the pages, turning the pages, unable to stand the disquietude any longer. I vaulted over some sentences, then went back and scoured them scrupulously, hoping they'd contain something that corresponded to my long-standing sense of the scene—I was searching quite desperately for resemblances, there was so much at stake after all—until, without any possible further delay, and as clear as anything ever can be, there it was—her voice, saying to him, "What did you throw in?"—saying to him: "What did you throw in?!" Perhaps there has been operating in me a belief that men do not throw anything into water besides hooks and stones. That the impulse to release a thing into the drift is a female one. Perhaps I consider that impulse to be exclusively female because I understand it to be an immemorial tremor, somewhere between rebellion and collapse. Not quite knowing how to rebel, but nonetheless wanting to, very very much. Or perhaps we are perfectly well acquainted with the available ways by which we might outwardly demonstrate dissent, but we notice in them the same stereotypical connotations that bind us to the very position we are desperate to cast off. Perhaps there is only the abyss. Formless and interested. "It isn't exactly that a man has died," says Emerson. Funny how in novels lives can be dispensed of, less problematically than postcards in fact, in order to facilitate a rising theme, a pressing campaign, the crossing of a spiritual boundary—the irrevocable expansion of an undeveloped heart. How was it that I came to believe, for so long, that it was her who threw them in? Was that what was in my head when I was in Florence, with my two unsuspecting friends, all those years ago? But at that time I'd only just read the book, and yet I think, even then, I very much had it in my head it was her, not him, not him. I think really I only thought of precisely where she stood as she recovered from seeing blood falling from out the mouth of a man who at that very moment seemed as if he had something to say to her, of the way her elbows were upon the parapet, and how it feels to stand like that, with the water wide beneath and someone like Emerson so near, almost matching my own position, and how tremendous that can be, yet also how utterly expected, so that in this moment of tremendous awakening one also ebbs a little, one is in fact quite abated, and so, not wishing for things to become realised just yet, one does something to upset this dreadful concordance—it is too soon, too soon— one quickly squanders something, a wineglass, a shoe, postcards, anything, just gives it up, throws it to the wall, just to ensure, for the time being, that everything, such as it is, remains askew. Nothing has been decided. Nothing has fallen into place. No, nothing settled yet. Look at how naturally, how instinctively, I toss it all up into the air. I want it, but I don't want it yet. No, not yet. Not yet. That is, I think, what I thought.

I hadn't yet read any Dante, but I had read Machiavelli and Marlowe and John Milton. One of my school friends had brought me a Penguin edition of *Paradise Lost*. She gave it to me before I headed up to London to begin a degree in English Literature with Drama and Theatre Studies and she'd written good wishes and some other things inside the cover. I think she'd managed to fill the whole page. I don't remember what she wrote, but I can remember her handwriting. It was quite big and the letters were very rounded, yet the words were bunched together, so even though there was a lot of space inside the words there wasn't very much space between them. It was probably fashionable to write that way. There's a fashionable way of doing everything at that time of one's life of course. For a while all the girls put a line through the letter "s" so it looked like a dollar sign, teachers hated that and forbade us from doing it—I did it for about a day and a bit and then couldn't be bothered anymore. And some people, though again probably only girls, did circles above the letter *i* instead of a dot which looked idiotic, I couldn't see how you could expect anyone to take anything you wrote seriously if you did that so I never did it. I have no idea where my copy of *Paradise Lost* is now. When I left England to move to Ireland

many years ago I put my books and the belongings I'd accu-
mulated up until then in boxes and I put those boxes in various garages and sheds for safekeeping. During the first few
years of living here I travelled back to England with my then
boyfriend two or three times and we collected a couple of his
boxes, a couple of my boxes, and brought them back in the car
to Ireland. I didn't get the books. I always thought I'd get
them the next time, that they weren't really essential, and
anyway if you're just renting places and you don't know how
long you're going to be in a particular place it doesn't feel
good to have stacks of books everywhere. Though having said
that I'm still renting and I have stacks and stacks of books by
now. They don't bother me anymore. I don't have any furniture really so I'm still fairly unencumbered, though the idea
of having to move again makes me feel sick. Perhaps if the
books I have were on shelves or in bookcases they might seem
more imposing and would weigh on me more but they are in
piles on the floor and on the arms of the sofa and against the
walls and beside the bed and so on. Someone who snuck up to
see me in my flat, at eleven o'clock in the morning on a
Wednesday of all days, and snuck back home at lunchtime,
never to return, said to me, with his stupid loafers back on
and his hands in his pockets by now, "You don't believe in
shelves do you?" "Do you?" I felt like saying "Do you believe
in shelves?" I don't know if those boxes of books I left behind
in England ended up in the dump or found their way to a

secondhand shop. I know I should say I'd prefer it if they'd gone to a secondhand shop and from there went to good homes with reclaimed floating shelves either side of the fireplace but to be honest I find it doesn't matter much to me either way. I know it's better if they didn't get thrown away, of course, but personally speaking, it doesn't matter to me, one way or the other, where they ended up. I remember only three of them distinctly—the Milton, *Zen and the Art of Motorcycle Maintenance*, which I hated the cover of and never read, and a big biography of Virginia Woolf that had a beautiful cover of course, though I hadn't read that either by the time I left England. A lot of the books I read when I was younger were library books so it's difficult to remember with any certainty whether one book or another that I know I've read belonged to me or was out on loan. Very probably I had my own copy of *A Room with a View* then. I've certainly had many copies of it since. The one I have now has fallen apart—pages are missing and the ones that remain aren't in order. I'm quite sure I owned several Graham Greene novels. *The Heart of the Matter* being one. I remember buying a couple of his books as well as a floor-length silver lamé skirt in a charity shop not too far from the train station in Brighton, just after I'd got off the train in fact. I remember coming out of the changing room wearing the silver skirt and saying to the woman working there, "I'm going to keep this on if that's alright" and she said it looked spectacular on me and hang on a minute, she'd cut off the price tag, and I turned around and faced a jumble of handbags and shoes and closed my eyes at once and awaited the scissors.

I'd gone to Brighton for the weekend. When I was a student in London it did me a lot of good to get out of the city now and then and be somewhere else on my own for a couple of days. Somewhere by the sea. At that time I hadn't read anything by a still not very widely known working-class writer from Brighton who I've since become smitten with, indeed it would be many years until a man who gave me a light for a cigarette outside a pub would tell me about this woman and I was so impressed by what he told me and amazed by the passion, the passion he had for her writing, and by the pleasure that recalling her writing so clearly gave him, that I vowed to buy *Berg* the very next day, but, the very next day, I could remember the face of the man who had lit my cigarette and the pleasure with which he had spoken about this author, this British avant-garde author, 1960s, yes, British, yes, female, yes, yes, but I could not remember her name, it was months and months after until I heard it again and I recognised it right away and wrote it down this time, and soon after that I did buy *Berg*, and of course since then I've nosed about online and read some things about Ann Quin, for that was her name, and discovered that she was born in Brighton and she died in Brighton, in the sea, but I did not know that then, when I went by that same sea on my way to the Regent Square in Brighton in order to find a place to stay for a night or two, wearing a silver lamé skirt that trailed along the pavement like the tail of a fish behind me. At that time I was going out with the man who had hectored me with the beginning of *Herzog* in the Town Gardens back in the town where I'd grown up and had lived all my life before moving to London to study literature and drama. I remember calling him from a phone box on the promenade and telling him I was in Brighton. I said to him, "Why don't you come?" "I'm standing right by the sea," I said, and he said he had a work do tomorrow evening and wanted to go along to it because a seller from Devizes whom he really didn't like was going to be there, he wanted to see "the little tosser," he said, and rub his face in the fact that he'd outbid him on some very covetable first editions the weekend before last. I found his reason for not wanting to come to Brighton really juvenile and unattractive and I said as much and hung up on him. Graham Greene. Gore Vidal. Nabokov. E. M. Forster. So many men for the simple reason I wanted to find out about men, about the world they lived in and the kinds of things they got up to in that world, the kinds of things too that they thought about as they drifted out of train stations, hung about foreign ports, went up and down escalators, barrelled through revolving doors, looked out of taxi windows, lost a limb, swirled brandy around a crystal tumbler, followed another man, undressed another man's wife, lay down upon a lawn with arms folded upon their chest, cleaned their shoes, buttered their toast, swam so far out to sea their head looked like a small black dot. I wanted to know the things they felt sad about, regretted, felt enlivened by, drawn towards, were obsessed with. I didn't want to read about women. Women were sort of ghostly and they put me on edge. I saw more of women than I did men, yet at the same time I felt I saw nothing of them. The way they managed to be practically omnipresent yet not really here at all was continually disquieting. And it wasn't as if they weren't occupied—they were always doing something, always seemingly immersed in some straightforward domestic way, chopping, mending, sweeping, wiping, folding, wringing, peeling, rinsing, but their eyes were fixed on something else, something I couldn't fathom. It is time to go and we are on our feet gathering our stuff—make sure you've got everything. Presents, scarfs, tissues, gloves, some unlovely souvenir from the fair conjuring up a bobbing whirligig of leering animals, ragged sacks, unsettled jars, stricken coconuts, and sudden leaping eyes. Come on then. Mother looked at herself in the mirror while her mother foostered in and out and back again with something else and another thing—do you want that, what about this—tins, bread, stamps, tea towels, iced buns. Tights, purses, magazines. She didn't want anything. There in the mirror her short jacket was buttoned up already by whose hand or perhaps all along, her face rising out of a black fluffy collar. There in the mirror that face all alone, the same and all altered but can't say how, as if she wanted me to know and not forget that I did not know what she was made of. I'd feel such a green twist of anguish looking at her looking at herself in the mirror. Should I look there too and try to catch her eye? I feel like I ought to, there is no one, no one else with her—but what if she quickly looks away? Where exactly would that leave me? She has taken herself off, vaulted just like that. By reflecting her gaze back onto herself she's flung herself a bridge and everyone else is falling away outstretched in their hats and gloves and scarfs. Caught in between I am torn. She is very high up on top of a strange kind of tower that has no inside, is all stairways, cloisters, courtyards, spiralling stalagmites of ice, curlicues of coldest mist, and narrow violet streams of the purest water in the world. All is silent here and then a bird. There are no windows to clean, no doorsteps to varnish, no tiles to regrout, no fences to creosote, it all pours through, the long long wind and its giddying sweep of breathless snow. My armpits and insteps arch, reaching for wings, flexing for hooves, some kind of instant apparatus that will launch me into flight and carry me to her. She is flanked by luxurious wolves, on her finger a mounted blackberry schemes, its beady nodes glisten tantalisingly like a behind-the-back teaspoon of caviar. She will not be my mother there and I will never find her will I. I will trail around the porticoes, clamber up the stairwells on and on, traipse back and forth across the small bridges, my hand scudding the dank wall always, scuff-blackened by the steely centipedes, the ivy berries, the moss manes, the slanting fungi. She is in here somewhere but up so high and faintly, so faintly. I find an eyelash on the crumbling ledge of a birdbath—it's already there, it's been there all along. A small and perfect scimitar. The birds come and go simply to bring it home that nothing else is moving. Down comes the sharpening fragrance of unrolling ferns and rubbed herbs for she has a huge circular bathroom does she not, right there on the very top, and copper pipes lace through the building like burnished sea serpents channelling thundering hot water, for he was a plumber was he not and he carried the windbreak did he not, the windbreak and the cool box. Hot and cold. Hot and cold. That's the way it goes. Her skin is flushed now. Her eyes are closed now. She is in her element now.

I'd read *The Bell Jar* in the bath in the first year of university but when Dale, who wasn't my boyfriend and never would be but often behaved just as if he were which now and then didn't bother me a great deal especially if for one reason or another I was the worse for wear, asked me in the second year of university if I'd read it I lied and said I hadn't read it. I can't remember if there was any particular reason why I lied to him about that. I think I lied to him and other men about a lot of little things on a daily basis or was at least vague oftentimes as a way of keeping something of myself back from them. I didn't believe it was a good idea to let them in on everything. Dale spoke about Sylvia Plath and Anne Sexton just as if they were two brilliant yet hell-bent girls who would be a bad influence on me if I had anything to do with them for even five minutes. He gave them their due, I mean he revered them both, but strongly intimated that I'd do well to give their high-octane poetry a wide berth for the time being. His familiar yet guarded way of talking about them amused me and he could see I was amused and I in turn could see that my amusement really riled him. He thought I was laughing at him, and perhaps I was. Sometimes he'd realise being wound up like that made him seem ridiculous and stuffy and his whole demeanour would abruptly change, become invigorated, boisterous even—in an instant he'd have his jacket halfway on and two cigarettes in his mouth and with a lot of jostling and hooting and a pair of gin and tonics to boot he'd bundle us out the door, and off we'd go, a couple of tots, off into town for hijinks. On other occasions, no, he would not shake out of it. On the contrary. His mood would blacken tighten harden and he'd stand there with heels dug in daring me to pit myself against him. And that amused me too, in a malign sort of way that was fearsome to endure yet impossible to overthrow. The pair of us stiffened just like that in a haunted impasse. There was no getting out of it. Centuries and centuries of mutual obsession and vengeance fastened us to the spot. We were not quite ourselves. We were not quite ourselves. We were the drama. Dale wrote poetry and read poetry and had plenty of poetry books, including volumes by Anne Sexton and Sylvia Plath—which he made sure to keep out of my reach. Probably if I got my hands on them and read them all up something terrible would befall me or else something terrible but infinitesimal already woven into me would get notions and take over and what on earth then? Women can't withstand poetry, seemed to be Dale's view. Women are beautiful and tender creatures and poetry breaks them, of course it does. Poetry rips right through you, makes shit of you, and a man can be made shit of and go on living because no one really minds, not even the man. The man likes it in fact, likes to be made shit of so that he can sit there and drink his head off and declaim one epithetical thing after another and all the other interminably taciturn men believe he is an exceptional man, a man taking a hit for them all, a hero really, a ramshackle hero they'd love to raise up upon their shot-to-fuck shoulders or else roll about in the muck with, for wasn't he a down-to-earth sort of a fellow after all? But it's dreadful to see a woman who's been made shit of due to her messing about with poetry. And what kind of a woman anyway is drawn towards poetry? Only a warped sort of a woman who wants to be made shit of, or else has been made shit of already and wants to lay out the nuts and bolts of it and in that way not keep it at arm's length any longer. Dale didn't think that that was any kind of rehabilitation so did not encourage me to read poetry by those women, showed me instead his own very neat handwriting and terse yet tender verses, and I remember that as well as being an acolyte of Bukowski he was a fan of e. e. cummings whose phoney lowercase initials and self-deprecating tone I couldn't stand—making yourself small really was the most sly and loathsome ploy for insinuating yourself into a woman's knickers—and there was that suffocatingly drippy line of his about such small hands, and that made me snigger, more than once, because Dale did in fact have very small hands and he often fell asleep with a cigarette in the left one—the right one being employed by a glass of beer around the clock—and he had burns in various states of slow repair all over that hand and if you said anything to him about them he would be satisfied you'd noticed yet look at you mock sternly as if you were only a daft goose who could never quite grasp what it was to be a poet and made shit of and on such occasions Dale would be inclined to call me "woman," which, I presumed, was his way of getting across that he was a man. Poor Dale and his two-litre bottles of dark ale and Columbo coat and neat handwriting and a suitcase full of band T-shirts pressed just so by mother. We were so very young then. It was a very long time ago and it's peculiar to think he has been alive ever since—that even now he is alive still somewhere.

How did he go on living, how have I gone on living, it wasn't at all clear to either of us then that we would go on living. I'm glad of course that I did go on living, not least because since then I've read lots and lots more books by writers such as Fleur Jaeggy and Ingeborg Bachmann and Diana Athill and Doris Lessing and Marlen Haushofer and Shirley Jackson and Tove Ditlevsen and Ágota Kristóf and Muriel Spark and Eudora Welty and Inger Christensen and Anna Kavan and Jane Bowles and Silvina Ocampo and Angela Carter and Leonora Carrington and Tove Jansson and Mercè Rodoreda. There came a point I don't know when exactly when I'd read enough books by men for the time being. It happened quite naturally—I don't recall deciding I'd had enough and wasn't going to read any more books by men for a while, it was just that I began reading more and more books by women and that didn't leave me much time anymore to read any books by men. All my time was taken up with reading books by women and the next thing I knew a year had gone by and I'd read nothing but books by women and another year went by and it was the same, then, from time to time, very occasionally, there might be something by a man, *Jakob von Gunten* by Robert Walser, for example, but mostly it was books by women I was reading, and that's the way it's stayed.

Admittedly, to begin with, many of the books I read by women were written when this or that woman was sad or was reflecting upon a time when she had felt sad and when I say sad I'm being coy of course, but what else can I say? Adrift? At odds? Displaced? Out of sorts? Out of her mind? At her wit's end? From another planet? Anna Kavan, for example, she doesn't want the day, she's not interested in all of that, because for one thing she went to school during the day and that wasn't where she belonged, there's too much reality in the day for another thing, everything is visible, on and on, for miles in every direction, and hardly any of it is especially engaging, that's how I read it anyway, that light in the wrong place can be a poison, that she felt quite at home in the dark—"Because of my fear that the daytime world would become real, I had to establish reality in another place"—the dark, where sleep has its house, yes, and I read that last October in my own bed when sleep could find no house in me at all, probably because of the loathing that crawled all over my unsheltered heart, so many creepy little legs tickling incessantly against my heart so it squirmed and shuddered, felt stripped really of any privacy at all, of any dignity, I felt so bad for it, yet there was nothing I could do, I sat up in bed helplessly my hands either side like small screwed-up paper balls and my tray beside me with its tea and its water and three or four toothpicks while my heart squirmed and shuddered not that far in, and there she was, Anna Kavan, or someone she had made up, a narrator who I suppose wasn't entirely unlike her, there in the dark, her dark strange words shining in the dark—"My home was in darkness and my companions were shadows beckoning from a glass"—giving dimension to the dark, such strange words, yet not at all unreal, not at all unfamiliar to me either, and as I read on those horrible little probing legs lifted away like the psychopathic teeth of a cartoon cog, no further molestation, just shadows, shadows then, slow and supple and overlapping, close and curious, companions really, yes, and not as sad as all that, perhaps sadness is not integral to the shades at all, it just feels that way because they have been neglected for so long because even now no one understands and welcomes them and no one ever will, they are misconstrued and distorted and feared, for so long and for evermore I expect—it's no wonder is it that they have about them an air, an abiding air, of sadness. No. No. No it isn't. Certain written words are alive, active, living—they are entirely in the present, the same present as you. In fact it feels as if they are being written as you read them, that your eyes upon the page are perhaps even making them appear, in any case, certain sentences do not feel in the least bit separate from you or from the moment in time when you are reading them. You feel they wouldn't exist without your seeing them. Like they wouldn't exist without you. And isn't the opposite true too—that the pages you read bring you to life? Turning the pages, turning the pages. Yes, that is how I have gone on living. Living and dying and living and dying, left page, right page, and on it goes. Sometimes all it takes is just one sentence. Just one sentence, and there you are, part of something that has been part of you since the beginning, whenever that might rightly be. The source, yes, you can feel it thrumming and surging, and it's such a relief, to feel you are made of much more than just yourself, that you are only a rind really, a rind you should take care of yet mustn't get too attached to, that you mustn't be afraid to let melt away now and then. Yes indeed, I am overall more or less satisfied with what the Doctor said to Tarquin on this matter—I'm especially glad he mentioned the greater imagination and referred to its correlation, the world soul. It pleases me a great deal to see words like that on a page. The Doctor seems to me positively handsome now I must admit. That speech has transformed him! He is wearing a thin grey suit now, and a white shirt, and he smells of Indian soap, it's lovely. It's lovely to think of him. Tarquin meanwhile is not in good shape, he really is very bloated-looking and has dark circles around his eyes and the ends of his fingers are all turned up where he has been chewing at his nails. On his way out of the apartment the Doctor sticks his head into the kitchen where the housekeeper is sitting on a low stool by the stove peeling chestnuts for purée and he tells her to make up a valerian tincture for Tarquin and to put him to bed right away. The housekeeper thinks how handsome the Doctor looks, his eyes are so beautiful and unabashed—she'd never really noticed them before. It's impossible to put an age on him, she thinks, and smiles, says of course Doctor, says goodnight Doctor. And for once I see the Doctor leave the apartment, he doesn't simply vanish into the air. I see the door close behind him and now he is on the stairs all alone. I see him go down the stairs, he doesn't use the banister, he has no need of it—he is light, yes, but no longer hollow, no longer empty. I see him standing on the street, it is completely quiet and dark of course, maybe there are one or two cats, but they aren't doing very much, they are blinking and curling and uncurling their sooty tails on top of a low rough wall, that's all. There are no dogs and no sounds of any dogs. The Doctor stands very still, there is a tree of course. A beautiful sycamore full of copper-edged leaves. What is the Doctor thinking as he stands there near the beautiful burnished tree? Perhaps he is thinking about Tarquin's mother, perhaps he is thinking of his own mother, perhaps he isn't thinking anything. Perhaps he is just standing there, looking up at the pale green clouds in the indigo sky, paying attention to the heart beating in his chest on and on and the breath moving in and out of his body on and on. At certain times, noticing these two procedures, the beating and the breathing, can be enough to bring tears into anyone's eyes, so miraculous, so precious, do they seem. Yes, there, I see the Doctor swallow, I feel it too. I feel it behind my own ears. The Doctor swallows and then he is gone, forever changed. Adieu. Adieu Doctor, I could have listened to you all night long.

The following morning, not terribly early, a barefoot Tarquin Superbus ventures into his library and, absolutely confident that he will have discovered this legendary sentence by lunchtime, takes down the first book he comes to, shoves up against the shelves with it, and starts turning the pages, turning the pages, turning the pages. This is easy, thinks Tarquin, after all of five minutes have gone by. This is a doddle—I'll have that sentence by lunchtime, then we'll see what's so funny! Then we'll see who's laughing! The thought of those despicable loose-lipped reprobates getting their comeuppance spurs Tarquin on, but not for very much longer, turning blank pages one after the other soon turns out not to be so easy in fact—in fact it is completely bizarro. Tarquin begins to feel horribly disoriented, the room has gone topsy-turvy, it's spinning madly and the floor lurches up and down, just as if he were standing in one of those floundering boats depicted in the ghoulish paintings above the fireplace. He takes the book and plonks down with it into one of the leather chairs, that's better, but in fact it is worse. The white pages crowd together and blot everything out, they bustle and jeer and conspire, and then they disperse, rapidly as rats, leaving one white face, completely without expression, without features even, yet it stares. It stares and stares, it's always been there, it has seen everything, everywhere! There is no getting away from it! Tarquin slams the book shut and closes his eyes, but that alters nothing. There's a meddlesome blankness flickering in his mind, creating havoc, pulling up memories and regrets and dreams, rousing exquisite moments from long ago. How pristine they all are. How much clearer now than they were then. What is white? White sheets, white lilies, white ribbons, white socks, white marble, white candles, white roses, white gloves, snow, snow coming through the window, snow on the ledges, the branches, the hills. And tears, tears are white. Aren't they, surely? Tarquin opens his eyes and sees his hand splayed upon the cover of the book. How weary it looks! The Medicis, the Borgias, the Gonzagas, the Inquisition. Yes, yes, yes. Who am I to them and who are they to me, he thinks and places the book upon the chess table. It looks nice there. Insouciant yet scholarly. Did he mark the page he had got to? No he did not—he has not devised any method whatsoever to help him navigate this enormous undertaking. And now he is hungry. Tarquin Superbus gets up and stretches, yawns in such a way that it seems he is chewing at the air, and pads off into the corridor, down towards the kitchen. Ah, the kitchen! He can already hear coffee percolating, eggs frying, the demitasse cup landing on its saucer, and the beatific clink of the apostle spoon nestling in beside it. He can already smell the divine triumvirate of butter and warm bread and sage—and, if he is not mistaken, the sweet gioioso aroma of chestnut cream. Tarquin can't get himself down to the kitchen fast enough! Grazie a Dio, there is the delightful blue bowl slap-bang in the middle of the counter! Tarquin practically collapses onto the counter, flings an arm around the bowl and hugs it to his chest, just as if it were a rock in the ocean, and starts spooning this most glorious coalescence into his gasping bocca. After two or three mouthfuls he tosses down the spoon in despair. Basta! He has had enough. He is full. He is full already! He hasn't even had his sage rolls and eggs but he feels absolutely stuffed to the gills. The very idea of raising another smidgen to his lips makes him feel bilious. He takes a sip of his coffee, but gives up on that too—he can hardly stay upright on the stool he feels so exceeded. The housekeeper lays a hand upon his forehead and tells him to get back into bed. Go on, Tarquin, she says, I'll make you up a nice fennel and burdock tincture with magnesium and Swiss honey. So Tarquin returns to his room, heaves himself back into bed, and lies there, feeling huge and heavy. So heavy. The housekeeper comes in with a bamboo tray upon which is the brewing tincture, Tarquin's favourite yunomi, and a wide-eyed blue delphinium gently rocking in a small red porcelain vase. She sets down the tray and asks him how he is feeling. "I am feeling heavy, Rosalia. I feel as if there is a great big stone inside of me, or as if I am myself turning to stone. I don't know which is better: to feel full or to feel empty. Please, won't you bring in the birds?" And no sooner has Rosalia closed the door than Tarquin is asleep. The tincture goes cold beside him, the honey collects at the bottom of the pot, the white eyes of the delphinium glance out in every direction, and the birds flutter from the top of the armoire, to the bureau, to the chair beside his bed, keeping the air moving, keeping it from going stale, ushering in the ghosts. He dreams of white sand. He is running. His feet are bare. He is completely naked. There are gulls careening above him, peeling away from the sky. His fingers are sticky with the juice from a peach. He runs down to the sea and crouches in the shallows, slaps his dimpled hands into the shallows, waves them about in the clear water joyfully, his hands are starfish—look! Then, suddenly, there are hands, bigger hands than his, wiggling in beneath his little armpits and he is lifted off his feet so fast, up, up, up into the air, he kicks out his legs and laughs his head off and she is laughing too, she laughs and swings him right down so that his little pink toes skim the water and up he goes again, laughing, laughing, laughing his head off, and she is laughing too, he can feel it, his mother's laughter, rippling like a wild breeze through his hair. When Tarquin awakens he feels substantial and clear. He sticks a foot out from beneath the covers and immediately a dove comes down off the curtain pole and perches upon his tufted big toe. "There you are," says Tarquin softly, "There you are."

The dove blinks and coos. Tarquin experiences that delicate yet absorbing sense of timelessness that often comes over one when one finds oneself stranded in bed in the middle of the day. He lies there and listens to the tender percussive sounds of clinking, scraping, coughing, peeling, mumbling, grinding, whisking, rustling. He knows he will get up and it's a nice thing to contemplate. He sees himself, Tarquin Superbus, getting up out of his bed fit for a king, striding into his bathroom, fit for a queen, he sees himself fastening his Chinese robe, fit for a prince, shimmying on his damask slippers, fit for himself, and down to the kitchen he will wend of course, where Rosalia will be beating a dozen golden egg yolks, which can only mean that Rosalia is making him English custard, and of course she is, of course she is making English custard—Rosalia always makes an ample bowl of English custard when Tarquin Superbus has had to take to his bed during the day. Tarquin knows all this and it's lovely. It is almost enough in fact—the contentment he feels from anticipating these impending procedures is so delicious that it almost renders getting up and getting on with them perfectly redundant. But then his stomach begins to growl with so much ferocity that it startles the dove upon his toe, she takes flight at once. The spell has been broken and Tarquin is no longer between worlds—his stomach has made itself heard. He is once more of the day and one thing he certainly won't be doing with it is going back to the library, he vows aloud to his changing reflection as he simultaneously powders his hair and performs his regime of facial exercises at the scalloped mirror. "I'm not stepping a foot in that god-awful room ever again," he proclaims. "To hell with it! What a lot of nonsense! One sentence indeed—whatever do they take me for?!" He doesn't doubt what the Doctor has said, he's willing to accept the veracity of every detail the Doctor relayed to him about the contents of his athenaeum, but he has no inclination, never mind about the Medicis and the Borgias, to go on with his search. Why would he when he has no desire in any case to transcend the world? He doesn't want to be above things! What for, when he enjoys so very much being right in amongst them? In the thick of it, yes indeed—that's where Tarquin Superbus likes to be. Rubbing shoulders—and earlobes, and clavicles, and posteriors, and whatever else he can get his hands on, right, left, and centre. He can live without that preposterous sentence, thank you very much. He can live without it rather splendidly in fact. To hell with it! Shut up the doors and throw away the key. He's never liked that accursed room and its infernal angles—every time he sets foot in that library Tarquin is guaranteed to stub a toe on this tricksy corner or else wallop his head off that itinerant beam—and the paintings—the paintings!—good god, to his eyes they're remindful of a supremely distasteful bad dream—a gone-off-Gorgonzola-induced nightmare—the noxious green-blue sea forever swirling and crashing and bulging, getting closer and closer, pressing in on every side until poor Tarquin falls back into a chair—and those red seats, prickling with scalding hot pins—weren't they devils' chairs? Yes, to hell with it, let the whole demonic abomination disappear beneath cobwebs and dust.

And so the carefree happiness that is Tarquin Superbus's typical condition is rectified to him once more. The doors to the library have been closed and the key entrusted to Rosalia: "You never know," she warned Tarquin, who, grinning from ear to ear, stood dangling it from its chain over the tazza del gabinetto. "Oh, but I do Rosalia! And what's more, what I know is all I want to know, ha!" But there was her prudent little palm, raised and outstretched—Tarquin could not disappoint it, so upon it the key was pressed and quick as a flash disappeared amidst a swift enfolding of adroit little fingers. Thereupon, silver-topped cohort in hand, off Superbus did go, buoyant and itching for merriment, into the streets of Venice. And how splendid it was, to trot this way and that once more! Up the steps, down the steps, coasting its many charming bridges, a tipple of young Friuli wine in every campo, a fishy cicchetti with the gondoliers behind the Bridge of Sighs, and whenever he heard laughter flocking about him, Tarquin would turn on his heels and laugh along too, he'd laugh heartily, and shrug, and roll his eyes to heaven, and they liked that, the Venetians, they liked that very much— they appreciated it when a man was able to laugh at himself, especially a man who had pots and pots of money like Tarquin Superbus did. Oh, yes, Tarquin Superbus had great style, he was fun, he could laugh at himself!—What need had he of books?! None at all, none at all, niente—everyone at last seemed to agree on that much.

Then, less than two weeks later, little things start to go wrong. Rosalia's soufflé falls flat. The lilies in the alcoves hang their heads, shed their pollen, and wrinkle at the edges as if they can't bear to come into contact with the air around them. Milk curdles in a heartbeat. Apricots go off without ever having ripened. Walnuts blacken meanly in their obdurate shells. The cats, after days of bumping their warm little foreheads into lopsided door jambs and swollen chair legs, have retreated beneath the sofas and won't come out. The birds are huddled against the alpaca blankets inside the wardrobe for similar reasons and they won't come out either. The Lady and the Unicorn tapestries in the vestibule are sagging—the carefully embroidered arrangements of bird and beast and mille-fleur are all in disarray, the spun leaves on the splendidly pruned fruit trees have withered and the vigilant rabbits with their pricked-up ears are conked out on their sides—indeed the vivid serenity of this woven paean to the senses is markedly disturbed and, correspondingly, Tarquin and Rosalia's own wits have likewise gone haywire. What's more, Tarquin's hospitable gut, which never turns away a morsel, has not a single vacancy now. Plus his limbs feel hefty and unwieldy, just as if he were wearing a cranky suit of armour—that's how he describes it to Rosalia, and she too, she confesses, has been beset by a pounding lassitude lately. Vexingly, the Doctor is out of town. He has gone to visit Josef Lobmeyr in Vienna's Weihburggasse in order, apparently, to view one of the great glass-maker's new decanters. Ordinarily Tarquin is thrilled to hear the Doctor has swanned off to Vienna because whenever he returns from Vienna not only does the Doctor have an entertaining bunch of vituperative stories about various scrapping composers up his sleeve, he also brings back with him a swag bag bulging with Tarquin's most favourite confection—a scrumptious ball of green pistachio marzipan snuggled inside a toothsome wodge of nougat which itself is attired in a slinky thick coat of the divinest dark chocolate. But Tarquin doesn't have an appetite for anything at all, not even gold-enfolded gourmet gobstoppers from Vienna—it's a horrible state of affairs. The days drag on, listlessly. One afternoon Tarquin wanders down to the kitchen to find Rosalia with her head dropped into a little nest made by her strong brown arms criss-crossed limply upon the counter. Tarquin has never seen Rosalia sleeping before. She has seen me at slumber so many times, he thinks, yet until now I have never seen her once in repose. I've never even seen her yawn! She is always busy doing something, always moving, always grafting away, always making things so lovely. But she is not a fairy for goodness' sake!—she must sleep more, he thinks. I will tell her that she can sleep whenever she feels like it, wherever she happens to be. It is unnatural that all this time I have never seen this side of her. She snores and snuffles sweetly like a baby boar. He scoots around behind her on his tiptoes, observes her Trojan shoulders rising and falling so steadily, it's very moving to see another person sleeping Tarquin thinks—then he notices Rosalia's hair and is alarmed because Rosalia's hair, which is always so beautiful and lustrous and full, is slumped, coarse and heavy, all the way down her back, like the useless dusty tail of a dead Ligurian she-wolf. Tarquin can't believe what he is seeing—is this even Rosalia? Oh god, it might not be—"Rosalia," whispers Tarquin, once, twice, three times, but to no avail. Then he tugs at the very end of the dubious-looking tail, he can't help it—there, it's done—and is elated at once to see Rosalia's dear sweet head rise up from her arms and turn to him. Rosalia! Before her eyes are open she tells him in an uncustomarily deep and croaky voice that she's about to make muffins and coddled eggs. Tarquin shakes his head mournfully and pats his tummy, "No room at the inn, Rosalia. Though I haven't the faintest idea where its present rather uncordial guests hail from." When he speaks his words sound slurred. When he breathes it feels as if Vesuvian lava is shunting into his lungs. Everything is slowing down. The air is thick and pestering. Rosalia's period has come early and is especially globuliferous and clingy. Heavy, heavy. Everything is heavy. Tarquin knows why, Rosalia knows why, though neither of them quite knows how they know why. They just do. It is the books. They are weighing everything down, and they must go. They must go! Enough is enough. They squat there darkly at the centre of the Superbus residence, full of eyes—full of eyes that have seen everything and pernicious blank faces that give nothing away. They are taking in the air of the living and secreting a stultifying miasma in return. It is like a tomb—a tomb at the heart of one's home! "They have to go!" announces Tarquin, banging a fist down onto the counter—"They have to be destroyed—every last one of them—we are being buried alive in here, Rosalia!" Without a word of protest Rosalia slips a hand into her apron pocket and takes out the key. She places it on the counter. It has turned red and appears to have a sparse white beard. Rosalia doesn't care. She pushes herself up from the stool and drags herself towards her own quarters. Her pantaloons are sticky with glistering blood and need rinsing out, pronto.

And so there is a fire. An enormous fire piled with thousands of books down in the square below. I can remember it very well. I can remember how I imagined it, all those years ago, when I first wrote this story. It was a very frightening fire. Big and black and burning. It made everything immediately around it appear dark and impenetrable. Shadows flickered and overlapped with the flames, seemed more powerful, more consumptive, than the flames. This was Milton's "darkness visible," and it was terrifying. The shadows raged and grew taller, they towered above the flames, and all around drums were pounded and strange recursive songs caterwauled to and fro. Had I seen at that time the photographs of the book-burning in the Opernplatz in Berlin on the tenth of May, 1933? I don't think I had. I don't think I knew that that evening, amidst singing and band-playing and a crowd of forty thousand or so onlookers, boys from the Hitler Youth and scores of university students, and SS soldiers, and police, and brown-shirted paramilitaries burnt thousands of books deemed to be "un-German," at the behest of propaganda minister Joseph Goebbels, who urged them on with the words: "You do well, in this midnight hour, to commit to the flames the evil spirit of the past. From this wreckage the phoenix of a new spirit will triumphantly rise." Amongst the German-speaking authors whose books were thrown into the flames in Berlin and in thirty-three more university towns across the country that night and on subsequent nights were Vicki Baum, Walter Benjamin, Ernst Bloch, Bertolt Brecht, Max Brod, Otto Dix, Albert Einstein, Friedrich Engels, Sigmund Freud, Hermann Hesse, Franz Kafka, Theodor Lessing, Georg Lukács, Rosa Luxemburg, Thomas Mann, Karl Marx, Robert Musil, Erwin Piscator, Gertrud von Puttkamer, Joseph Roth, Nelly Sachs, Anna Seghers, Arthur Schnitzler, Bertha von Suttner, Ernst Toller, Frank Wedekind, and Stefan

Zweig. Books by French, American, Russian, Irish, and British authors were also destroyed in the fires, including works by André Gide, Émile Zola, Victor Hugo, Romain Rolland, F. Scott Fitzgerald, Ernest Hemingway, Helen Keller, Jack London, Upton Sinclair, Fyodor Dostoyevsky, Ilya Ehrenburg, Vladimir Nabokov, Leo Tolstoy, James Joyce, Oscar Wilde, Joseph Conrad, Radclyffe Hall, Aldous Huxley, D. H. Lawrence, and H. G. Wells. Amongst the millions of words of poetry and philosophy and theory and prose that were desecrated was a sentence by the nineteenth-century German poet Heinrich Heine, who in 1821 had written in his play *Almansor* the words: "Dort, wo man Bücher verbrennt, verbrennt man auch am Ende Menschen"—"Where they burn books, they will, in the end, also burn people." It is a very well-known aphorism, and it is probable that even if I had not yet seen the photographs of the book-burnings when I first imagined the fire down in the square outside of Tarquin Superbus's home I would already have come across this famous line. Then again, it is one of those lines one feels one has always known, was perhaps born knowing. Because of course I've always known deep in my bones that it is a very bad business to destroy books, that burning them is especially appalling, is undoubtedly a sacrilegious act that stirs up and unleashes malignant and merciless forces in humankind which twist and maim and sully and eventually eliminate everything they search out and drag callously into their abominable sphere of methodical humiliation and unsparing processes of eradication. And so this image I have of the Superbus book fire is very dark and very strong, and I don't believe it has altered a great deal since it first cast its diabolical shadow over my mind more than twenty years ago. I see the same hapless faces gasping and grimacing between shadows and flame. Grotesque faces blistered from the heat and dripping with acetous sweat. Faces that look as if they are melting yet the unhinged lips are thick and protruding. All the features are deranged, all the mouths are giurning and leering, all the bulbous snot-bubbling noses grunt and snort, all the eyes are agog and bloodshot, all the ears are creased and discrepant and bristly. Short-arsed men with stumpy legs jolt over the burning books, back and forth, back and forth, hup, hup, scalding the soles of their stunted feet. I can see the ragged edges of their sleeves, their shit-splattered coattails, the brims of their grimy hats, licking the pyre and catching alight. I hear their wild shrieks. They are doused in liquor. Women bare their breasts and jiggle them in front of the flickering pages with heads thrown back, hooting for the devil. Boys expose their carbuncled backsides and let rip and howl as the foul gas lights up bright blue. They toss live pigs and tortoises and jackdaws onto the fire, they swing screeching mice by their tails in and out of the blaze, they throw chairs, jugs, one another's hats, whatever they can get their hands on, it's vile. Oh, it's flagrantly vile. I see Tarquin's balcony and the long lightless windows of his drawing room. He has shrunk back, observes the debauched commotion from behind a dark purple drape with terror. He had no idea. He had no idea. He just wanted them away, gone; he wanted to remove the terrible weight that had entirely quashed his appetite for food, for joy, for life, for pleasure. What is a man without desire! Why, oh why, hadn't the Doctor been here? He would never have acted so rashly if the Doctor had been here. The thick black smoke rears upwards and hangs in the air where it starts to swarm and twist into distinct and terrifying shapes, one after the other, like a monstrous changeling. A dragon, a crucifix, an ouroboros, a swastika, a phoenix, ears of corn, an ankh, a scarab, an eye. Tarquin slides out from behind the curtain and stands on the balcony with his hands gripping the red-hot railing. The searing pain and the tears that immediately flourish in his eyes are responses which are familiar to him, they are like friends that go way back, way back, and so he is soothed and fortified by them. The awesome shape-shifting shadow goes on swooping and swarming and amassing suddenly into bewitching figures and uncanny faces. One sentence. Just one sentence! But sometimes one sentence is all that it takes. And now it is burning, burning. Perhaps it will never stop burning. Perhaps its fire will never go out. Perhaps it will carry on burning for all eternity, sending out thick black smoke up into the sky, emitting its rebuffed and squandered wisdom in an unrelenting litany of mesmerising recondite signals. Perhaps I will stand here forever, with my hands welded to the balcony, in a kind of necromantic trance. And it's as if the phantasm has picked up on Tarquin's morbid ruminations. It hurtles across the square and hangs directly in front of where he stands on the balcony and though quite featureless Tarquin can feel it looking at him, studying him, weighing him up. He breathes in and it comes closer. He breathes in a little more and it comes closer again. Closer and closer it comes until Tarquin realises he is drawing this strange inquisitive beast into his body with every inhalation. He can feel it, curling around itself in the pit of his chest, a burned-out dragon gone home. He breathes in. He breathes in. And he can see before him the darkness disappearing. He breathes in the final wisp, the zigzag tip of its tail, and it is gone from the air. It is quite gone. Everything in fact has gone. He looks down, down into the square, and it has all gone. All of it! No fire, no ashes, no charred books, no half-burnt piglets, no scorched bedknobs or broom handles, no gummy patches of melted toffee, no smashed apples, no singed hair or fur, no stewed vomit, no smouldering trotters, no dribbling flagons, no punctured drums, nothing, all gone. Just leaves, just some leaves from the sycamore tree drift over the empty square. My god! Oh, mercy! Tarquin starts to laugh and cry, his whole body is shaking. There he is, Tarquin. Just before daylight. On his balcony, and the square below quite empty. All gone. Just a few leaves—a little cat pads gingerly through maybe. The first birds are rustling up a note here and there. And he is laughing and crying and his body is shaking and the blackness inside him is shaking too and with all the shaking it starts to break up into recalcitrant lozenges of bile sending up dust and soot into his oesophagus, into his larynx, aggravating them both, so that Tarquin's laughing and crying turns to coughing and spluttering—yes, here it comes, he can feel a nice big lump of phlegm, yes, here it comes, once that is dislodged I'll be clear as a bell he thinks, up it comes, yes, and my god it tastes foul, and straightaway Tarquin spits it out, expels it completely, up and over the balcony railing, and down it goes, landing with a triumphant splat down on the street below. Tarquin, feeling utterly purged—hasn't the whole ordeal in fact been absolutely cathartic—goes back inside and wets his whistle before taking to bed for a few hours, and he looks forward so much to being awakened by the ferocious rumblings of his ravening stomach once more. But that is not all. Down below in the street, while Tarquin Superbus is sleeping soundly, the disgorged blob of phlegm grows. It grows little limbs and on the ends of these little limbs are tiny digits, and once these tiny digits have become sufficiently unstuck from one another and the little blob of phlegm coalesces into a firmer substance, it stands upright. It is very tiny. Yet it can walk, and, what's more, it can climb. Climbing in fact is its forte, it is aided after all by a natural stickiness. So up it goes. Tiny little thing. Up the wall of the residence of Tarquin Superbus, and in through the balcony railings. Yes, there it is, tiny—you can hardly see it—but it's there. There on the balcony while Tarquin Superbus sleeps.

It was yellow, a horrible pale yellow. The yellow of a primrose. And in fact it grew no limbs or digits, it slid along and in darkness dragged itself up the stairs, right the way up to Tarquin's apartment. What was it? What was it made from? Was it the sentence? Yes indeed, something like that, but I was not sure what the intentions of this potent extraction were, or what its nature was, whether good or bad— something beyond both perhaps. My memory of it is, first, splattered on the street below, yellow like a primrose and throbbing steadily, and then, sliding up a very gloomy, utterly silent staircase. And it stopped there. Outside the door of Superbus's apartment. I believe there was more to come—I don't think I was done with the story. I would write more and in doing so I would discover the nature, the intentions, the fate, of this replete amoebic entity. That's what I would do. No, it wasn't finished by any means—it was perhaps just getting started. And then one afternoon I came home to the bedsit I was living in with my boyfriend at the time. Our room was on the ground floor at the front of a two-storey house near the canal. We hadn't been living in it long, just a few months. We were still trying to find our feet in Ireland. There wasn't a great deal in that room because we didn't have very much stuff—we hadn't at that time made any trips over to England to collect some of the separately stored-away boxes that contained our belongings. Even now, all this time later, I feel so relieved that I'd had the sense to suggest we put our things in separate boxes when we packed everything up, because although my boyfriend was affronted by the idea and huffed about it for days and days it saved us a lot of trouble later on. When I opened the door, the first one on the left, and entered our room that afternoon I saw right away a heap of torn-up paper in the middle of the floor. The sun fell on it directly and made it look very delicate and white, like a top-pled snow-covered lantern on a snow covered rock. I knew immediately what it was. I went closer and crouched down beside it and ran my fingers through the shredded pages of my notebook, just as if it were the hair of a dying lover, and I winced as I recognised a fragment of a word as it dropped from my fingers. My boyfriend liked me being a writer, but didn't very much like me to write. Writing took me away from him, to a place he didn't understand and couldn't get to, plus he was convinced I was writing about men all the time, and perhaps I was, some of the time. Was he threatened by Tarquin Superbus, did he perceive him to be a rival—is that why he destroyed him, is that why Tarquin Superbus was laid out on the floor of our bedsit all in tatters? My heart broke. I felt very sad. I had so enjoyed spending time with him, it's true. And the Doctor, the mysterious yet kindly Doctor. Rosalia I didn't miss. I was spared that for the simple reason that she didn't exist then—it is only now, in this retelling some twenty or so years later, that Rosalia has come to be. Indeed I have augmented and finessed the original tale of Tarquin Superbus in so many ways, yet I can't extend it—it's impossible—I can't take it beyond the point at which it was when it got snatched up from my side of the bed and was irreparably taken apart. "I'll stick it all back together again," my conscience-stricken boyfriend said, later on that evening. I rejected the offer, so then he asked if perhaps I could write the story again. "Maybe I will one day," I said. I've never written anything like that story since. I don't know where it came from. From being young and at a loose end and wanting company I expect. For a long time after whenever I recalled the heap of ripped-up paper I saw it burning brightly and it was as if each little shred was a whole page. It was as if the entire heap was in fact an enormous pile of pages, wrenched out of many many books, not just one, not just my notebook, and all of them despised and aflame. I would see grey smoke quickly filling the room and the windowpane darken, and sometimes I would see my incensed boyfriend's face in the glass, rippling with shattered reflections. The startling sudden vision of my decimated notebook, there in the afternoon sun, overlapped with the horrifying image of books burning and that huge profane fire which the torn-up tale itself contained. The two images fused, were inseparable, their meanings conjoined too, and I couldn't recollect one without seeing the other. It was all the same. From time to time it occurred to me that probably my story hadn't been very good anyway, probably wasn't something worth showing to anyone else, was merely a thing I'd conjured up to amuse myself and pass the time in a new country. Yet I couldn't quite discard the idea that in it somewhere there might have been a sentence, just one sentence, of such transcendent brilliance it could have blown the world away. And that idea burned in me, on and on.

IV.

UNTIL FOREVER

The Critique of Pure Reason, read under 60 watts
in the Beatrixgasse, Locke, Leibnitz and Hume,
befuddling my mind with concepts from all ages
in the dismal light of the National Library
under the little reading lamps . . .

—*MALINA*, INGEBORG BACHMANN

At the beginning I wrote on unbound and unlined A4 sheets of paper my father brought home in blocks from work. Although he didn't work in an office, from time to time my father came home from work with office supplies, such as the neatly enveloped blocks of paper I just mentioned and slender twisty-up stainless steel ballpoint pens—red, black, green, blue—and staplers and staples and paper clips and bulldog clips, and I feel sure there were also small boxes of drawing pins that I liked to shake back and forth either side of my head. The main thing, or so it initially seemed, was the different kinds of embossed leatherette folders that smelt like the inside of my grandparents' seldom used green Rover and were all very smart-looking but turned out to be not especially practical and so fell by the wayside soon enough since they were obviously designed to contain just a handful of specific documents to be presented and discussed on specific executive occasions across a wide oblong table. Sometimes there would be bottles of Tippex too which was always exciting even though we couldn't do much with them—we weren't allowed to use Tippex since the teachers wanted to be able to see all our workings out so that if our answer to something or other was wrong they could see whether somewhere along the way we'd hit upon the correct solution, or had at least got within a hairs breadth of it, and if we had they'd give us some credit for that. So the Tippex remained at home, as did all the other items of stationery my father brought back from work from time to time, though where exactly at home they were kept I cannot now recall since generally we were not encouraged, my brother and I, to familiarise ourselves with the various cabinets and drawers of the mahogany furniture. It was better of course if the things you wore and brought with you to school—stationery, bags, hair-slides, lunch boxes, socks, and so on—looked more or less the same as everybody else's stationery, bags, hair-slides, and socks, and lunch boxes, etc. Anything even marginally different would like as not attract a lot of derisive attention and asinine fuss, and that could go on and on for weeks, and that is the reason why, I suspect, these items, which issued a distinctly EEC vibe, remained somewhere at home, possibly in the drawer of this or that piece of mahogany furniture.

The A4 paper stayed at home too since it was in loose sheets which would get crumpled and grubby if I were to shove them into an already crammed-to-the-brim school bag. And anyway we had exercise books to work in at school, which we had to cover front and back with wallpaper as soon as we were given them. Consequently, at the beginning, as well as writing on loose unlined sheets of A4 paper, I also wrote in the back of school exercise books because while I was at school that would be the paper I had readily to hand. Teachers didn't look in the back pages of your exercise books, although my maths teacher did—I don't know what she was looking for, but of course she came across something mean I'd written about her and when I happened to turn to that page during maths class a week or so after having written it I saw that she had written a textbook teacherly retort beneath, something like "I don't like you either." When I looked up red-faced she was smiling at me. I don't know what bothered me most, what she wrote or the sight of her hand-writing, there in an area of my book I had considered out of bounds. I quickly drew a caption bubble around her comment which immediately made it less offensive. It was in the back

of another exercise book that my English teacher discovered
a story, possibly my first, which I'd written during a very dull
lesson when someone else was filling in for him. It was a very
small story, about a girl who is sewing her sisters' dresses by
candlelight in an underground chamber—a cellar—a dun-
geon even—since the stone walls are thick and bare and glisten in a way that suggests they are perpetually wet, though
never dripping, and the floor is flagstone and clearly very cold
and probably damp right the way through also, and the window, which is not ever in view, is tiny, square, impossible to
fully close and so high up it's impossible to see out of or for
any light to come through it in a way that would make any
discernible difference to the room's resounding gloom. I didn't
describe the room at all in the original story, but now that
I am thinking about it again I am easily reacquainted with
the dank enclosed image that was in my mind as I penned
those few lines one afternoon during school hours many years
ago. One possible reason why I offered few details pertaining
to the girl's immediate surroundings is because it would seem
her predicament is straight out of a fairy tale—as such most
people would already be familiar with the sort of confined
and pitiful settings these kinds of scenarios typically make
use of in order to convey the unjust suffering our heroine is
obliged to endure day in day out. In any case, from what I
remember my starting point wasn't the room, or the girl, or
even her grim situation and the inevitable twist of fate that

surely awaited her. It was the white cotton thread she moved, with the aid of a sharp needle, in and out of the stiff cloth of her sisters' preposterous gowns, one stitch at a time, until forever.

I had been doodling familiar arrangements of clustered petals, arrows, antennae, and small dotted spheres in the back of my exercise book during an aimless lesson led hither and thither by a floundering supply teacher and perhaps because this aimless lesson could itself be described as a kind of doodling I became dissatisfied and irritated by my own doodling and perhaps that's why the face began. Unless I was cheerfully coerced by the aggressively jolly art teacher I would not attempt to draw anything that belonged to the world of actual things and real beings. It soon became my custom to devise, via a concoction of the patterns described above, made-up entities that were partly plant partly creature and resembled those sliding will-o'-the-wisps that move with all the juddering grace of stage scenery at the edges of one's vision and vamoose entirely like ascending cardboard angels if one tries to fast-darting capture them in the black circle of one's amphibious pupil. The pupil is of course the rimmed abyss out of which we are pushed and around which we array our unfurling selves, so naturally when the face began it was the eyes that first appeared. I'd noticed on more than one occasion one or another classmate approach the task of depicting a face by sketching its outline first of all, within which the features—brows, eyes, nose, mouth—were subsequently arranged, just as if they were the sloppy toppings of an extravagant pizza. Sometimes I saw that there wasn't enough room for all the features and so quite often the mouth for example would exceed the face's perimeter and thus there would be no estimable chin to speak of. And, for similar reasons pertaining to the googly eyes, thus no winsome forehead to speak of either. Despite knowing that this was certainly not the correct way of thinking about and portraying the dimensions of a face and the features that surely determine them, I was incurably bad at achieving a likeness whenever I drew anything that had its place in the surveyable scheme of things. Nonetheless, my insurmountable inability to create a credible resemblance did not deter me from this impromptu undertaking for the reason that, although this face occurring upon the page did in fact correspond to a face that really did exist, a human male one that I had seen with my own eyes on countless occasions, creating a credible likeness of the man's face and the unique features that made it his alone was not my aim. I did not become cognisant of my aim until I embarked upon the second eye of the man's face, which was turning out to be quite distinct in size and shape from the first eye and would have looked perfectly at home on the face of any creature—real, fictitious, or mythical. Its remarkable lack of accuracy and specificity didn't matter to me one iota however—as I went on with the second eye's unparalleled iris my true aim made itself felt in parts of my interior that I'd never before been especially aware of. And so I came to understand that the real purpose of my impromptu undertaking was not to depict this man's likeness, but to bring him to me.

Previously and for some time I had only thought about this man and thinking about him was a lot like looking at a photograph of him because for as long as I thought about him he did not move and was always more or less situated in the same environment more or less standing in the same way each time with more or less the same things around him and so in fact I was only remembering the man which meant he existed in my mind merely as an artefact from the past and not as an animate and evolving entity that could thus entwine and perhaps even combine augmentingly with my own evolving self. So on I went with this uneven yet enfolding portrait, even though I could see I was making a very poor job of it. I had outgrown that inert and impersonal image which could just as well have been a photograph, and was right now discovering that making marks on a page with my own hand could play with distance and get things moving. When it came for me to do the man's hair however I wasn't sure what sort of marks exactly I should make. He had such beautiful hair it seemed to me I ought to at least make an effort to attest to its allure in some way. The pressure was quite unbearable. Should I render it as a single mass with just one confident undulating stroke, or as a textured accumulation of individual strands—with lots and lots of quick little dashes? Clearly if you're besotted with your subject you'll want to spend as much time as you can on this, as such a microscopic approach would seem to offer more in the way of gratification. One hair at a time. Repetitive. Minuscule. Painstaking. Devotional. Small as stitches. As previously implied I hardly cared a jot what the depiction looked like in the end. Once I'd finished my creation I would very likely find some way to expunge it entirely. Though by what method exactly might prove to be problematic, since, as previously mentioned, we were routinely discouraged from eliminating any mental emanation we'd committed to paper since it was felt, I presume, that we did not yet know enough about one thing or another to be in a position to discriminate which items of thought and expression were of value and which were not. Ripping a page or pages out of an exercise book was forbidden categorically and I recall that on the few occasions when anyone was heedless enough to flout that rule they were admonished with what seemed to me a perplexing degree of solemnity that would have been commensurate to the maiming of a canonical text but which in relation to the destruction of this or that school exercise book belonging to this or that undistinguished pupil seemed disingenuous and excessive. For there surely was a

significant and demonstrable difference of calibre and conse-
quence between the two, was there not? The idea that there
might not be was, I sensed, related to the ongoing preoccupation with the notion of individual promise, and as such it was
as seminal as it was confounding. In this case it seemed obvious to me however that the finished work inside the back of
my exercise book would not and would never be worth the
paper it was written on. It was the activity of drawing and not
the drawing itself that was of any value—I was not drawing
for posterity, certainly not. I was drawing each human male
feature down into my deepest mire. Where they did not reas-
semble pure and neat as a face in a photograph, but scattered
like charms right the way through me. Let him sink into me.
One hair at a time. Until forever. It soon became apparent
however that biros aren't a very suitable implement for this
kind of conjugating endeavour, the feeling's all wrong—the
feeling's connected to maths and a crack in the protractor
snagging the insensate nib, time and again. I lost all connection with what I was doing and so became distraught and got
manic with the oafish pen. Very quickly the whole thing
scrawled up into a tight frenzied bundle of steel wool that
obliterated the man's every feature. There was nothing left of
him. Exhausted, my vexed little fist relaxed, but the pen
would not be downed. It was not quite done. With the nib
still on the catastrophic page I allowed the line to trail and
meander for a while and in the absence of my inclination to

resume doodling it tapered off. Like a stray length of cotton thread I felt its frayed tail between my teeth, came back through and onwards went with no particular place or subject in mind or so it seemed when somewhere along the way a shift occurred as from the aforementioned depths of me there issued a strange reverberation, the thread threw out a few exuberant loops then broke off into words and the words set forth the story, as if it had been there all along, of a girl who repairs the broken dresses of her sisters by the fluctuant light of a solitary candle, just a few lines in the shape of words whose sequence told about a girl sewing in the semi-darkness of a cellar for so long and so diligently that her fingers become thin and flimsy as cotton thread, the needle falls, gets absorbed into the gloom, the girl jumps to her feet, throws her arms up into the air, she cannot take hold of a single thing now, nothing at all, her fingers cascade into growing lengths of thread that flail around the room with the electric energy of a lasso until at last they whip the increasing flame of the candle and are instantly set alight, fire sprints up the girl's swirling arms and blazes, brilliantly, across her chest and whole body, a magnificent conflagration she pounces jubilantly into a dust-dry basket nearby where the clothes she has mended for her sisters are carefully folded and piled high, and together they burn in a bright disc of white fire before collapsing softly to a pale heap of softest ash.

And then the pen was done, spent, happy, and lay there now, smouldering on top of the closed exercise book.

Spent, yes, but I knew now what it was capable of.

It was the afternoon many years ago and I was sat at a table with three or four other girls and though I more or less went along with the things they liked to talk about in a more or less spirited fashion I felt no natural accord with them and their schemes whatsoever.

I suppose they knew this or sensed it. Beyond the classroom we quite naturally went our separate ways.

Oh is it any wonder at all that the story that wound its way out of me during that pointless lesson on that lacklustre afternoon many years ago brought upon its tail a girl devoured by flames? Indeed, there was something gloriously sating about the coruscating vision of her body being engulfed and consumed.

The image's blaze lit through me, again and again,

one and the same as the fervid blood that
crackled beneath my pristine skin like wildfire.

A few years later I attended what were now referred to as seminars and these took place on the sixth floor of a much maligned building between the casino and the library slap-bang in the centre of a much maligned town. There was a lift which was exciting at first because most buildings I'd had reason to go into with any regularity up until then had been probably no more than three or four stories high and in the event that there were more floors than that and a lift shunting up and down between them we were most likely told for reasons I couldn't get to the bottom of not to use it. The lift at college was small and did not run especially smoothly. I loathed waiting for it anyway. Standing near the lifts waiting for a friend to come out of one or the other was fun—waiting for the lift itself was none at all. Not long after starting college I realised the schooling I'd received prior had been pretty woeful for it was soon clear that everyone else had already read a lot of important books and knew a great deal more than I did about all kinds of things I barely even knew existed. Everyone else had gone to other schools throughout the borough and seemed to know one another and many things. From my school I was the only one and so knew no one and nothing much. Ergo my mind was quickly set upon by the mercilessly figurative nature of all manner of profound formulations including Syllogistic Ravens, Fearful Symmetry, The Five Ways, Hume's Fork, Ockham's Razor, Lucretius's Spear, Vegetable Love, The Golden Mean, A Cat in a Drawer, A Pampered Swelling Flea, A Tree Falling in a Forest, A Cave of Shadows, A Ship of Fools, The Myth of Metals, A Drop of Dew, The Death of God, The Opium of the People, Time's Winged Chariot, and The Tables Turned. These capital ideas and sublime conceits conspired to unfold in me an awe-inspiring and loaded landscape of mostly grassy dunes and clandestine groves and fragrant bowers and minarets all bronze and brass and gold, with many precise ornaments here and there such as a topsy-turvy hamlet of small bamboo cages cradling tortoises tugging at the crimpled edges of bright green lettuce hearts, a filing cabinet skew-whiff in the sand, golden grasshoppers abounding in pairs, a bowl of lemony lemons on the leaf, ball bearings on the move, a stone-cold anvil naturally going nowhere, a skein of thick coral-coloured rope, a river far off and unfinished, a long pair of scissors reflecting the clouds, streaming at speed, across a blue sky. The aura, the tone, of these penetrating visions intimated a sophisticated universality while my homegrown innermost entities, which had hitherto seemed illimitable and sacred, were now shown to be by contrast naïve and uncomposed, consisting of some other less cogent material, and as such were vulnerable it seemed, quite vulnerable, to being wiped out by the mood, the aura, the tone, of this most consummate conceptual influx. So, for example, the girl, the girl so far in who sews until her fingers are reduced to threads and her body goes up in flames, lost her spark. Was nothing more than the third element of a pitiful trio along with the weakling candle and crooked basket. Insipid shadows now flinched beneath this futureless creature's eyes and her hair hung limp and greasy. Her wrists ached and her nose ran. Unclean splinters beset her paltry thighs and measly behind. And the darkness, the darkness itself, too was downgraded, was no longer the active metaphysical dark of a bodegón painting but was now only flat and inert.

Wall-to-wall and nothing further.

And because there was no dark, no real darkness to speak of, there was of course no light, no real incandescence to speak of, just a rapid dousing of a miserable thing, nothing glorious at all, merely a routine extinguishing, inevitable and unremarkable.

Par for the course.

She no longer leapt in gleaming Blakean splendour but was snared in the scored lines of a grim grisaille from a Marxist pamphlet that gravely expounds the dire consequences of having no stake at all in the means of production. For wasn't it perfectly clear that the merging of the girl's fingers with the tools she day in day out worked with showed that she had no existence independent of the labour she was enjoined day in day out to go on with? Only the most menial and repetitive of activities are dictated to her, her life and destiny are not directed by her own volition—indeed she has no opportunity whatsoever to cultivate any goals, is utterly deprived of power, and this powerlessness has alienated her from the world she is apparently living in.

Once her fingers have become threads she cannot touch nor grasp a single thing.

But what in any case is there for her to take hold of? There is nothing in her immediate environment to reach towards.

There is absolutely nothing for her to strive for.
The sight of her flailing around a dark sunken room is made doubly horrible by the fact that the room is entirely empty.

Is there anything worse that can befall a young woman than to be robbed of impulse? Than to have her pounding promise laid to waste?

V.

ALL THINGS NICE

The truly faithless one is the one who makes love
to only a fraction of you. And denies the rest.

—*THE DIARY OF ANAÏS NIN*, FEBRUARY 1932

Many years ago a large Russian man with the longest tendrils
of the softest white hair came to live in the fastest growing
town in Europe which at the time happened to be in the
southwest of England. Very little is known about why he
came there or what he did with himself but one thing relat-
ing to his daily round that can be set down with utmost confidence is that whenever the Russian man needed groceries
he'd fold himself into his small maroon car and drive to a retail park in the suburbs to get them. And probably the reason

he went to that retail park and not another was because there was a very pleasant supermarket in that retail park which aside from Saturday mornings naturally never got too busy and as such there was always an available parking space, up near the exit and entrance doors, and this in all likelihood suited the Russian man very well because he would likely have had tremendous difficulty finding his own car, if it was only shoved haphazardly in there somewhere amongst all the other cars parked one after the other with cracking midday sunlight spreading out all over them, diluting their already indistinguishable roofs, in the practically endless car park. The Russian man's car was fairly distinguishable for the reason that it was ancient, which meant it was a distinctly vintage colour and had the finish, furthermore, of an old immoveable garden gate which meant it could hold its own against the suburban sun's brash emanation. But in all likelihood the Russian man did not in any case know what his own car looked like so the only way he could find it was to be certain of where he'd left it and this perhaps explains why the Russian man liked to park his small maroon car up near the entrance and exit doors of the supermarket which despite its commodious proportions had the familiar feel and botherless charm of a corner shop. Right there on the perimeter of this booming yet visionless town in the southwest of England. Once inside the supermarket the Russian man would seize a basket from the pile that could always be counted on to be neatly stacked and regularly replenished right there on the left of the entrance and immediately he'd taken the basket he'd look alarmed and off-balance just as if it were a grim pail full of headstrong and incompatible eels swinging perilously in his hand. Holding the basket at arm's length, off he'd career, light on his feet, orbiting the aisles at full tilt, the empty yet possessed basket swinging to and fro out in front of him, ghostly wisps of white hair tapering off into the air behind him. Round and round the Russian man went. Making frantic laps of the store's circumference. Plunging headlong through the shining fruits and scrubbed vegetables, hurtling past the bakery the deli the butcher the fishmonger, bypassing all the little paper plates perched up on the respective counters offering samples of gluten-free kaiser rolls scamorza affumicata award-winning blood sausage special offer undressed spider crab, barrelling back up the booze aisle then rushing by the checkouts 1 to 19 at such a terrific rate they might very well have been checkpoints as far as the Russian man was concerned. There he was, back at the start, up by the entrance and exit doors, right where the baskets were stacked. And off he went again, faster this time. And again, and again. Faster and faster. Plunging headlong through the shining fruits and scrubbed vegetables hurtling past the bakery the deli the butcher the fishmonger bypassing all the little paper plates perched up on the respective counters and all the while the captivating basket swinging wire only out in front of him until at last it steered him off down one or another aisle and on into the next and here and there along his lurching passage grocery items predominately of the long-life variety found their way into the Russian man's basket and he would stand the large Russian man with the now pacified basket swung up and out to the left right in the middle of this or that aisle facing the shelves on one or other side half-bowed just as if the splendidly arrayed shelves of pickled vegetables were in fact the stalls of a magnificent Viennese auditorium and he stood before a prestigious audience who had travelled especially from the grandest domiciles of Europe to witness him perform an exquisite sequence of sublime prestidigitation that of course the Russian man would execute with vigorous precision and a rhythmic tenderness so perfectly pitched that the gentlewomen in the audience bolt upright and agog would hold their breath would part their lips would follow hungrily through narrowed eyes every miraculous yet seemingly inevitable turn of his astonishing hands would think my god what this man could do for me he could turn it all upside down and it would simply feel like everything was at last the right way around and I would flourish flourish yes attain a fullness at last of flesh and spirit experience at last the divulging pleasure I suspected was there somewhere all along all along but have so far myself never twined with directly and the man seated beside her would look down involuntarily at his wife's hands and see that they are squeezing the long burgundy gloves that he did not notice her remove but which are now nevertheless being twisted this way and that between her pale ensorcelled fingers. The man clears his throat to get her to stop that at once but the wife is uncharacteristically oblivious to her husband's characteristically tactful prompting so the man somewhat reluctantly casts a hand over to her lap. Settles it down around her agitated fingers. Bringing them together easily. Pliant yet stilled. There, there. Like the tapered petals of a pair of cool fresh tulips.

The man's hand relaxes, he does not withdraw it, why not leave it there. His hand stays heavy in his wife's placid lap upon his wife's motionless fingers as if it were no longer attached to him at all. And that was precisely how it felt to her in fact. As if a hand belonging to who knows who from who knows where had dropped willy-nilly into her lap. Soon her fingers begin to stir again. Like rippling laminaria digitata they turn over and reach through the unflappable fingers of this unsuspecting hand and lift it up to where she can see it. Before he can stop himself the man turns to look at his wife and that is a mistake—too late—already his head is turned in order to search out his wife's eyes. The eye contact which he impulsively sought would have surely only made these strange matters worse, had it been established, but eye contact with his wife was not established in fact for the reason that she is peering quizzically at his hand, which she is holding there in mid-air between them. What is she doing now? She is tilting her head to one side now. She is looking around the hand at her husband as if to say, is this yours? There is nothing he can do except let her have the hand and watch as she pushes the first two fingers back and her mouth opens wide. Keeping his hand exactly where it is in mid-air between them and her mouth wide open she brings her head towards the hand and draws her mouth around the two extended fingers without touching them, and when at last she feels the tips of the fingers come into contact with the back of her throat, sending sudden fluid up, up, to revel in the crescents of her eyes, she closes her mouth around them both. Right down to the base. The man can do absolutely nothing except watch his two fingers disappear into his wife's head and be appalled at how hot the inside of her mouth is. It is practically industrial and this is very disturbing. It is like a furnace in there and who, who exactly, is responsible for stoking and tending to and maintaining this furnace? Her tongue is nowhere. Her tongue is lying low. Waiting. Waiting for what or who exactly? Between the underside of the man's fingers and his wife's lurking tongue is a torrid vacuum that pulls at him. His gut his ribs his perineum the backs of his arms are particularly susceptible to the abysmal demands of the shockingly insistent and accusatory void brought about by the smouldering abeyance of his wife's tongue.

His wife's tongue.

Where is it? Where is it?! The edges of her teeth behind her lips press down on the base of his two fingers and he detects a jolt, a spasm. She presses down firmly, trying to stifle this engrossing bout of cadent gagging. Or perhaps she is pressing down firmly in order to bring it on? He attempts to inch his fingers out, but it is impossible. In addition to her lips clamping the base of them her hand hampers his wrist with the indolent strength of a nothing-else-to-do-in-the-world constrictor. She will never let go. She will perhaps discreetly choke to death on his fingers. Slump down into his lap. And he will perhaps push his left hand into the amaranthine coils of her fastened hair. Come into contact thereupon with the unearthly beauty that is surely immediately emitted by a shapely cranium no longer stippled by the hell-bent drub of sequestered and unfathomable yearnings. And perhaps while the unearthly beauty of this smooth and peaceable skull permeates his fingers and moves onwards unperturbed towards his chest where it will collect into a propitious pool within which the man's heart will be bathed and anointed the man will look about the auditorium and see that yes the head of every wife has come to rest in the lap of the man beside her and he will also note that every man has one hand pushed into the elaborate updo forever fastened upon the stilled head, there in his lap, while the other hand reposes on the narrow velvet armrest, there to the left of where every man sits. And look don't the first two fingers of every man's hand glisten upon the velvet armrest, there to the left? And look, hasn't the Russian man come to a standstill at the front of the stage? Doesn't he stand there, smiling, triumphantly, and aren't his two fingers held aloft for all the men to see? As the man's heart makes its decorous descent into the scintillant pool of unearthly beauty siphoned from the recently molli-fied dome lolling heavy and unloaded upon his knees he ex-periences lapping waves of awe and gratitude at the sleight of hand this Russian man has performed which has surely un-furled all the riddles, all the riddles, all the riddles have been unfurled. Their intractable convolutions thrown to the breeze, the sphinx at last is laid to rest, and how beautiful she is. How very beautiful. More beautiful now it goes without saying than she has ever been.

She is letting go.

The man's wife drags her lips away from the base of his two fingers. Pulls them along their renowned length. Just as she is about to run out of finger her tongue rises from its dip and flickers between the two tips. Fleetingly cajoles the two fin-gertips with lubricious delight before the tongue and the lips, her whole mouth, depart from the hand completely. The winding grip around his wrist eases. But she does not let go. Her hand moves upwards. Glides over his hand. Clasps the two long embrocated fingers. The man's wife holds his fingers up in front of him, she flashes her dark sparkling eyes in mock surprise, and mouths the word "Voilà." And still she does not let go. She leans in towards him. She looks directly into her husband's eyes. She presses his two fingers against her stretched throat and with her vocal apparatus thus slightly impaired she says very quietly, "It's all yours." The Russian man comes to a standstill at the front of the stage. He stands there. Smiling, triumphantly. His hands moving slowly through the tumultuous air.

Caressing the air in fact.

For it is absolutely altered. It is mottled mercurial aflame. The gentlewomen in the Viennese auditorium are on the edges of their seats, their ductile kidskin gloves of various regal shades squirm and slide like tossed offal beneath the small heels of their small encrusted boots, they are beating their unclad hands together with so much ferocious excitement their hands sting, their hands are burning, their hands are on fire, and all at once they begin to sing, feel my breast, how it burns, brilliant fire, holds fast my heart, it twists within, and surrounds me. Wagner—of all things! The Russian man runs his hands all over the air's beseeching currents and indeed he can feel oh so clearly that the women are emboldened, that the women are ready for anything. Anything! Is this why the Russian man is smiling so triumphantly? Because he knows very well that the most distinguished women of Europe are primed, yet at the same time they do not have the faintest idea what it is they crave? Because he knows very well that they have

preserved and finessed a diaphanous and titillating clueless-
ness, and in doing so have foregone developing the natural
wherewithal and cultivating an unflinching curiosity that,
between them, might surely have conducted the unbridled
appetite that is tearing hell for leather through their breast
towards an expedient and gratifying erotic scenario? There
will be one or two here and there who are perfectly capable of
course. Those débrouillarde women however would have
been sitting in the Viennese auditorium with something or
other up their musky sleeve from the off. Doesn't the Russian
man know very well that for most of them all this has been
rather too much, all at once, and as such their urgent and
blind fervour will be coaxed and exploited in all manner of
abominable ways? Ways that will thrill and send them over
the edge of course—the impulse for transgression and a taste
for abasement is not so difficult to locate and arouse. Because
of course it is thrilling to be astutely defiled. To have every
revered trait and inimitable asset compromised, undermined,
and subverted. Yet the Russian man knows these fine demure
women cannot abandon themselves completely. Once and
for all. It is not possible! Reality will right itself, roles must be
resumed, and all things nice must take their place once more.
Oh, and all things nice! Lace, opal, gypsophila, rose oil, meringue, gardenia, pearl powder, mink, sugared almonds, pas
de chat, beeswax, tarot, orange blossom, Liszt, calisthenics,
Venetian talc, parakeets, baklava, cameo, amber, calamine,

broderie anglaise, whalebone, honeycomb, rabbit, polka, damask, potpourri, crystal, Chrétien de Troyes, lavender, mahjong, gymkhana, tortoiseshell, squid ink, filigree, silk, saffron, liquorice, curling tongs, terrapins, vanilla pods, pineapples, bathwater, plumes, tinctures, tazze, candelabra, banana shampoo, maidenhair ferns, gold-plated taps, manicure sets, iced buns, tan tights, lapsang souchong, avocados, minty chocolate, the cherry moon—and what then, what then? Surely the Russian man knows very well that they will be mortified by the unspeakable acts they were complicit in carrying out and will henceforth be cowed and contrite to the core of their besmirched bodies and chequered hearts? It is quite impossible to know in fact which side the Russian man is on as he stands there, smiling, jubilantly. Stirring the fractious air, smiling, smiling, now reaching forward. One irrepressible hand coming to rest first of all on a jar of pickled cucumber then moving impishly along to a jar of pickled cucumber containing dill and the Russian man is very fond of dill especially in his pickled cucumber because he likes to eat pickled cucumber as an accompaniment to red salmon and red salmon and dill are natural bedfellows and it is this very jar of pickled cucumber containing dill in fact that the Russian man is settling into his basket when I enter the condiment aisle with a pen in my hand and my hair twisted back into a french plait on my way to checkout 19 where I will sit myself down upon a lopsided swivel chair and commence yet another nine-hour shift because these are the summer months and in the summer I work all the hours the devil sends so I have a sizeable wedge squirreled away for when I return to the college equidistant from the woeful library and the marooned casino slap-bang in the centre of the fastest-growing town in Europe in order to resume my studies in three subjects pertaining to the humanities come September. The Russian man is alone in the aisle. His hand is again moving deftly through the air and I cannot get past him because in an instant he has pulled a book from out of nowhere and delivered it directly into my path. "Here—all yours!" he exclaims, and I take the book from the Russian man's hand without stopping and say thank you kindly and keep walking to checkout 19 with my head up and the book held close against my thigh and when I get to the checkout I immediately stash the book on a shelf beneath the small beige machine that prints out receipts all day long. There it is next to the till rolls there it is next to my obdurate seat there it is brooding beside me until I take my lunch break and I don't give it a single glance in all that time. Whether I look at it or not makes no difference—I've seen the title, I know what it is. The book the Russian man has seen fit to give me is by Friedrich Nietzsche and the name of it is *Beyond Good and Evil* and I am beyond unnerved because it is abhorrently clear that the reason why the Russian man has seen fit to give me this book is because despite time and again rolling his jars of pickled vegetables and tins of omega-rich fish across the scanner deliberately without uttering a word more than the amount due, a minor yet far-reaching aspect of my disposition wavered in the periodic presence of the Russian man nonetheless and has given me away, unveiled a secluded modicum of my deeper substance, for there is the proof, right beside me, that the Russian man has seen through my ruffled yet unbroken flesh. Straight into the quickening revolutions of my supremely aberrant imaginings.

VI.

WE WERE THE DRAMA

The strands are all flying, quivering, intermingling
into the web, the waters are shaking the moon.

—"THE POETRY OF THE PRESENT," D. H. LAWRENCE

Now and then I'd take the train when I couldn't stand it anymore, which was more often than now and then but it wasn't
often that I had the money for the train then, or the wherewithal for the station my god which was always, whatever the
time of day, very chaotic and noisy noisy noisy, it was noisy
wherever you went from start to finish and it was the noise
ongoing I couldn't stand I couldn't switch any aspect of it off
never could and one day while I was on the train the noise
was there too, which wasn't always the case at that time—quite

often people on the train didn't make much sound at all because at that time none of us had a phone and we were used to sitting quietly like that with a magazine and a tea and some biscuits not making much sound at all beyond pulling at the wrapper and breaking the biscuit, for dunking in the tea, generally this I believe was what it was like on the train except one day when it was, on the contrary, very noisy because of all the schoolchildren, and they were all moving around, all boys I believe, in bright blue jumpers and grey trousers heading down to Brighton I believe, that's where we were bound in any case though they may well have disembarked sooner than that I wasn't there to observe where exactly they got off, I left the carriage practically straightaway before the train had really picked up speed the reason I was on it in the first place was because I couldn't stand it any longer, the noise that seemed to find its way into every corner yet I couldn't quite distinguish from where exactly it came, on it went and there it was in the carriage, which was no good, no good to me at all—there was nothing to deliberate—you're just doing what you have to do by now, which in this case meant of course going out of the carriage down those lovely narrow corridors where there are lovely pairs of doors that slide open, and there you are, in a neat little perfectly silent compartment all on your own, no first-class ticket of course not. Never mind that. Yes, never mind that. This silence. This silence. Now everything in me could stop straining could settle down as much as it ever could settle down and stretch out and even perhaps bask a bit. I had a packet of ginger nut biscuits with me and two of those lovely slim cans of gin and tonic from Marks & Spencer. I've a feeling I was wearing a green hat but I might be wrong about that, that might have been the woman I made up years later who takes a train to see friends of hers a day earlier than they expect, that's to say she arrives a day early and they are surprised but that's only something she feels—they in fact don't express surprise in any way whatsoever, they are very welcoming and jolly nice in fact though somehow or other one of them, the wife probably, does of course say something about the woman being there like that a day early but it doesn't matter, of course not, and we don't do anything much these days do we Drew and it'll give the two of us a chance to have a good natter before everyone else turns up, and she is mortified of course and does what she can thereafter to not be there as much as possible starting with taking a walk around the grounds which go on and on and there are some very old enormous trees, Scots pines and so on, and that's where she goes, up to where the oldest Scots pines are. The Beatons are well off naturally and she came a day early and no one in fact is surprised and that's the awful thing. She had a lovely time on the train. Hardly a soul on there. She had grapes. The seeded kind. I remember that bit. "I much prefer the seeded kind," she says. "They seem entire and you eat them more slowly." "As for the seedless variety," she says, "it's as if someone's already made a start on them." Those are the sorts of things she said, and as she went on saying them I knew she was Charlotte Bartlett so it gave me a great deal of satisfaction, later on, to disclose, after several intimations, that she'd had a brief incredibly passionate affair with Mr Beaton, Drew, that did involve, more than once, an assignation against one of those very old Scots pines. "What if it falls?" she said. "It won't fall," he said. "It's been there for over five hundred years, and I doubt we are the first." No grapes for me on the train. I wouldn't dream of going into a shop like that and putting a couple of bunches of grapes seeded or otherwise into a small white plastic bag like that and taking them up to the grocer at the till like that because that's what you'd have to do and you'd think it would be straightforward but it seldom is—I can give you three peaches for a pound they'll say, or how about two liquorice sticks for fifty pence, how is it possible to know, how likely is it that what they are offering you is something you have a fancy for, but perhaps it might be nice, later on, later on you might be glad of three peaches and one or two sticks of liquorice but no thank you because as it is I've absolutely no idea how much the grapes are going to cost no idea at all, could be five pounds for all I know, no grapes then and no first-class ticket, though funnily enough that sort of thing I had no difficulty at all handling. I tucked my gin and tonic behind my bag twisted up the biscuit packet and took my legs off the seats just before the inspector came into the compartment, proffered my standard billet and told him I'd moved in here because of a sudden terrible headache—it was terrifically noisy in second when I boarded but perhaps it's a little calmer now—and naturally he wouldn't hear of me returning to second because for one thing I was young not even twenty or perhaps just about and either way I didn't look it and for another thing people didn't seem to mind as much then as they do now, they seem to mind very much now, they're too afraid not to mind or don't have the mind not to mind, the system won't let them etcetera. At one point the train stopped between stations just came to a halt. Outside the window was wet trees and hedgerows. It was the end of autumn. There were shrivelled berries and the last leaves were hanging by a thread. Nothing moved. I didn't move either. Perhaps I didn't even breathe. Once we got going again after I don't know how long I burst into tears. I cried and cried my shoulders shook. Shaking the tears out of me big fat cold autumn tears fell straight down into my lap, down they went, into my lap into my lap into my lap into my lap. I was on the train. Bound for Brighton. On a previous occasion I'd gone to Cambridge and that long road from the station nearly killed me I didn't know where I was in the wrong place I thought should have gone the other way—I walked up and down looking for a suitable place to stay or anywhere at all in fact because that's how it was then and not one B&B did I see along that road from the station. You are silly I thought and went into a pub that had a pool table and fruit machines. I always enjoyed going into a pub wherever I was, Marlborough, Bristol, Bath, Oxford, Malmesbury. I'd have with me a notebook and pen and at least one paperback classic and a packet of cigarettes. I smoked all different brands. Marlboro Red of course. Rothmans which were a strange brand because on the one hand they were generally seen as a bit rough but on the other definitely had a certain cachet, because hadn't I seen a photograph of Bianca Jagger dressed in a white catsuit at a round table in a club that had on it cocktails of course and packets and packets of cigarettes and at least one of those packets near Bianca Jagger's sheathed elbows was a blue and white box of Rothmans. Dunhill International was another favourite. Also the Dunhills that came in a bevel-edged box. Lucky Strike but never for very long because they just didn't suit me. Gitanes though again not for very long because although they did suit me they were too short and too strong. Gauloises occasionally. Sometimes Camel though it became annoying how people kept on saying they gave money to the KKK and other people said they contained fibreglass that made your lungs bleed I don't recall that anyone ever alleged both of those things, it was either one or the other, and always said just as if you'd never heard it before which was ridiculous since nearly everyone said it, one or the other, on and on. I smoked a lot. I loved it. I loved it whenever someone bought me a packet of cigarettes I remember getting sent packets of cigarettes through the post now and then and it always cheered me up. The feel and look of an unopened pack was a glorious thing the day was taken care of. I smoked in bed all day long one smokes wherever one happens to be especially back then when one could smoke more or less wherever they wanted I was often in bed day after day so that's where I did much of my smoking. Sometimes I smoked in the bath. If I wasn't in bed chances are I was in the bath. Down to the bathroom, legs aquiver, head compressed, sometime in the afternoon. Smoking in the bath with wet fingers. I don't suppose I'll do that again.

I had a pint in the pub in Cambridge it was on a corner and rounded and that's the reason I went in that pub and not another because the walls were rounded. Do you have rooms I said while I stood there after ordering a second pint and he said not as such what are you looking for there is a room up there but we don't usually have guests staying it's fairly basic— how long would I want it for would I like to have a look? It was a very plain room not very big and the bed to the left against the wall was a single and I was still quite used to sleeping in a single at that time and even now all this time later I must say I don't mind a single bed as long as it's moored up against a wall and there aren't a lot of things crammed in underneath it. He showed me how to lock it from the inside and said I wouldn't be able to lock it from the outside was that OK it was five pound a night alright. I phoned Dale the following day or perhaps even the day after that. He was very annoyed but made it sound like he was concerned. I might have done anything. Why hadn't I let him know? Very occasionally I felt it in me to do something and it would be such a rare but exceedingly strong impulse that I'd determine to stay as close to it as I could did nothing to endanger or sabotage or undermine or diminish or distort it if I had the impulse to pack a few things into a holdall and to check if the gas was off before heading to King's Cross those things would happen with little thought with no thought at all hardly any effort even, one thing then the next as if it were all a familiar sequence that needed no discussing, it needed no discussion, what for, what did I need to tell Dale for, just so he could say what's wrong and where are you going to stay and who are you going to see down there and have you got enough money and again what's wrong, what's wrong, because there was nearly always something wrong with me, and why did I want to go off down there, and why should I explain to Dale, why, when all Dale would do is talk me out of it in order to keep me close because that was the point wasn't it, Dale wanted to keep an eye on me, I might do anything, and is not best pleased with me at all not saying a word and then full of excited chatter on the phone in Cambridge about a pub with rounded walls and a room that's not a room for only five pounds. "I'll come and get you," he says. "There's really no need," I say. "I'm going to come back tomorrow anyway." "Then I'll be there at the station to meet you off the train," he says. "Alright then," I say. Dale would hate it in Cambridge, and he'd have to show it too. Dale hates it when I put my sunglasses on my head when we're walking down the street he swerves away from me as if from a wasp and says "Jesus Christ take those fucking things off your head." Quite often I put my sunglasses on my head purely so that Dale will scrunch up his face and say that. Dale thinks I am damaged. Dale thinks I've been with all the wrong men. Dale thinks there might be something of a self-destructive nature in me that draws me towards terrible men again and again though whether I was born that way or whether it came about because of the first terrible man who was probably just a misstep but nonetheless inaugurated a pattern I cannot overthrow remains a mystery. Dale thinks I need protecting either way. He lent me *The Bell Jar* then quickly changed his mind. Took it back at once and wiped it with his sleeve. He hides his Anne Sexton books from me even though I'm not looking for them. I am not interested in reading books written by women who killed themselves. I think it is very likely that I will one day kill myself and if I do I want it to be all my own idea. I don't want to lose myself in their shadows their darkness might swarm in and drench mine so that I won't be able to tell them apart and what then? I knew only what I'd experienced and although I didn't know why I felt the way I did I could know at least that it wasn't due to anything I'd read. It was all mine. All my own doing. And I was afraid that if I read if I became immersed in the writings of Virginia Woolf and Sylvia Plath and so on I'd become horribly self-conscious and it whatever it was my own little bit of occasionally all-consuming darkness would drift away from me because perhaps my own shadows were only very flimsy and wayward and away they'd go once these inequivocable much more established shadows swooped in and I'd be left estranged somehow with no option really but to simulate what had once been so integral and from then on I wouldn't know would I if I truly felt up the walls or was merely putting it on in order to be once more what I once was and so to guard against all that I mostly read books by old white men such as Graham Greene and Edgar Allan Poe and Robert Louis Stevenson and that man who wrote *Heart of Darkness*, whose name escapes me. I hardly ever saw so much as a glimpse of myself in any of their books and I didn't care to. I didn't want to exist in books. I liked how the men talked to other men and I liked the places they went to. I liked being able to go with these men wherever they went and they went everywhere of course, all over the world, hardly ever really liking each other, so often paranoid, so often out on a street near the water last thing, or walking first thing down avenues churning with blossom, dying, dying weakly beneath a thin lapel, dying on the vine. Their shoes and their watches and the small scissors they used to trim their nails first and their nose hair after and I loved to think of them shaving though that was a rousing detail that barely got mentioned was quite often passed over then when I got older of course I saw it for myself and loved leaning against the side of the bathtub or sitting on the end of the bed watching a man's face in the mirror as he stood at the sink shaving himself. I didn't think much of *A Room with a View* when I first read it why would I it was just a book we all had to read so I read it dutifully three chapters a night and then it was on to *King Lear*. Sometime later near exams we were advised to go back over it all to revise as they call it so out it came again and this time it was late spring, a whole year had gone by. I will read it in the garden, a sheltered spot, no one will be home. I'll go in and out all day long getting water, cups of tea, fetching a peach, a scone, a satsuma, cleaning off the soles of each bare foot each time, left then right, left then right, and it will be as if I hadn't read it before, and the exercise book I've bought especially to make notes in will fill up in no time. I'll write pages and pages, the words teeming out of me, the pen hardly able to keep pace, then turning back to the text, and it won't be long before something else sets me off again, and I'll write pages and pages more. Lucy Honeychurch would have been about the same age as me I expect but we were not kindred spirits. I didn't dislike her though perhaps her spoilt ways did irritate

me slightly—it was her aunt I was drawn to. Charlotte Bartlett. She had a secret it seemed to me. That's right—she was
the only one out of all of them who had a past. Her life was
not a well-made thing, one instance causing another and on
and on—somewhere along the way something immense had
broken off, floated away, never to be retrieved or rectified, yet
everybody in the book and outside of the book makes the
classic mistake of supposing that she'd never been any other
way than the way she is now, with her broken boiler and peculiarly convoluted way of procuring change for the cab
driver, but isn't it also true that she kept George Emerson
alive in Lucy's obstinate muddled heart? On every single
possible occasion after Italy she says something to Lucy about
the Emersons at least—and quite often about George Emerson specifically—and doesn't she even take to calling Lucy
"Lucia"—and what's that if not an effort to revive the memories and spirit of Florence, and while they were still in Italy
didn't she tell Miss Lavish all about what went on in that blue
field, she won't let it go—and isn't that because she feels in
her heart that Lucy shouldn't let it go either? No, Charlotte
Bartlett is not at all what she seems. She has spent a lot of
time on her own and certainly that makes a person susceptible to overthinking simple transactions and occasionally losing perspective. You will overreact it seems from time to time
because getting by on your own steam day after day plays on
your nerves, you've no buffer, nothing, just your own head,

on and on, it all builds up. When they withdrew into their separate rooms at the pensione at the end of the day it was into Charlotte's room not Lucy's I went and I lay down in the dark and remembered things for her, alongside her. Her secret glimmered and shone obscurely and edgeless, like moonstone. She is never without it. The briefest love is also sometimes the longest love.

When you leave the station in Brighton it's much nicer than when you leave the station in Cambridge. Almost right away I found myself in a charity shop looking at books and bought several of those classic Penguin ones with orange spines and yellow pages, probably fifty pence each. Perhaps it was in the same shop that I bought a silver skirt. Somebody had made it you could tell that from the zip and the way it had been put in. It was very long much too long for me but you don't let things like that put you off when you're barely twenty it didn't matter to me at all that it trailed all over the ground soaking up all the puddles and flinging freezing-cold dirty rainwater across my ankles it fitted me perfectly around the waist, and it was silver lamé. I'll keep it on I said handing her the dainty handwritten price tag and off towards the sea I swooshed orange spine and silver tail a right turn towards Regency Square where it was all B&Bs and up and down and all along I went eyeing them up carefully and hoping to wake up my third eye because I had a picture in mind already of course of how my room should be. Of course what they do these places is set up a very elegant and enticing reception you can glimpse from the street. You look up the steps see a chandelier and an aspidistra and polished brass and black and white tiles and a plush red carpet or perhaps pale blue and there's velvet or damask curtains either side and a little shiny bell and you think that looks nice that looks up together and not too stuffy and up the steps you go and then you notice the stand-up calendar with the fat red numbers and daily proverbs on the desk and a clock made from a cross-section of varnished wood on the red and cream and gold striped wall but the old chap is already taking a key off a hook with a liver-spotted tremulous hand and you're already following him up the stairs and up more stairs and the next set of stairs is much narrower and steeper and the carpet here is much thinner and more gaudy and cut very badly the walls are marked here and there and the ceiling is much lower and the lights are fluorescent and the doors aren't old and painted white they are new and dark brown veneer and the old man opens one of the doors that seem awfully close together and gestures for you to go ahead and enter because if he enters there won't be any room for you and so just like that you're in this tiny fusty room and there's far too much furniture in it the curtains at the window have come away from the rail in places the mirror is mottled and on and on what can you say you start to panic you are so cross what's the big idea you think bringing me up here what on earth do I look like that he brings me up here to this do I look mad is that what it is is that why he's brought me all the way to the top and the very back of this towering Regency building does he think this is all someone like me could possibly hope for and you stand side-on in your recently acquired silver lamé skirt and green peachbloom hat stinging with indignation and shame and you don't know how you're going to get out you just want to get out of here as quickly as possible but how there's nowhere to move he's standing at the door "I have no money," you say, "I forgot to bring money, I'll come back," you say, "I'll keep it for you then," he says, "do you want to take the key," he says, "no," you say, "no, that's alright, I won't be long," you say and you walk back down all those creaking stairs, holding on to the banister, trailing silver. That was awful. I sat in the square quite bewildered and then thought it was funny it already seemed so long ago. I had a cigarette and it was delicious I was free. Looked down the square towards the sea. The pebbles. All banked up. I hadn't even heard of Ann Quin at this stage, it would be years. Years and years until I'd stand outside a pub smoking a cigarette and the man who'd lit it for me would lean against the window beside me and tell me all about Ann Quin and then I'd forget her name and then it would come up again and this time I'd write it down and of course when I looked her up to find out the titles of the books she'd written I discovered practically straightaway that she'd died at the age of thirty-seven in the sea near Brighton Pier on August Bank Holiday, 1973. A man named Albert Fox saw her go into the water and contacted the police. Her body was found by a yachtsman the following day, near Shoreham Harbour, approximately seven miles away. I wonder what Albert Fox did after that, probably toddled off home, stood at the kitchen sink for a bit and kept stumm—certainly wouldn't say a word to his wife about it would he. No. No. No fear. And then it would be in the paper. Body found by yachtsman near Shoreham Harbour later identified as writer Ann Quin, or perhaps there was no mention at all of her being a writer and the books she'd had published. Probably not. The coroner gave an open verdict and I took that at face value but then I went on to read several articles and essays that stated without any ambivalence at all that she'd killed herself, that Ann Quin committed suicide, and that annoyed me, and I didn't quite know why it annoyed me more and more the more times I read it, it seemed thoroughly presumptuous I suppose, and then I read some of her work and the sea is referred to so often in her writing, the sound of it, the smell of it, the waves, the weed, the rocks, that it's quite clear she had some kind of relationship with the sea, to the extent that she felt she was of it perhaps—"Is it her body I hold in my arms or the sea?" asks a character in *Passages*. Again and again the sea is evoked as a majestic expression of powerful mutability, it flows, it surges—it's fluid, yes, yet at the same time it retains its shape, its currents, its integrity—"Half cylindrical waves kept their direction when intersecting. Movements of the water's impressions penetrated each other, without changing their first shape." The waters of the shifting oceans give palpability to the ultimate ontological fantasy—that it is possible to be boundless and permeable while holding on to one's essence, one's "first shape." Perhaps, according to how she saw and took part in the world, Ann Quin wasn't so much killing herself when she went under the waves as luxuriating in her primary generative contours—"Death reunites us with ourselves," said Sartre, a quote Quin apparently knew and approved of. On the other hand perhaps her own unique cosmology had fallen away. Perhaps she was only where she was—back in England, back in Brighton—back in her hometown. Sometimes there is nothing worse—you'll never get away from it, you'll never get it out of you. "Oh that grey, grey thing creeping from the sky, smoke, buildings, into the pores of skin. Grey faces. No she could not go back to that." New Mexico with the post-Beat poets is where she felt at home. She had a place in Placitas for a few years, and travelled around a lot, to New York, to Iowa, to Maine, to the Bahamas, to San Francisco. At a party on an estate in Connecticut she met Anaïs Nin—"who is exquisite in Dresden fashion," she wrote in a letter to friends in New York in September 1965: "tho 60 looks 30" (which just goes to show you, doesn't it, that Nin's ongoing bid for continued existential freshness was tangibly efficacious). She also met Rothko; "who looks like a Wall Street broker." England? No—she could not go back to that! But back she went. Money had to be earnt no doubt, and Quin writes incisively about the terror of menial work and the toll such employment took on her nerves—her menaced account of a hotel job in Mevagissey, Cornwall, has an especially gothic volatility: "The setup there consisted of three other girls, a Welsh chef with medieval face, round eyes, who followed me on my solitary walks along the cliffs, and jumped out from behind the bushes. The proprietors were always having rows. She lived on drugs. He on drink. Work consisted in making beds, peeling potatoes, washing up, hoovering, and serving thirty/forty British holiday-makers lunch, tea and dinner." The situation worsened and one morning Quin collapsed: "I reached the point when a moonlight flit seemed to be the only way out. I arrived at the railway station in utter terror of being discovered, made to return to the hotel. I reached home speechless, dizzy, unable to bear the slightest noise. I lay in bed for days, weeks, unable to face the sun." In addition to her suicide, it is also pointed out time and again that Ann Quin was working-class—and an "avant-garde" writer. To be one or the other in addition to being a woman would have been sufficiently indecorous, to be both was downright impudent, and incurred suspicion and snobbish disdain from some critics at the time who proclaimed that her formal experiments were mere imitations of the writers of the nouveau roman such as Nathalie Sarraute and Alain Robbe-Grillet. This reluctance to credit her with the ingrained capacity to quite naturally write in an atomized fragmented style that shifts effortlessly between registers demonstrates the pitfalls of criticism written more or less exclusively from the lofty perspective of posh white blokes who have no grasp whatsoever of the lived experience of a working-class woman in the 1960s. When I read Quin I recognise her fidgeting forensic polyvocal style as a powerful and bona fide expression of an unbearably tense and disorienting paradox that underscores everyday life in a working-class environment—on the one hand it's an abrasive and in-your-face world, yet, at the same time, much of it seems extrinsic and is perpetually uninvolving. One is relentlessly overwhelmed and understimulated all at the same time. Is it any wonder then, that such a paradox would engender a heightened esthetic sensitivity that is as detached as it is perspicacious? Quin mentions somewhere in one of her shorter pieces the "partition next to my bed," how it "shook at night from the manoeuvres, snores of my anonymous neighbour." If your immediate locale doesn't offer you very much in terms of dependable boundaries it's not entirely inconceivable is it that you'll end up writing a kaleidoscopic sort of prose that is constantly shuffling the distinction between objects and beings, self and other, and conceives of the world in terms of form and geometry, texture and tone. The walls are paper-thin. You rarely have any privacy. And neither do you have the safety nets, the fenders, the filters, nor the open doors which people from affluent backgrounds enjoy from day one. When you are living with no clear sense of a future, day-to-day life is precarious, disjointed, frequently invasive, and beyond your control. Voilà. Quin's pithy dispatch, "One Day in the Life of a Writer," does not offer up that familiar slightly nauseating scene of the shawled scribe pottering off to her wisteria-strewn shed at the bottom of the garden in order to write in hallowed seclusion. There's a landlady hollering up the stairs about kippers and lamb stew, a window cleaner up on his ladder peering in, burn holes in the carpet, burn holes in the lampshades, unemployed men along the Front, spitting and muttering. Just up the road in Regency Square was where I sat quite oblivious to all that, twenty odd years after Ann Quin went into that same sea and did not come out again. Puffing on a cigarette my overnight bag jammed between my feet. Fancy being taken in by all that ostentatious hostelry bric-a-brac, a load of old rubbish, it's subtler than that you little bumpkin, and in the end I fell for the way the number three was painted upon a pillar like a ribbon, just as if it were a ribbon and might well blow away in the next breeze, and in I went and the same thing, stairs and more stairs but not quite so many as before and the manner of the place didn't decline so much the further up we went, remained pretty well consistently so-so, and she went on in and stood by the window looked out, it's not much of a view I'm afraid but it's quiet and the sun comes in in the morning.

When she left I stood where she'd stood rooftops and rows and rows of enormous chimneys and there were seagulls overhead and pigeons on the sills and that was all I wanted, to see rooftops and chimneys. I knew the sea was nearby I could feel it when I lay on the bed you can't be that close to the sea and not feel it. There was an extractor fan somewhere but apart from that it was quiet. A single bed a locker beside it a lamp on top of that. A wardrobe in one corner a sink in the other and the window in between. Alright then. I snoozed for a bit and when I awoke I was really very pleased to be where I was. I went for a walk of course along the Front and looked out to sea. I noticed a telephone box near the steps and that got me thinking about Billy I hadn't thought about him much lately. I went for a drink down the end, at the end of the pier perhaps, it was all decked out with nets and starfish and when I read *A Single Man* many years later a murky memory of that place came to mind during that later scene when he goes to the bar and meets the student and they drink beer together. It's strange that it was that bar my mind came up with since my memory of it at the time was no better than it is now that's to say so irresolute, as if in fact it were underwater. He is underwater by then though I suppose, the grief washing over him, what does he say at the end, something extraordinary, his grief by then has gone above and beyond, I must find it, what did I do with it? You phoned Billy on the way back it was dark but not late you'd had a couple of gin and tonics—what did they drink the man and the boy, bourbon probably—never mind that—"Why don't you come tomorrow?" you said, Billy said, "There's a work thing on and that prick from Trowbridge will be there and I'm ready for him this time." "Really," you said, "getting the better of some little shitehawk from work is more important" and Billy laughed, "Oh ratbag only when it suits you, eh?" Didn't cross my mind to call Dale it didn't really cross anyone's mind to contact anyone then in the way it does every five minutes now. I probably went back to my B&B and on up the stairs all cosy and lay on the bed with a cigarette after all that disgruntlement with Billy. And that was all there was to it me on the bed no texting no emailing no one knew where I was it wasn't as if I told my parents or my housemates, perhaps I'd told Dale. Probably I had but quite often people didn't know where you were what you were doing nor how you felt about it either. You just had to lie there oftentimes, that was all there was to it. And I loved that feeling of no one knowing. And went on loving it. Treasuring it. I treasured it really. Privacy. Secrets. But it became more and more difficult to get that not-knowing and the deeply glamorous feeling that came with it and now it doesn't exist at all the outcast minutes of the day gently claw at you, over here, over here, and it's harder to know where you are or what you're doing and how you really feel about any of it. One's on tenterhooks nearly all the time and there's nothing remotely glamorous about tenterhooks.

I went straight to Dale's when I got back to London I felt very well and had my new skirt on and I had my books it was the afternoon. Perhaps I'd telephoned him to let him know I was on my way though that wasn't necessary—people weren't in the habit so much then of telephoning before calling over you could just turn up out of the blue no one was put out and if you were put out you usually wouldn't be for too long. Dale was drinking a bottle of ale and a bottle of whiskey at his desk. He had a typewriter. He poured me a beer and lit me a cigarette. I lay down on the sofa with my cigarette and glass of beer and I felt very relaxed. I'd been away and now I was back. Dale said I looked like a beautiful mermaid and I smiled as I always did whenever Dale said the word beautiful because his Yorkshire accent sounded very vigorous when he said that word and also when he said the word music. Then Dale said "I'm going to come over there woman, I'm going to come over there and I'm going to fuck you." Dale had never said anything like that before, I couldn't believe my ears. His voice sounded so much deeper than normal—I presumed he was joking around doing an impression of someone—I could tell he'd been up all night at his desk smoking and drinking his head off hitting it hard communing with his sacrosanct panoply of hell-raising booze-addled poets, what on earth was he saying? I shot my eyes upwards and looked back over the arm of the sofa at him and even upside down I could see he was all worked up and as single-minded as a revenant but I didn't have to go along with it did I—I didn't have to go along with whatever derivative scenario he was trying to initiate nor the shabby roles that that drama designated, just who did he think he was, a shambling badass laureate of the dispossessed who would one day show them all, he who laughs last laughs longest, wasn't that what he always said, a roguish chain-smoking barfly whose storming intellectual prowess and devilish wit made beautiful women weak at the knees—and who was I exactly, a woman under the influence, some tragic spun-out waif all togged out and light-headed in silver lamé on the knackered-out sofa in this dark smoke-filled room with the curtains closed in the afternoon, no, no, no, that wasn't me or where I was at all—I'd barely had a sip of my beer, I was relaxed and clear and feeling generally hopeful—we were not on the same page at all—"Oh, Dale," I said, "not now, not now," and he said, "Yes now, of course now." And so that's what happened. Whatever rebounding sunbeam I'd managed to catch hold of down by the sea was promptly and unceremoniously snuffed out by the slummy contemptuous world Dale was right then bloody-mindedly trajecting. Dale put out his cigarette and took a long drink from his umpteenth glass of beer set it back down on his writing desk and over he came. "I don't really want to, Dale," I said, and I said nothing more because Dale was undoing his belt and I'd upset myself more if I started saying anything, it would just be an awful scene and I had no desire for any sort of scene just then. I'd just got back I'd been away and now I was back and Dale went in me and I kept my eyes open because if I shut my eyes the outside world would be gone and all I'd have to be aware of then would be my interior and my interior was being invaded in and out in and out and I preferred not to be aware of that as much as possible, so I kept my eyes open and glanced around the room with the kind of nonchalance one has when one lies on a couch on a Sunday afternoon moving a cigarette, nonchalantly, in and out, in and out, of their mouth. I could look at things like the curtains, the curtains were behind him and they were pulled, they were always pulled, and I could hear the pigeons on the balcony, they always had so many pigeons on that balcony and they must have been roosting, bundled all in together, all warm and diseased, and all that shit everywhere and all the feathers, shit, and feathers, and husks, all sticking together. Dale was very sweaty, I didn't like that I didn't want it dripping on me—was he enjoying it?—I don't know I don't know what it must feel like to be right the way inside a woman who likes you a great deal but really doesn't want you to be doing that and has said so and isn't moving a single muscle, is just lying there, maybe he thought that that's what women did, protest a bit then just lie there, staring into space wincing now and then when they felt a drop of sour booze sweat land on their delicate female skin, poor Dale. Poor, poor, Dale. I went home soon after that, though not before I'd finished my beer and had a cigarette and showed Dale my books and he'd said how lovely my skirt was, then I went home after that. Dale said, "Woman I'm coming over there and I'm going to fuck you." "Oh Dale," I said, "not now, not now, I'm ever so sleepy." "Come off it woman," he said, "you don't have to do very much." and I thought, perhaps he's right about that, perhaps I don't—don't say anything more now, don't push him away and don't wriggle down the sofa, if you start doing that, if you start wriggling about and trying to stop him that'll make it into a dreadful scene and you don't want that you don't want a dreadful scene do you, of course you don't, so don't do anything, it's Dale fucking you and you're just so tired, that's all, that's all it is, Dale, poor Dale, what does he think is happening as he goes in and out of me in and out and me here not doing a single thing, what does he think, does he think that I can't be bothered, that I'm lazy, that I'm just too tired? Afterwards I finished my beer and had a cigarette and showed Dale my books wanting things to be normal wanting very much for the day that had been and the general feeling of hope it had given rise to to return for the silver skirt to still be shimmering the books in my bag to still be vital and enticing. It was almost dusk when I left and walked the few streets over to my house. It was quiet when I got there nobody else was in. I changed into baggy things possibly had a wash but very quickly because the water wouldn't have been warm and went downstairs to make a cup of tea. What I wanted was to stand at the back door with a cup of tea and a cigarette and see it get dark and feel it get chilly. And it did. And I stood there. With a mug of lapsang souchong and a Rothmans. And I was leaning a bit against the door frame because as it turned out the insides of my thighs were trembling terribly. If you don't do much at the time it all goes on afterwards. Of course you join in, of course there is no not doing very much, you can't switch your body off—how did I not know that? Will I eat something? Cheese on toast maybe? Do you feel awful? Is this terrible? Are you going to cry? Well are you? Or are you going to make yourself cry because you feel you should cry? Was it really awful or was it merely unpleasant? Make up your mind now and stick to it—are you going to get into a state about this or not? And then I got irritated with thinking about it since thinking about it seemed to invoke some other voice, a carping busybodying sort of voice, belonging to precisely the sort of person I more often than not disliked, and avoided.

I had some cheese on toast and later on since no one was in I had a bath and I smoked in the bath and read one of the books I'd bought in Brighton *Vile Bodies* I think it was and then I went to bed and then it was the following day and not long after that it was the end of term and then there was Christmas back home and disgustingly busy shifts in the supermarket and after that a new term and new modules one of which was "The Great War and After," which, apparently, according to the lecturer, Dale had signed up for, but there was no sign of him the first week, or the second week, there was no sign of him anywhere because apparently Dale wasn't coming back for the final term, apparently he'd deferred and was staying up in Yorkshire. I moved into a much nicer house near Clapham Common my room was very spacious had a bay window looking out onto the street and a high ceiling and I was over the moon. I would sit for a long time, smoking and looking up at the pipes that slipped through the walls into my room, moved along the wall and disappeared out of it, onwards, to somewhere else I did not see and could not get to. Shifting in and out, up and down, throughout the building—not really ending here, not really beginning there—showing only a little of their passage. They seemed so important sometimes, and so graceful, the most graceful resolute entity in here, and they were so high up and opaque that sometimes their indifference was unbearable, and I wished in a way that I was a spider so I could see the ghostly dust upon their backs and perhaps make something of my own up there. Next to my room was a small kitchen with a long window and down the hall a bathroom and Bettina's room. Bettina was from Poland and rarely to be seen. Occasionally when I was in the bath I'd hear her all of a sudden just there on the other side of the wall and a picture of her room would immediately come to me, dark and bereft and everything draped with scarfs with metallic glints, like tropical fish in a grim nightclub aquarium. Upstairs were sisters who were more or less twins, they had trailing plants and Hodgkin posters from the Hayward Gallery and their own small kitchen which was handsomely festooned with onions and garlic. Downstairs were two girls from Ireland and they also had a kitchen which was actually very big but then since it was downstairs it was obviously the original kitchen, whereas the ones upstairs had obviously been added much later. I've never minded overmuch about the size of a room. What I liked about mine and Bettina's kitchen was that it was above the hallway which meant I could push up the window and sit out on the ledge with my feet on the porch roof which was flat and had small stones all over it and sometimes I used to toss those stones down into the middle of the street while I smoked a cigarette and waited for example for my pasta to boil. Bettina never used the kitchen though from time to time a large dried sausage would appear in the fridge and it would brood away in there for days and days before vanishing entirely. Sometimes I worried about Bettina, sometimes I hoped she was alright. Sometimes I heard her talking on the phone late at night downstairs. Sometimes she didn't sound alright. But who did really—I was hardly ever alright, not when I opened my mouth anyway. I found it better to stay in the house. There was a shop around the corner that had most of the things I ever wanted. Wine, crackers, pistachios, sardines, humous, flowers, yoghurt, apples, chocolate, cheese, and cigarettes of course. Everything really, yet it was only a tiny shop and if you went in around lunchtime it would be jammed with construction workers holding rolls and waiting for coffee, some of them were really nice-looking. I couldn't think where they'd all come from though because everything around here had been built already. I mentioned this to a friend of mine one day and he called me a berk and said they're probably not even construction workers—"they're probably laying cables, you berk," he said, and I said I didn't think so. I moved everything around in my room, I always do that, even in hotel rooms though that's really not so possible anymore since in hotels now everything is fastened into place. I remember there was always a lot of books on the bed and in the bed. Most of them were heavy and it made my body feel amorphous, to have all these books pushing in, here and there, upon and beneath it. They were nearly all library books and now and then I'd get up to wash my hands because the pages were coated from the touch of so many other hands making my own feel sullied. I started masturbating once without really planning to and I hadn't washed my hands all morning but it was too late now and it was as if a hundred sordid fingers were all over my vulva and though I made sure to wash my hands after that the image of all those filthy dirty hands all over me often came back to me whenever I masturbated. There was lots to do in bed really so my staying in it for days on end isn't so surprising. There wasn't a great deal going on outside of it that would interrupt me—the final year was beginning to wind down, so there were exams but I didn't mind that because it was in and out, you didn't have to talk to anyone, and workwise by this time I still did the occasional champagne waitressing event at the Lord Mayor's Banquet Hall and St. James's Palace, and I'd probably sign up for Lords again because that was a lot of money, but I was getting more and more hours at Riverside Studios and I liked working there and had got friendly with a girl called Beth who wrote feminist plays and lived in a nice flat practically opposite. The work was easy, and interesting—I spent most of my shifts sat wide-eyed in the back of a cinema auditorium watching films from all over the world. Then one afternoon the phone downstairs in the hall near the door will start ringing. It will ring and ring and ring and then it will stop. And then it will start up again. Ringing and ringing. I will realise that no one is home. Neither the sisters, Bettina, nor the Irish girls are here and I'll realise the phone will not stop, it will go on, ringing and ringing, until I answer it—so out of bed I'll get, much too fast, my head will spin, spin back towards the bed—the centre of the universe—and the ringing will go on and on and I'll plunge forward, grab my dressing gown from off the hook I'd banged into the side of the dresser, and I will stand unsteadily near the sink for a minute. Hello, I'll say to the corner of the room. Hello, I'll say again, in a louder voice. Hello, I'll say again, and there it'll be—more or less—my voice. "Hello." I will open my door and step out onto the landing and of course the ringing will suddenly be much much louder alarmingly loud and I will fly down the stairs towards it wanting to make it stop. "Hello," I will say, in my voice more or less, and it will be Dale's voice I hear back and Dale will say without any preamble at all, "When you came back from Brighton last year I raped you didn't I?" And then there will be a pause and I'll cagily move some letters around on the floor near the front door with the toes of my left foot and then I will look up at a dark cobweb in the coving and I'll hear my voice say to Dale, "If you're asking me did you have sex with me when I didn't want you to then yes the answer's yes Dale," and Dale will curse, Dale will say "fuck, fuck," and I'll hear him saying things about how I'd already been treated so abysmally and how angry that had made him and how he couldn't bear it the way I'd been treated so badly by the most disgusting arrogant men and yet it turned out that he was worse, worse than all of them put together, and he'll sound very emotional and I won't feel emotional at all, I'll feel embarrassed, and I'll say "Perhaps I bring out the worst in men" and I'll be joking actually but then it will be a notion that occurs to me frequently and persuasively for the next fifteen years or so and Dale will tell me how awful he feels, how awful it's been, and I'll say, I'll say to poor Dale, "Look Dale don't dwell on it, I don't, I hardly ever think of it—I think it's OK," and he won't say anything and I've wondered since if somewhere in him he hated me for saying that because if he had behaved worse than those men he had castigated and tried to keep me away from, if he had done the worst possible thing yet still hadn't managed to get under my skin, what did that mean, what on earth did that mean exactly? I hadn't so much absolved him as obliterated him. I should have cried perhaps. I ought to have cried really. He'd witnessed me coming apart in reaction to far less serious misdeeds and contraventions—but there isn't a fail-safe index for these things is there, that reliably instructs us as to what will thrust a knife through us and what will be water off a duck's back? I ought to have cried but it's too late for that I am quite monstrous and Dale is lost for words. I will hold the telephone receiver so tightly. I will hold it hard against my ear as if trying to push the big black telephone receiver all the way into my head as if the brain inside there is an almighty sponge that will absorb the cold gaping silence of Dale's humiliation. I will push the receiver so hard against my ear on and on. Willing my ear to envelop and vanquish Dale's humiliation. Willing my brain to soak up every last drop. And then I'll feel it, my voice, there again, warm and round within my throat and my hand will relax its grip on the telephone receiver and the horrible black silence will slither back down the coiled telephone wire and I'll open the front door as I often do while I'm talking on the telephone and I'll stand in the hall in my dressing gown holding the receiver with the door wide open and I'll look at the very elegant light fixture in the beautiful living room in the beautiful house directly opposite and I'll ask Dale if he is still in Yorkshire and he'll say yes he is, he hasn't had a drink for nearly three months now he'll say, and he'll ask me how I am and I'll say not very good, still drinking too much but not all the time—"It doesn't look like I'll be able to stay on in London much longer," I'll say, "I owe so much rent, I don't know what's going to happen," I'll say, "I'll probably have to go back home. Perhaps I should take a little trip," I'll say, "clear my head a bit, I haven't been anywhere for ages," and Dale will say, "Why don't you come up here, tomorrow—I'm away the next day," he'll say, "I've to go down to London to sort out a few things, and my parents are going to Nottingham for a few nights—you'll have the place all to yourself," he'll say, and I'll say, "Alright then, that sounds nice, thanks Dale, thanks, see you tomorrow," and I'll hang up and I'll stand in my dressing gown in the hall in the middle of the afternoon with the front door wide open and I'll go on looking at that beautiful light fixture that looks like a wreath of lilies until my body bristles, as if it can't understand why it's not in that beautiful room in that beautiful house, is only ever over here, looking in at it.

Dale and his mum meet me at the train station and we immediately go to the supermarket. I've got my sunglasses on my head and Dale can't say anything about them because his mum is there. Perhaps he wouldn't say anything about them now anyway. It's hard to know if Dale still feels awful or if he's on his best behaviour because his mum is there. I remember the white lines in the car park, they were extremely vivid, almost writhing, and I walked along them with my arms out which probably really annoyed Dale too but he didn't say anything about that either. Perhaps he wouldn't be able to say anything to me anymore about anything. Perhaps I was being a little cow on purpose. Once we were in the supermarket it became apparent that we were in there for me. "We probably don't have the kinds of things you like," said Dale's mother, and I wondered what exactly Dale had told her about me. I felt uncomfortable with the idea of her buying things especially for me but she egged me on in such a gleeful sort of way that I was soon lobbing all sorts of stuff into the trolley that Dale was pushing up and down and around the corners so as not to be a great big spoilsport. Earl Grey tea—they didn't have any lapsang souchong—strawberries, pineapple juice, grapefruit, minty chocolate, crackers, yoghurt, sardines, avocados, iced fingers, humous, cheddar, blue cheese, Camembert, grapes, pickle, fig rolls, Jamaican ginger cake, tomatoes, pistachios, baked beans, wholemeal bread, vanilla ice cream. "Don't you eat meat," she said, "oh yes" I said, "I'm quite partial to a Peperami." When we got to Dale's house his dad was sitting in an armchair in the living room reading a newspaper and he didn't move, he didn't even look up. It didn't bother me because enough had gone on already and I needed a cup of tea before getting into the next round of introductions, but I did think perhaps it would have been nice for Dale's mum if his dad had said something when we came into the house. Dale's mum was bustering about in the kitchen, she wanted to show me where everything was and where everything went. It was a small very well-organised kitchen and I could tell Dale and his dad didn't have much to do with it. There was no door on the kitchen so I could look straight through into the living room and see his dad sat in a chair in front of the window reading his newspaper. After a bit he folded up the newspaper, put it on the arm of his chair, took off his glasses, and rubbed his face before leaning over slightly in order to peer into the kitchen at me.

"How are you then?" "Yeah, I'm alright, thanks." "Enjoy the train?"

"Yeah."

"Fantastic isn't it? We'll be getting one tomorrow—I suppose Dale told you."

"He did mention it, yeah—are you going somewhere nice?"

Dale's mum told me I could sleep in the guest room at the front, or in Dale's room at the back and Dale would take the guest room, and she was disappointed when I chose the back room which was tiny and not the front room, which was quite big and weirdly lavish. She'd probably put a lot of effort into making that room nice and ladylike—I really would like to know what Dale had said about me—there was lots of little hard shiny cushions, and a covered box of tissues and things and things, so many little trinkets, a wardrobe with mirrored sliding doors, and a double bed. Maybe that's what put me off. At the time it didn't occur to me at all that she'd likely spent a bit of time making it nice for me. Or perhaps she hadn't—perhaps the room was always like that and she was proud of it. It was the best room and then I didn't want it, so what did that mean exactly? Dale's room had a sloping ceiling and a single bed. There was a grey and red cover on the bed and beside it a gigantic hi-fi with stickers on it which I thought probably didn't work anymore. When I asked Dale later he said the CD player was fucked but the turntable and right tape deck worked perfectly. "That just goes to show you doesn't it," he said. Dale and his parents left the following morning. Probably at the same time. They were probably taking the same train. I felt left behind when they all departed. London seemed very appealing all of a sudden and I had to make myself be quiet as the three of them walked off towards the station. I could do what I liked but I couldn't really. I was being done a good turn. These were decent people. I had everything I needed. Dale had been a bit full of himself the night before. Sliding back into his role of my saviour. I remember an occasion when we went to a gig and someone kept pulling my hair. "Dale," I said, after a song had finished, "someone keeps pulling my hair." Dale's eyes immediately widened with incredulity and he looked all around but at no one in particular and said very loudly, "Who pulled the hair? Who pulled the hair? Who?! Who pulled the lady's hair?" Another song started up, one of our favourite ones, and then, about halfway through, the hair pulling began again and this time I turned to Dale right away and said to him, "They're doing it again!"—"Who pulled the hair?" Dale roared, "This is an outrage! I demand to know who dares to pull the lady's beautiful hair." The third time it happened the penny finally dropped, I couldn't believe how dumb I'd been—I turned to Dale once more, grabbed hold of his lapels this time, and said

"Go on, do it again—I dare you." There is a lovely photo of us somewhere. Probably it ended up in his possession after going back and forth between us. If I had it he'd want it and if he had it he'd want me to have it because we are both smiling in the photograph, we might be laughing, and that was proof wasn't it, that we got on terrifically well, that we always had a marvellous time together, that being with him made me happy. You hold on to it then. It was taken in The Bread and Roses. Dale is looking at the camera. I'm looking at the floor. We are both smiling. We might be laughing. Yes, we are laughing a lot. I'm wearing a lilac blouse and he's wearing a three button jacket with a grey Joy Division T-shirt underneath. There are cigarette boxes on the table and an ashtray and gin and tonics. I drank an awful lot of gin then. One Sunday I locked myself in my room and drank a bottle of gin until it came back up into my mouth. I was amazed at that. It was just as if I really was filled to the brim. I swallowed it back down and it came right back up again and fell into the glass with a funny plop. That's that then. I was cutting up overexposed photographs and making a collage. It was very geometric. And then I painted on it here and there. Big red circles and calligraphic black lines. I thought it looked Japanese. Sitting on my bedroom floor. I'd had the paints for ages my mother's mother had bought them for me from the pound shop. Tubes and tubes. Why on earth it seemed like a good idea for me to be in that house in Yorkshire I don't know. The village was dreary—there was nothing beautiful or transporting about it. Even the mountains were unpleasant and begrudging. They did not soar upwards. They had no business with the sky. No, they were embroiled with the comings and goings below on that mile-long road. Huddled together like debt collectors blocking out the sun. I walked up there in any case. Nothing else to do was there. Dale's dad had told me how. Head towards the station, cross over the bridge, etc. And it was alright to begin with, for the first half hour or so. There were trees, lots of them. I saw a woman with a white dog. Upwards I went and the trees stopped and the mood altered. It was terribly bleak and loveless, sort of derelict. A ruin. A natural ruin of something that had never amounted to very much in the first place. There were no seasons here. No time of day either. Just this, and night. The light was on. The light was off. On and off. On and on. I've written about what happened next many times—though not at all in recent years. I gave up on it. Every time I tried to write about what happened next it invariably turned out horribly overwrought, because what happened next came as a shock, which meant that my cognition was immediately fractured, and because this fracturing effect was such an integral part of the experience, I tried too hard to recreate it each time I wrote about what happened next. That's right, part of me registered what had happened right away, while the rest of me, unable to take it in, was pulled back and forth, again and again, by uncertainty and a preoccupation with peripheral details. For goodness' sake spit it out.

A log is a fine place to sit. Feels like a proper place to sit. As if there could be no other place to sit. No matter how wrong everything might have been up to now the sitting here on this log seemed to mean everything was how it should be. Little by little I found the log a good place to sit.

I wore lace-up canvas boots.

The grass was long and still soaked through with mountain dew that drenched my shoes as I walked towards the swing. The ground was uneven so I swung at a tilt, head thrown back. Take and leave the world, take and leave. Nothing escaped me.

All this time I'd been reading the world.

Seen the log through the trees, nothing yet had been welcoming, no it was not heavenly. All that pressure to think things through, but wondered instead, who lives down there, who lives in that valley. For whom is that valley home every day, every day? Sat on the swing, take and leave the world, take and leave.

I saw a young man hanging from a tree.

Get so high the chains become slack and the momentum's fucked. Get so high the chains become slack and the momentum's fucked. Get so high the chains become slack and the momentum's fucked.

I saw a young man hanging from a tree. His dark hair was in a ponytail.

After looking down at the valley and wondering about it all, got off the log got on the swing. Swing. Swung. Easy come, easy go. Threw my head, back, back. Saw the world upside down. The whole thing. Got so high the chains shook either side. The trees, the sky. Back, back. Saw him upside down. Once. Twice. Three times. Leapt off into the grass. Wet long grass. Mountain dew. My hands. My hands splayed out in the wet long grass. Wasn't sure what I had seen but didn't dare turn around. Stayed down in the grass. Shaking in the grass. Held on to the grass.

Children were at school, otherwise they might have been here, what with there being a swing, and a log, they would know that those things were here, perhaps this is somewhere they come, after school, and that must not change, they will see faster what is clear, prevent that, standing next to the swing looking back now over the long wet grass, ready now, ready to believe, got to believe somebody.

Standing in the hall in my dressing gown on the telephone in the middle of the afternoon with the front door wide open looking at the elegant light fixture in the beautiful living room in the beautiful house directly opposite.

Bristling.

It was a car park so the ground was uniformly flat and divided up into equal spaces with vivid white lines, they're painted on, if for some reason you should put a foot wrong, there's no need to panic, you will not fall and once inside the supermarket you can roll down the aisles on a trolley until you get your breath back.

Oh ratbag, only when it suits you, eh?

He will raise his head and he will look. Look at me. Looking at him. I had to look. He had to be seen and I had to see him. But went no nearer. It was a private thing. He was dead. He'd done it. I went no nearer. He will raise his head. Wait. His dark hair was pulled back into a ponytail.

Easy come, easy go.

Look at me.

He will raise his head.

———

Wait
Wait

My god, woman, Dale may as well have said, you were only there for five minutes. He'd lived there his whole life and had never seen such a thing. He was envious, I could tell. Envious and annoyed and resentful and scared. Scared of me. Something morbid within me drew me towards dreadful things, one after the other—I was beyond hope. It's not exactly that a man has died, Dale may as well have said. We stood beside the main road around the corner from my house back in London. No, there was no river, no postcards, we were not in Florence, I did not get to put my elbows down upon the parapet. But something had happened, nonetheless. I had been in my dressing gown in the hall miles and miles away and then I had got dressed and packed a bag and then I had taken a train then another train and another train after that to a place I'd never been to and then in the morning I had walked, out of an empty house that someone else had grown up in, down a street I'd never walked down before, passing houses lived in by people I didn't know and would never meet, over a bridge I hadn't known existed until the previous day, passing a white dog walked by a woman who was a stranger to me, up a path that was also every inch unknown to me, all the way up a baleful unchanging mountain that meant nothing to me at all and down the other side where again everything I saw I saw for the very first time, getting closer, closer, every single move bringing me closer, to this man, this young man, who lived in the valley, had grown up in the valley, down in the valley where his family lived, all of his family, for generations going way back, way back, out of his house in the valley the young man walked and down the street, passing the houses of his neighbours, knowing who lived in every single one, and onwards, across the bridge and up a path that he had walked, up and down, thousands of times, getting closer, getting closer, up to where the log is, up to where the swings are, up to where the tree is, the log he sat on as a teenager with other teenagers drinking cans and passing spliffs back and forth, the swings he swung on as a child, the tree, the tree he climbed, they all climbed, children, teenagers, it has good strong branches, good strong branches, that took their weight without a creak and will take the weight of him now, a young man, a young man now, his dark brown hair pulled back into a ponytail, walking up the path towards the log and the swings and the tree, getting closer, getting closer, holding a long blue rope, and there I was, not far behind him, getting closer, getting closer, to the log, to the swings, to the tree, the tree, and then there I was and there he was too. One. Two. Three. I threw myself off the swing. I got up from the grass and turned around, and I saw the young man, it was me who saw him but he did not see me. Would see nothing more now. It was me who walked the mile and a half to the police station and it was me who walked the mile and a half back with two policemen on my heels because the station only had one car and it was out on another job miles and miles away. It was me who showed them where you were, it was me who stood again in the long wet grass and it was my finger that pointed towards the tree, and I don't know why it was me, I don't know why it worked out that way, had you got there very long before me, I didn't dare touch you, it didn't seem right to get too close, I didn't know you, I wouldn't have crept up on you if you were alive would I, so why would I now, I wanted to give you some space, some privacy, the way your head hung, you looked like Jesus, and in fact when I try to remember you now that's who I see, the way his head hangs, so sadly, for the sins of the world, the sins of the world, and the world had let you down, had squandered you, and I am so sorry and ashamed, ashamed that the kind of world we live in is such that in the end all that society managed to do with you is hang you from a tree, not that any elected person will ever take any responsibility for your death of course, the authorities will point to the fact that you were using heroin, you will be referred to over and over again as a "heroin addict" and that will be all you are, all you've ever been, all you'd ever be, and what more can a heroin addict expect to hope for than to wind up hanging from a tree? I leant against the frame of the swing while one copper cut the rope and the other copper slung the young man's untethered body over his shoulder. When the sawing knife ripped through the rope at last I threw up onto the small footprints all smashed into each other in the mud just in front of the swaying faded seat of the swing.

We were students of literature but we didn't read in order to become clever and pass our exams with the highest commendations—we read in order to come to life. We were supremely adept at detecting metaphors, signs, analogies, portents—in books, and in our immediate realities. We confused life with literature and made the mistake of believing that everything going on around us was telling us something, something about our own little existences, our own undeveloped hearts, and, most crucially of all, about what was to come. What was to come? What was to come? We wanted to know, we wanted to know what lay ahead of us very very much, it was all we could think about and it was so unclear— yet at the same time it was all too clear. He was from the valley. I was from the fastest-growing town in Europe. Where we came from people left school and found a job, often in the same trade or firm where at least one close relative worked already, and then, soon after, you got married and moved into a starter home and had two or three children, and you'd work all the overtime going and after a while you'd have the house extended or you'd move into a bigger one, and there would be nice things, TVs and barbeques, and a fortnight's holiday abroad once a year, and it's not bad, it's not a bad lot, yet we couldn't say why exactly but neither me nor Dale were cut out for that. We could tell, had always known it—the encroaching inevitability of that life path had been a source of anxiety to us both since we were approximately eleven years old. We tried to keep that anxiety at bay with reading, with writing, with alcohol, with fantasies, with all the strength and imagination that those things gave us, and were on the lookout, always, for signs, proofs, indications, merest hints that we had promise, that we were special, that our lives would take a different turn. And just days before the end of the final year of university Dale had flung out a hand and I had taken several trains to his hometown in the valley and found there a young man hanging from a tree. What did that mean? What exactly did that mean? Dale didn't tell me the young man's name. I presume he had been told. Don't give me his name then. Don't let him become human. Don't give him a life. Have him forever remain a symbol. Only and always the dead man. The Hanging Man. First seen upside down. Just like on the tarot card. One. Two. Three. What did it mean? Whatever did it mean? How could we regard a man's death as a grim motif in our own lives, and then again, how could we not? We barely said a word to each other. I gave him back the key to his house and he walked off up the main road and I went into the tiny shop to buy fags and a bottle of wine and when I came out I looked up the road and Dale was waiting at a bus stop smoking a cigarette and I waved and he waved back and I turned the corner then and went back up to my room to pack up my things because I was returning to the fastest-growing town in Europe, a booming yet purblind place, and Dale was going back to that slag heap of a village far off in the valley, and I would never ever clap eyes on him again. Our story had come to an end, as far as he was concerned, no more pages left to turn—and who was I to disagree?—his sense of narrative after all had always been much stronger than mine.

VII.

WOMAN OUT OF NOWHERE

I am her ghost, I inhabit her vanished being.

—*A GIRL'S STORY*, ANNIE ERNAUX

There was a very large rug in that room, and beams. Rafters probably. Rafters, that's right, and a desk. A brand-new desk with a white surface which she'd got for us especially. We'd talked on the phone about it. We'd never spoken to her before. We didn't know her. No, we didn't. Someone we knew a little bit knew her very well and that's how it all came about. We asked on the phone didn't we if there was a desk because we had to make sure. Yes we did, it was on our mind and we had to make sure. And she said she'd get one because we told her we had a lot of work to do. We have a lot of work to do, we said. I'll sort something out, don't worry, she said. We thanked her, said "great," that we appreciated it very much. See you in a couple of weeks then, we said.

We were going to London. We were.
For about a month. Maybe longer.
Maybe longer. Yes.
After all these years.
And we were very pleased and looking forward to a change of scene.

We'd visited many times of course.
That's right, in the twenty years or so since we'd packed up our things we'd visited London now and then.
Stayed here and there.
Yes.
In this spare room, on that pull-out bed, etc.
In hotels even.

Truth be told we did not pack up our things twenty years ago.
No.

No.

No, we didn't.

We didn't want to.

No we didn't.

So we left them where they were.

That's right.

We sat on the floor in the middle of our room with a bottle of wine and all our things were in their places all around us. Exactly where they always were. The dressing gown on the hook. We wanted more than anything for our things to stay where they were. Yes we did. We wanted to stay where we were. That's right, we didn't want to leave did we. No, of course we didn't. We wanted to take our dressing gown off the hook we'd banged into the side of the dresser and go down the hall and have a long hot bath in the bathroom beside Bettina's room. We were just getting the hang of living in London. That's right. Now that we weren't a student anymore, now that that part of our being in London had ended, we felt much better about being there. Yes, now that that monumental disappointment was done and dusted we felt quite optimistic. We did. We did. We felt light as a bird and fairly upbeat in fact. But we didn't have any money. No, we didn't—we owed money. We did actually. So what we felt and wanted was neither here nor there. We had to get real.

That's right, we had to face up to reality. Get real. Get real. We didn't want to. No. No. No we didn't.

When our father arrived he was irate that we hadn't packed a single thing. He was expecting us to be ready to go. But we weren't ready. No we weren't. We were just sitting there drinking wine in the middle of the room. He'd brought a van. That's right. A large white van that belonged to his girl-friend's dad. It was parked just outside on the street below. We went over to the window and looked down at it. He went off to the tiny shop around the corner to get some big black bags. That's right. The tiny shop that sold everything our tiny heart desired. Wine, pistachios, cigarettes. And now our fa-ther was in there impatiently scanning the chock-full shelves for a reel of big black sacks. And when he came back we snatched them off him and tore around the room. We did. Emptying all the things out of the drawers and off the mantelpiece into the big black bags. Coins, postcards, Blu-Tack, stamps. Knickers, necklaces, shells, lipsticks, tights, marbles. Tapes, creams, notepads, scissors, contraceptive pill. Photographs, tea lights, pinecones, books, incense, bones, shoes, hats, tampons, sunglasses. Scarfs, pens, Booboo, lapsang souchong. Camera. Camera. Jeans, eyeliners, collages, blouses, diaries, cotton wool. Lighters, conkers, skirts, towels, knife, crystals, nail varnish. Earrings, brooches, razors, candlesticks. Bubble bath, records, hairgrips, paints. And when the bags were full we threw them out of the window. We did, we pushed open the sash window as far up as it would go and tossed black bags full of our belongings down into the street where father stood with his hands on his hips below. Father caught the bags and stuffed them into the back of the white van. It didn't take long to clear the room of everything. No it didn't. We were upset and intoxicated so did it all in a fuelled-up frenzy. Throwing our things into rubbish sacks. Throwing our things out of the window. Throwing our things down into the street. The street full of beautiful houses. One after the other. Streets and streets. Of beautiful utterly still Victorian houses. One after the other. Nothing moving. On and on. And when it was done we shut the window back down with a slam and brought the wine with us. We did actually. We needed it. We sat up in the van and drank wine while father drove full throttle down the M4. The M4. The M4. With all our things bundled up in black sacks behind us. That's that then.

Down

Down

The ignominy.

The ignominy.

What if once we get to London, all these years later, we just end up staying in our room in the attic, drinking two bottles of beer from the express supermarket on the corner and eating cheese and Jacob's crackers night after night? And then we wondered, didn't we, if that would be so bad after all and concluded it wouldn't be so bad at all, if we were twenty or even ten years younger. But not now. No, not now. Ten or twenty years ago that's probably precisely what we would have done night after night and it wouldn't have bothered us one bit and indeed there would have been nothing much wrong with it, but at this stage in our life carrying on like that would be utterly unseemly.

Abject.

Dismal.

Weird.

We couldn't help but think of the two young daughters and we didn't like the idea one bit of night after night being up in that attic with two bottles of beer and a block of cheddar and cream crackers sliding off a plate onto the nice rug while the two daughters were in their pretty single beds just there on the floor below us. And surely they'd soon wonder why a woman of our years had come out of nowhere and installed herself at the top of their house and creaked around late into the night. Perhaps they'd see her, this woman out of nowhere, now on the stairs, glassy-eyed and slightly woozy. And the re-cycling box downstairs in the pantry, suddenly filling up with brown bottles. They'd soon put two and two together. And why had this woman come out of nowhere to sit up there at the top of their home, drinking bottles of beer night after night, and trampling crackers into their lovely pastel-coloured rugs? All of that seemed to us very bleak. Yes it did. So even though on the first night buying two bottles of beer and a block of cheese and a packet of Jacob's crackers from the express supermarket on the corner was exactly what we did we didn't do it again did we or we did do it again but only once or twice and we were there for what, five weeks in the end, which meant didn't it that it was quite impossible for the two daughters to think of us as an unseemly abject dismal weird woman who'd come out of nowhere only to sit at the top of their home drinking two bottles of beer and gorging pleasurelessly on great lumps of generic cheddar night after night, probably without ever even using a knife.

The desk was really big and we moved it so that it was no longer flat against the wall. We wanted to face the window. We could see a red-brick block of flats through the bare silver birches at the end of the very long back garden. A woman would come out of her flat several times over the course of an evening and puff on cigarettes in the dark with her arms folded. We don't really smoke anymore do we. No. No. Hardly ever. One or two. Yes, one or two. One or two, hardly ever. We stood and smoked one or two cigarettes before bed once or twice at the bottom of the very long garden. Between the bare silver birches. Yellow eyes. Yellow eyes. Blink. Blink. And gone. As it turned out we went out nine nights in a row.

We did actually. All over town. All over town. And everywhere we went people assumed didn't they that we lived in
London. If they didn't know any better, then they would as-
sume, that's right, that we lived in London, just like they did.
Which is understandable. Yes. We were flattered that they
thought that—flattered that they believed us to be capable of
living there. Of having the wherewithal. Yes, the wherewithal
and the means. The means. It's funny how, when we are visiting it is presumed we are at home, and when we are at home it
is frequently presumed that we are visiting. We belong in neither place do we. No, not really, and perhaps that suits us.
You haven't lost your accent, people often say. They do often
point that out and it's true, isn't it, we still have our West
Country accent. Yes. Yes. Yes we do. After all this time. If
we'd stayed in England we probably would have lost it, and
that's the funny thing. If we'd stayed it's very likely, yes, that
we would have toned our accent down. People do, don't they.
Yes, they do, lots of people do. Our brother, for example, said
he felt he had to smooth his accent out a bit when he moved
to London approximately six years ago. That's right, he had a
job in Mayfair to begin with and didn't want to sound like a
right bumpkin in meetings he said. A bumpkin. A bumpkin.
A bumpkin in Mayfair. Whatever next! Stuff my old boots!
Arrives at the office on a donkey. In a wheelbarrow. Bits of
barley poking up out of his buffed brogues and breast pocket.
He took us to lunch one day in The Little Square. That's

262

right, we met him outside Green Park station. This is the A4, he said, pointing up and down Piccadilly with his big work brolly. Goes all the way to Marlborough. So in fact we have a stronger West Country accent than he does, even though we left England over twenty years ago. We don't feel the need do we to tone down our accent in Ireland. No. No. Once or twice at the start we did and for a completely different reason from why English people find it necessary to tone down their accent in England. At the start one or two people took voluble exception to our accent but not anymore. Not anymore. Not for a long time. Though never say never. No. We still have our accent and it's funny to conjecture that many people who have left England are in fact preserving its regional accents. They're dying out on their own turf. That's right. And that's hardly surprising is it since people who don't have an accent are inclined to make all kinds of obnoxious presumptions about a person's background and intelligence and ambitions and sense of esthetic if they do have an accent. They might not even be aware that that's what they are doing. They might not—yet there are others who are very aware of what they're doing, and seem to think they are quite justified in behaving so invidiously. Only yesterday we read a newspaper article about how students are bullied at universities in England simply because of the way they speak. You won't get anywhere talking like that—that's what a teacher said to a student with a Northumbrian accent, for example. It makes you sound stupid. Stupid, that's what the teacher said. I flattened my accent, the young woman told the newspaper. Flattened it, yes, every day for four years, and she's not the only one is she. Of course she isn't. Thousands and thousands of bright young people from all over England are deliberately mangling the astute and witty and imaginative words that come out of their mouths in order to fit in and be heard and taken seriously. Or else they just keep their mouth shut altogether. A student in Durham for example said the fear of ridicule and judgement from other students meant she didn't dare say a word during seminars. Not a word. She'd get looks and smirks otherwise, she said. It made our blood boil to read that. It made our blood boil. Imagine someone day in day out purposely making you feel ashamed of the sound of your own voice. Imagine what that would do to your confidence. How could you believe that anyone would ever be interested in listening to anything you have to say? How could you believe that anything you thought was of any significance or value? How would you be able to write freely and expressively and fearlessly? How much are we not hearing? How many words are just not getting through? People sometimes ask us, don't they, what we think would have happened if we'd stayed in England and it seems very likely we would have got more and more incensed. We suspected that back then didn't we, when we still just about lived there. We did. We did. We were already angry. We were. And we didn't want to spend our whole life being angry did we. No. No. It takes too much out of us. Yes it does. Much too much. It is nice to visit England though, from time to time. Yes. Yes. To be a visitor. Yes. We had a lot of fun in London didn't we. We certainly did. Nine nights in a row. Nine nights on the town! Having fun. That's right. And then we were frazzled. Completely. But we couldn't sleep. No, not a wink. Unbelievable. Yes it was. Our eyes got really puffy. We bought a brightening cream for them in Boots on the Holloway Road. We did actually. And much to our chagrin they wouldn't accept our Irish loyalty card would they. No. No. How parochial.

It was a nice bed. It was a nice bed. It was a nice room. The ceiling sloped and there were rafters. There was plenty of room. There was. It was spacious but cosy. We had plenty to read. Of course we did. We'd brought books over with us. And of course we acquired lots more very quickly. Everywhere we went people gave us books didn't they. They did. They did. Everywhere we went. Very soon we had stacks of books. Stacks of them. We don't much like stacks of books do we. No. No. Not really. We liked one book then and we like one book now. That's right. We lay awake in bed all night long with one book on the duvet beside us. Wide awake. Yes. We couldn't sleep could we. No, and our eyes were still ever so puffy. One book. That's right. Open and facedown on the duvet. It wasn't our house was it. No. No it wasn't. One evening the woman whose house it was said she felt a bit guilty about having such a big house. We told her she was very kind and did lots of good things and had nothing to feel guilty about at all. Enjoy it. That's right, enjoy it, we said. They all went to bed early because of school the next day and the house was very quiet then. The house was very quiet all night long. We couldn't get to sleep could we. No. No. And in a way we didn't mind. No, we didn't really. We remembered a lot of things without even trying and the things we remembered didn't upset us did they. No, not really. We felt very relaxed. We felt ageless in fact. In fact we felt all the ages we've ever been all at once. That's right, all at once. All of the ages we've ever been all at the same time. Yes. Now and then we picked up the one book beside us and read for a bit. We did. Talking to women. That's the title of the book. It is actually—*Talking to Women*. That's right. Nell Dunn went around to friends of hers and talked to them about love and sex and babies and money and all of that in London in 1964. Ann Quin is in there. She is—she's not dead yet so she's in there. She's in there but we didn't read her interview, did we, not until later, not until after we'd returned to Ireland. That's right, we read the Ann Quin interview back at home. Sylvia Plath is dead so she is not in there. No, she isn't. And she might have been in there mightn't she. Yes. Yes. She lived in London. She did. She died in London. She did. The year before.

She died in 1963, that's right. The year before. Janet Malcolm said that all the photographs of Sylvia Plath disappointed her. She looks bland, she says. That's right, according to Janet Malcolm, Sylvia Plath looks bland and then she looks like a housewife. Janet Malcolm finds this disappointing: "of her *Ariel* persona—queen, priestess, magician's girl, red-haired woman who eats men like air, woman in white, woman in love, earth mother, moon goddess—there is no trace in the photographs." Basically what Janet Malcolm is saying here is you wouldn't think so to look at her. We quite enjoy it, don't we, when a woman feels and behaves in ways that don't have any obvious accord with her outward aspect. We do. Why not. Yes, why not. Keep them guessing. That's right, keep them guessing. Isn't that why the surrealists loved Alice so much—because despite her golden-girl looks and hairband, which of course is not unlike Plath's hairband, she was willful and intrepid and went where she didn't ought to go. And kept going. And kept going. The surrealists delighted in contradictions. Yes. It's a form of rupture in reality and there isn't anything the surrealists like more is there than a rupture in reality. Nothing more. Edna O'Brien is in there. Yes she is, right in the middle in fact. It's unlikely anyone looking at a photographic archive of Edna O'Brien would feel shortchanged. That's true. She was very good company on those quiet sleepless nights. She was. We didn't dare play any music quietly or call anyone did we. No, we didn't. We didn't even bother texting. No. Edna and Nell are talking about love and sex and money and babies and so on and very near the end of the interview Nell asks her what makes her go on living, and Edna says: "Well, it varies from day to day. Sometimes I'm just waiting for a telephone call or the next meal, or to pick my children up, but when I think about it and pose the question to myself I imagine that in time I would've become a different person and the world around me will be different too. There is this constant desire to break out of one's own skin and into another reality. Sometimes you see paintings of rocks or ocean, or wilderness, and you think not only will I go there but I will partake of a whole new kind of experience. I will be born again through those rocks or in that ocean and the I who now suffers and laughs will do it in a different and possibly richer way."

Quite often we'd still be awake when the two daughters got up for school. They'd run about wouldn't they, up and down the stairs. Yes, they would, up and down. Where's this, where's that. And their mum shouting up to them from the hall. Hurry up. Hurry up. Have you got this, have you got that. That's right. It was nice. It was actually. It wasn't our house was it. No. They weren't our daughters. No. But it didn't matter did it. Not really. We enjoyed lying in bed after being awake all night, listening to the two daughters running about, up and down the stairs, asking about this, that, and the other, and their mother calling up to them. We've discovered haven't we that something or other doesn't have to belong to us in order for us to enjoy it. That's right, it doesn't matter does it, if whatever it is isn't ours. An ostensibly permissive and uncommon attitude that got us into a lot of bother, once upon a time. Once. Yes. And only once. "You don't believe in shelves, do you?" No. No. And where, exactly, did believing in shelves get you? When they'd left for school the house went quiet again and we'd go on lying in bed, thinking about the kitchen downstairs and making coffee and after a while we'd get up and go down all those stairs and we'd go into the kitchen and we'd make ourself some coffee. Yes we would, we'd go down to the kitchen that wasn't ours and make ourself a pot of coffee, then we'd bring it back up to the attic on a tray that was ours. It was ours actually. We'd brought it with us. We'd packed a tray. The one from the museum in Amsterdam with white egrets in the snow on it. Since our room was in the attic we'd foreseen that it would be very useful to have a tray. We were right about that, it was very useful. Up and down the stairs. Up and down the stairs.

There was sun in that room in the mornings and around ten o'clock it would hit the desk directly and the surface of the desk was white. So white. It practically gleamed didn't it. It did. It did. And we'd be there wouldn't we, we'd be sitting at that big white shining desk first thing. We would, we'd sit there with puffy peepers and a second pot of coffee. Writing. That's right. Writing something in the light of day. The light of day, that's right. Full of the night in the light of day. We were writing about how it all began. Yes. Yes. The blocks of plain A4 paper father brought home from work and the verboten mahogany drawers and the smell of our grandparents' seldom used Rover. Tippex. Yes. And never tearing out a page. Never ever. And drawing a face in the back of our exercise book which quickly became a horrible ball of tangled thread that straightened out and then by some larval impulse took on the form of specific words one after the next. And the words set forth a story. As if it had been there all along. Of a girl sitting all alone in a cellar repairing by the fluctuant light of a solitary candle the sheeny cloth of her sisters' frothy gowns. And the girl does not sigh or grimace or sing or curse or weep. She goes on in just the same way. Hour after hour. She does not seem the least bit put out and so strangely it is a kind of tranquil scene. But one that nevertheless cannot be sustained. Something has to change and something does change. Very quickly. There is no fairy godmother. No. No prince charming. No. No castle. No white horse. That's not it. No. No. No one is going to save the day. No, of course not. It's something inside her. The girl's fingers become very thin very quickly. They elongate and lose rigidity. They become thread. The needle they held so diligently, so devotedly, falls away. Is wolfed up by the scabrous dark that presses so very ravenously up against her bluish ankles. She gets to her feet. Leaps up. The long lengths of thread cascading from her hands whirl about the room with the electric energy of a lasso. Around and around they whirl. They cannot take hold of anything. Not a single thing. Around and around they flail. And it is only a matter of time of course before they come into contact with the flame of the candle. Which until now has been meek and miserly but now leaps up bright and proud as a trumpet. A trumpet. And the threads delight in this brazen little flame and kindle its appetite further. The emboldened flame divides. Bounds up the ten lengths of thread like awakened red squirrels bounding ecstatically along the budded branches of a beech tree before striking at the chest of the girl. The girl's chest explodes. Bursts into flames right away. Bright roaring flames. Yes. Yes. The flames burst out of her just as if they've been there all along. All along. Waiting all along. Biding their time. She burns. She blazes. A magnificent conflagration. A bright disc of white fire. Leaps dives plunges into the dust-dry basket of preposterous dresses. Jubilantly. Yes. The whole thing goes up in flames. Flames. Roaring. Yes. It all burns up so quickly. Every inch of her included. Yes. Leaving behind an iridescent pile of the softest ash. The sort of ash you want to stir. Softer than feathers. Run your fingers through. Run your fingers through. It tingles doesn't it. Yes. Yes. Yes it does. We can feel it. Our fingers. Our fingers are tingling like mad aren't they. Yes, they are. Tingling. We can feel it. Tingling like mad. Our fingers tingle, madly, madly yes, just as if they are coming to life.

"Dazzling . . . exquisitely written and daring."
—O, The Oprah Magazine

Shimmering and unusual, *Pond* captures the interior reality of its unnamed protagonist, a young woman living a singular and mostly solitary existence. Every sentence and scene is suffused with the hypersaturated, almost synesthetic intensity of the physical world that we remember from childhood, pulsing with hidden truths. The effect is of character refracted and ventriloquized by environment, catching as it bounces her longings,

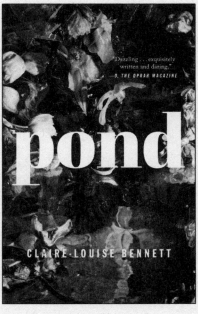

frustrations, and disappointments—the ending of an affair, or the ambivalent beginning with a new lover. As the narrator's persona emerges in all its eccentricity, sometimes painfully and often hilariously, we cannot help but see mirrored there our own fraught desires and limitations, and our own fugitive desire, despite everything, to be known.

"A sharp, funny, and eccentric debut . . . *Pond* reminds us that small things have great depths." **—The New York Times Book Review**